Guinevere the Queen AD494
ISBN 978-0-6480789-1-3

Aenghus Chisholme

Connect with Aenghus Chisholme: www.aenghuschisholme.com

Cover by Andjela Vujic (Varvara11 on guru.com)

Also by Aenghus Chisholme

Merlin the Sorcerer AD491

Guinevere the Queen AD494

Sir Gawain and the Green Knight AD499

Arthur the King AD517

Murder on the Mary Celeste

Jack the Ripper: The Murder of Madam Athalia

The Best Things in Life Begin with the Letter B

This book is dedicated to everybody who has discovered the joys of books.

Contents

Chapter 1: AD 494-Outside of Caerleon Village; Midnight

He had consorted with beasts to see that his devious plan would come to fruition; one, the foulest creature he could have possibly imagined. But now it was done. He had successfully stolen Excalibur from King Arthur. He looked down at the sword sheathed and tied to his horse's riding bindings. A sense of malevolent satisfaction poured over him that manifested itself as a twisted smirk upon his face. He was ambling along at a lazy cantor. There was no need to tire his horse by riding her at great speed. There would be no pursuit from Caerleon Castle. Everything had gone exactly according to his plan. Even if one of the guards on the watchtower had spotted him, unlikely as it was, he would not be a figure of interest, riding slowly away from the village. Time was on his side. He had ample time to complete the remainder of his intricate scheme. It would eventually be the undoing of Arthur, Merlin and their reign over the native people in Briton. With nobody to oppose them, the Saxons could invade in even greater numbers than they had already.

He began to visualise the future, heralded by his people as the man who rid the land of King Arthur and the Knights of the Round Table. He pictured himself as a newly crowned King; a ruler by his own hand, not by birth right. He would be majesty of a huge land holding, one that included a castle. Perhaps he would take Caerleon as his own. He turned to try and glimpse the castle upon the hill. There was no moon tonight, but he could make out its shape by the stars that it blocked from view. Yes, he would make Caerleon his castle. That too would have to be part of the bargain that he was to strike with his fellow Saxons. Looking ahead once more he began to laugh. His destiny lay before him now and he could hardly wait for it to be fulfilled.

Chapter 2: Arthur & Gwenhwyvar's Chamber; Morning

Arthur awoke, somewhat startled. There was something familiar about this feeling. It was broad daylight. He would have normally awoken just before the sunrise. Sleeping peacefully between him and Gwenhwyvar was Amhar. He must have crept past his Chamber Maid and come in at some time during the night. This raised the feeling of suspicion that something was wrong even more so within Arthur. They would have both normally been awakened by Amhar crawling into bed with them. Why had they not this time?

"Gwenhwyvar" he called to the prone form of his wife. He could see her chest moving up and down to the sound of her breathing. Much like Arthur, Gwenhwyvar's eyes shot open and a look of confusion covered her features as she looked first at him, then Amhar, the window and the bright blue sky that it framed. They both sat up in unison.

"So late in the Morning" said Gwenhwyvar pointing out in a single sentence the conundrum that they both found themselves in. The motion had stirred Amhar who yawned himself awake stretching and rubbing his eyes before opening them. "Ma, Da" he smiled looking from one to the other of his parents. Gwenhwyvar kissed him on the head. The entire court had spent the cold months this year at Cellewig castle in Dumnonii. Since returning to Caerleon, Amhar had taken to sneaking past his Chamber Maid and tried on a number of occasions to secret himself into bed with the two of them. If the noisy unlatching of the door did not betray his efforts, then the act of squeezing in between his parents always did, but not this time. It was quite a puzzle.

Arthur rubbed his hand over Amhar's scruffy head of hair. "Return to ye Chamber Maid little one, have her prepare thee for the day" Pleased by the fact that he had been successful this time in sleeping in the same bed as his parents, Amhar made no argument, instead he wriggled free of the blanket and raised his arms in a gesture for him to be lifted from the bed. Arthur hoisted him over the side of the bed and deposited the little Prince gently on the floor. He turned and scurried to the chamber door, reached up and deftly unlatched it. Opening the door just enough for him to squeeze through sideways he pulled the door noisily shut as he left. Arthur looked at Gwenhwyvar "Ye did not wake when Amhar came in during the night?" he queried. "No; did ye?" she responded. Arthur shook his head.

Clearly something was wrong, but they did not know exactly what. It was unusual for them both to sleep so soundly. Unable to explain the unusual circumstances that they found themselves within, there was nothing more to do but prepare for the coming day. Gwenhwyvar put into words what they were both thinking, "There is much to do in preparation for ye journey to North Rheged mine love; best that we hasten to do so". Arthur loved the clarity that his wife was able to bring to any situation. He leant over and kissed her on the lips tenderly. "Aye mine Queen" he smiled as they separated.

The next few minutes made their unusual awakening experience seem distant as they got ready to face the coming day. The absolute normalcy of getting out of bed and beginning the usual daily routine almost washed away the feeling that something was amiss. Arthur glimpsed the area by a stool where he rested Excalibur every night when disrobing. The sword was not there. In a horrifying moment he felt the pupils in his eyes first dilate then constrict so completely that it actually hurt. The space was empty! "Excalibur!" he wailed at the top of his voice. Completely startled Gwenhwyvar spun around to see what was wrong. She took in the scene in an instant. Arthur crouched over legs spread as though he was ready to run, but unsure in what direction. He was looking at the place where his magical sword should have been resting, but it was not there. A fear gripped Gwenhwyvar as the realisation of what had happened enveloped her. Somebody had been in their chamber and removed Arthur's sword whilst they slept.

It was almost inconceivable. Who could have the courage or the ability to steal the symbol of Arthur's Kingship from the royal chamber? Here in the King's castle, surrounded by a host of Knights and foot soldiers. Surely there could be no way that it could be done without the thief being apprehended? And the thought that they were lying there defenceless as the bandit removed the sword. Was Amhar already in bed with them by this time or did he enter after it had been taken? Gwenhwyvar felt the hairs on the back of her neck rise at the very thought that her child could have been in such a perilous position. Arthur snapped her attention back to reality. "Merlin will know what to do". She shook her head free of the image of the brigand malevolently towering over the sleeping forms of herself, her husband and child. Arthur was already striding toward the door. With an overzealous amount of strength, he flung open the heavy wooden door. It crashed against the stone wall of their room. A servant who had been walking past at the time looked in alarm at the King standing in the doorway. "Fetch Merlin; quickly!" bellowed Arthur. This sent the servant continuing on his way but now practically running, so accelerated was his gait.

Arthur turned back to look once more at the empty space where Excalibur should have been. He looked the room over, in a hopeless attempt to locate the missing sword. Gwenhwyvar could see the look of torture upon his face. She searched for some words of comfort to offer her distressed husband. "Surely Merlin will hath ability to locate Excalibur?" It was a question filled with both hope and uncertainty. Arthur looked directly into Gwenhwyvar's eyes. She could see that he simply did not know the answer. "There is that hope" he said. There was an unmistakable note of urgency in the reply, as though he were wishing it to be true, but was uncertain if it was. The minutes that they waited for Merlin to arrive were taken up with conjecture as to how the burglar could have possibly perpetrated such a crime. Who it could have possibly been, and where might they have secreted the magical sword?

Merlin eventually appeared at the still-open doorway. His features portrayed the puzzlement of being summoned to the King's private chamber. "Excalibur hath been stolen!" Arthur's words pierced Merlin's ears. His vexed expression was replaced with a look of absolute horror. "How could this be?" he fumbled, completely flummoxed. Hurrying into the room he repeated Arthur's previous search for the missing sword. "No vision of Excalibur being stolen hath ye?" queried Arthur. "No mine King, no vision" answered the old sorcerer. This gave Merlin an idea. He would consult with the only other person in Caerleon that also had the power of such sight. "Morgan" he said resolutely to nobody in particular. For a brief moment both Arthur and Gwenhwyvar thought that Merlin was somehow implicating Morgan in the events that had transpired. Gwenhwyvar was the first to pick-up on what Merlin was in fact doing. He was calling for Morgan. She would be sure to hear his call no-matter where in the Castle she might be.

Although no longer lovers, they still had an eerie connection that most in the Castle had at some time witnessed. There was clearly still a good deal of mutual respect for each other's abilities in the magical arts. Arthur too realised that his sage now wished to consult with his sister about the incredible matter of Excalibur's robbery. Merlin despised the feeling that now engulfed him. He felt helpless, adrift, with no idea how to proceed. But that would not help their current situation. The wise old man knew that he needed to show Arthur that he somehow would remedy the situation. "Between us, we shall see to its safe return" promised Merlin. It felt like an empty promise, but Merlin hoped that Arthur would not detect the underlying doubt that he was riddled with.

In a scene that echoed the one previously whilst waiting for Merlin, the three of them engaged in conjecture as to who in the Castle could have perpetrated this evil doing. Merlin was sure that somehow Aelle of Sussex was behind it. Impossible as it would be for him to walk in and take Excalibur, he may have instead planted a spy in their midst somehow. Arthur was not his typical level-headed self. Normally he would listen to an idea and weigh it up against logic, in this case such as opportunity, motive and ability. But this time he just looked at Merlin almost wild-eyed and agreed with him. Gwenhwyvar could see that the two of them were fuelling a fire of wild conjecture instead of tactical discernment. She skilfully put an end to it by interjecting, "What of thine journey to North Rheged? Will thee cancel and send word to King Rhydderch?" The reality of the situation that they all faced put an end to the pointless supposition that they two men were engaged in.

Arthur looked firstly at Merlin then Gwenhwyvar. There was a long pause. This pleased Gwenhwyvar, she could see that it marked the return of Arthur's usual demeanour. Well considered and careful deliberation before making any important decision. Eventually after what seemed an age, he replied to them both. "No. King Rhydderch needs assistance with the problems at Vallum Hadriani. Merlin, ye shall remain at Caerleon and uncover what hath happened here this night." Merlin shook his head. He would not disagree with a Royal command unless he felt strongly opposed. In Merlin's mind he had abandoned Arthur two and a half years ago to face Aelle at Anderitum, a battle that Arthur lost and was lucky to escape from with his life. Never again would he leave the King's side. "No Arthur. The thief will be revealed by their absence from Caerleon. We shall know soon enough who it is..." Merlin's train of thought was interrupted by the arrival of Morgan.

She almost floated into the room, her movement was so graceful. "Arthur, Gwenhwyvar, Merlin, good morning" she smiled. It was an uncertain smile. She could sense that something was wrong. Not just from the vexed expressions on the three but from the 'tone' of Merlin's call to her. She was busy making a new set of clothes for Mordrede when she heard the summons from the old sorcerer. It felt urgent, almost panicked. But that would be so unlike Merlin that she felt that she must have misinterpreted the bid for her to join him. It only took a moment after she entered the room for her to realise that the situation was indeed extraordinary. Merlin summarised the state of affairs and set her a task in a single sentence. "Excalibur hath been stolen; can ye unveil the thief or the sword's location?" She drew a breath in readiness to ask a barrage of questions about the shocking news, but cut herself off. It would do no good to state the obvious, nor tread upon ground that had without doubt already been covered by the trio before her arrival.

Merlin could see her disciplined resolve to respond to his question instead of further interrogating them on the details of the theft. He was pleased with his former student's focused mind and restrained curiosity. They could see that her eyes were now focussed far away and not upon any of them. Morgan turned her head slowly in a miniature arc to the left, then back to centre and to the right. Looking back to Merlin she dashed his hopes of an immediate end to the dreadful circumstances. "Nothing", her answer was brief and apologetic.

Arthur addressed Merlin once more. "What more can be done?" his tone betrayed the helplessness that he was feeling. Merlin thought quickly. "Should a vision of Excalibur come to either of us we must be ready to act". It was Gwenhwyvar that managed to organise the plethora of thoughts that were pouring through them all. "Mine love. Should Merlin have a vision of Excalibur's whereabouts whilst ye are journeying to North Rheged, then he may send word to Caerleon through Morgan. If Morgan is the first to be granted such a vision she may let Merlin know. Either way there must be Knights ready to retrieve Excalibur." This was the clear thinking that Arthur loved his wife for. He built-upon her plan of action. "Mine force shall be divided equally between Caerleon and the quest to North Rheged." It was all coming together. Merlin was nodding in agreement, already finding the good sense of the plan being outlaid by the King and Queen. He completed the strategy, "We shall be ready to act when the whereabouts of Excalibur is known. However, the knowledge that thine sword hath been taken should not be made known to the court."

This was an almost absurd idea and took Arthur completely by surprise. What reason could his sage possibly have for such secrecy? Anticipating the King's question Merlin answered it before Arthur had the chance to put it into words. "Since the battle of Anderidae, thine kingdom hath been shaken with uncertainty. This could add weight to those that hath lost faith in ye." Now Arthur could see the tactic behind Merlin's plan. It would not do to have more of his kingdom fall away. News of his defeat at Anderitum had spread like a fire in a dry forest. It was an irony that in the successive two and a half years, Arthur had increased the number of Knights that had pledged their loyalty to him, but the many lands that had previously made up his kingdom had diminished. There was a general fear that he was not the legendary king that was to unite the land and drive out the invaders. That single defeat had done more damage than he could have possibly envisioned. Arthur could only imagine what news of the theft of Excalibur would do to those lands that still remained faithful to him.

"A sword shall be fashioned to look exactly as Excalibur. Only the Knights charged with the safe return of the real Excalibur shall know of the subterfuge." There was a general feeling between the four of them that the situation was somehow now manageable. It seemed less daunting that it had appeared only a short while ago. With a sigh of relief, Arthur nodded and gave his approval to Merlin's proposal, "Aye Merlin; good advice mine old friend'. He put his hand on Merlin's shoulder. "See to it, whilst preparations are made for the journey to North Rheged". A silent pact was made between them. Knowledge of the sword's theft would be made known only to the knights charged with its safe return. To the rest of the court, it must look as though nothing was amiss. Merlin made to exit the room and begin his new task. Morgan took her brother's hand and gave it a reassuring squeeze. She too turned to leave the room.

There was a sense of an unanswered question between Arthur and Gwenhwyvar. "Aye" responded Gwenhwyvar, "If Excalibur can be found, Merlin or Morgan will be the ones to do it mine love". Arthur smiled at the typical amazing perception that his wife had of his own mood. He took both of her hands into his, gratified by the comfort that he was offered. "As wise as ye art beautiful", he complimented her. In a gesture of thanks he leant forward and kissed her deeply upon the lips.

Chapter 3: Merlin's Chamber; Noon

Merlin straightened himself from hunching over the fireplace. He had taken a sword from the armoury, much to the amazement of Sir Brumean who was on duty at the time. The knight knew better than to question the old Sorcerer, so had allowed him to take any sword the old man may desire. It was this plain looking sword that Merlin had taken to his chamber and began to re-fashion. He had agitated the fire to the point where the flame was intense enough to soften the metal that made up the hand grip. He was levitating it in the flame watching for the signs that the metal was ready to be re-moulded. It was taking a good deal of his concentration, but he couldn't help but think about the events that had transpired overnight. Someone must have put a lot of thought into this act of treason. Was there more to it than just the theft of Arthur's symbol of power? Of course there was. It must be a prelude to a challenge of Arthur's rightful place as King of Briton; but by whom?

Aelle was the obvious mastermind behind this; perhaps too obvious. It was also possible that this was the work of a previously unknown challenger to the throne. The Saxons and Angles and Jutes would all benefit with Arthur out of their way. Wales, Dumnonii and Northumbria would be able to be invaded without the unifying presence of Arthur Pendragon. Merlin's thoughts were interrupted by the task now at hand. The hand grip had begun to glow white and soften. Now he could begin. In what would have looked an act of madness to anyone who had they witnessed it, Merlin stretched out his left and right index fingers and began to trace into the metal the intricate patterns that made up the decoration on Excalibur. With equal dexterity between both hands, he pushed and pulled the metal re-creating the ornamental embellishments of the sword's trimming. He felt no heat, although it would have boiled the flesh from a normal man's fingers. Drawing back his hands he flipped the levitating sword over and repeated the process on the other side. When he was satisfied that he had indeed successfully replicated the adornments on Excalibur he gripped the sharp edge of the sword and dunked it into a nearby bucket of water. It hissed and spluttered loudly as the metal contracted and hardened.

Lifting his reproduction to the light of the window he studied his handiwork. A faint smile painted his until now, dour features. It was a perfect imitation. Now all that was needed was to secret it to Arthur. It was a difficult task. The king was busy with preparations for his departure. He would be surrounded with people all taking orders and loading horses with provisions for the journey northwards. "Hmm" he said to nobody. Concealing the duplicate beneath his robes, he left his room and made his way towards Arthur's chamber. He would deposit the copy there and make it known to Arthur.

After completing his task, Merlin descended the great staircase and hurried into the main courtyard to locate Arthur. It was a sunny day; perfect weather to begin a long journey. Now that the colder months were behind them for another year, it was certain that the expedition to North Rheged would not be hampered by inclement weather. He found Arthur exactly where he expected to, in the stables, loading up a horse with provisions. He smiled a little at seeing the King's attire. In order to circumvent any reason for not wearing Excalibur, Arthur had elected to wear a simple tunic rather than the more ornate garments that he normally wore. It would have raised a few eyebrows, but the outfit clearly was meant for work rather than show, or even battle. The absence of his magical sword would not seem out of place.

He approached the King who looked up expectantly as Merlin approached. "Mine preparations are complete Sire". The coded message was received and understood. Merlin glanced backwards toward the tower that held Arthur's private chamber. Arthur gave his wise sage a knowing look of acknowledgement. He called over to the nearest of his round-table Knights. "Sir Alynore, signal the readiness for departure". The general flurry of preparations now took on an immediate urgency as the king had decreed that the expedition to North Rheged would now depart, ready or not. Sir Alynore could be heard in the background repeating the King's orders. Servants, knights and soldiers scurried this way and that at the sudden notification. "Best to change into mine Royal garb" announced Arthur, seemingly to Merlin but in fact to anyone within earshot. Merlin bowed slightly in agreement and took a step back in order to allow the king to pass him and make his way toward the entrance to the castle. Arthur had taken to travelling in his full regalia since his defeat at the hands of Aelle. It was a strategic manoeuvre to show that he feared no reprisals at showing himself to the lands that he travelled, whether they were a part of this kingdom, or otherwise.

***

When Arthur entered his room he saw the substitute sword in the place where the real one would have normally stood. It was uncanny, the forgery was perfect, and Arthur could see that even at a distance. He walked over to the sword and picked it up. It was heavy. That was something that he would have to become accustomed to. The real Excalibur was almost weightless in his hands. Other knights had commented that it felt as heavy as their swords on occasions when they had the privilege to wield it. But to Arthur, from the moment he pulled it from the stone during the spring time six years ago, it had been easy to brandish about with a minimum of effort. He recalled the moment with absolute clarity.

***

The usual festival surrounding the attempts by virile young men to free the sword from its resting place had begun. Arthur had heard about it even though he was raised in Northumbria by Merlin. He was deliberately kept far from Dumnonii where the sword was imprisoned in its stone sheath. Arthur was raised knowing that he would one day attend the festival with Merlin and pull Excalibur from the stone. The word had spread far and wide throughout the land over the years. It had become an annual pilgrimage by pretenders to the throne, to boast about how they were the missing child of Uther and Igraine Pendragon. Stolen away by Merlin the sorcerer at birth and raised by nobility from Rheged, Kent, Mercia or wherever they professed to come from. There was always much promised of these young men and never delivered. Accordingly the toddlers that had first been pushed up to the sword by their hopeful parents those many years ago had given way to boys, then to young men in the ensuing years.

This was the scene that Merlin had witnessed when they arrived. Innocuous travellers, they did not display any royal standards or armour. They almost disappeared in the throng of people that had come this year, the seventeenth year after Uther's dying hand thrust the sword into the stone. An old man was loudly bragging about how his boy was surely the lost son of Uther, "Show thee all, that mine adopted son shall claim the Kingship by freeing Excalibur before thine very eyes". This was met by a roar of laughter from the gathered crowd. They had seen it all before almost countless times now. Clearly angered by the response and eager to vindicate his arrogant boastfulness, he waved to his boy toward the sword. "Hurry boy" he impatiently ordered the young man. Looking like a doe in the sights of an archer, the wide-eyed boy clambered up the rock and gave the sword a worried look. He looked as though the sword may somehow jump up at him at any moment of its own accord. Gingerly he stretched out his hand, his fingers closing gently around the grip. He could be seen visibly straining as he at first pulled a little and then as hard as he could to attain his prize. There was a moment of expectant silence from the crowd then a sudden eruption into a combination of laughter and vocal ridicule. Embarrassed and eager to leave the scene as quickly as he could, the young boy ran away as fast as his legs would take him. The previously cocky old man wasn’t far behind.

Merlin led the way through the crowd with Arthur following close behind. There was a loose kind of queue that had formed which they were not a part of, to be the next in line to make an attempt. The throng of people unaware of what they were doing parted to allow the old sorcerer and his ward access to the sword. A small troupe of four men was clearly annoyed at the intrusion of the newcomers. They were the next to attempt to free Excalibur. One of them began to object only to find his voice trail away into silence at the impassive stare from this menacing bearded old man. "Mine name is Merlin, and this is thine King, Arthur Pendragon" An absolute silence covered the assembly. Never in the history of the attempts had anyone ever claimed to be Merlin. Who in their right mind would make such an assertion? Nobody would try to pass themselves off as the sorcerer in fear of what may befall them if they did. Merlin's legend was as great as that of the missing son of Uther. The magical feats that he had performed in the service of the King were the stuff of stories told throughout Briton. Imagine what the sorcerer would do to somebody that dared impersonate him.

Arthur could see his destiny only a short few steps ahead of him. He couldn't feel his legs as he climbed the rock and stood beside the symbol of his entitlement. Transfixed by the sword, he was unsure of whether he had heard Merlin's brief introduction or not. There was no sound of bird in the sky or wind through the trees. The hordes of people were deathly silent. All eyes were upon the dark-haired handsome young man standing on the rock. He reached down and wrapped his fingers around the sword's grip. It felt warm. A shriek of metal being freed from stone cut through the air making people's skin tighten and hairs stand up. With an effortless flick Excalibur was raised above Arthur's head. The sword was absolutely new, and showed no signs of age or weathering. The light reflected upon its mirrored finish, and the crowd collectively gasped.

Merlin raised his right arm and pointed toward them, "Kneel before King Arthur!" He used Arthur's name a second time to ensure that it would be remembered, “And spread forth from here throughout the land.” In droves the gathered people fell to one knee in awe and respect for their new-found King.

***

Arthur shook the memory from his thoughts. He needed to don his royal robes and get back to the main courtyard. The expedition to North Rheged was important. He could trust both Merlin and Morgan to use their otherworldly powers to recover the real Excalibur. In the meantime, King Hael needed his help. Arthur set about getting ready for the journey.

Chapter 4: Caerleon Battlements, One Hour Past Noon

Gwenhwyvar joined Morgan upon the battlements of Caerleon Castle to watch the journey of Arthur and half of his Knights through the village and beyond. He only had a small band of soldiers with him. Arthur did not want to take a full force, simply because this was a diplomatic mission rather than a looming battle. Amhar was in tow; he could not see over the high walls and begged his mother to lift him so that he could view the procession. The three of them watched as the villagers waved and cheered the men on their way. Gwenhwyvar could tell that Morgan's thoughts were elsewhere. She studied Morgan's face. Her eyes were not focussed upon anything now; she had a faraway look upon her beautiful features.

***

Morgan could see him. The man that had stolen Excalibur, it was Lyal's replacement as head of stables, a relatively new addition to the Royal staff. Garlon had come to the court with impeccable references from the township of Mynyw to the west of Caerleon. The noble family there was loyal to Arthur; there was simply no need to suspect treachery. But now it was laid bare for all to see. Garlon's absence was keenly noticed by all during the preparations for Arthur's departure. Many comments and questions had arisen from his sudden disappearance; but Arthur, Merlin, Morgan and Gwenhwyvar had remained resolutely silent on the whole matter. Now that Morgan had a focal point for her amazing abilities the veil was beginning to part. She could see Garlon upon his horse, Excalibur strapped to the beast of burden. But the countryside which he traversed was unrecognisable. Wooded lands, no distinguishing landmark that would give away his location; the vision faded. Gwenhwyvar's expression posed the question to Morgan and the sorceress dutifully replied, "Yes mine Queen, 'twas Garlon, but where…." She left the sentence incomplete. Gwenhwyvar was magnanimous with her assurance in Morgan's abilities, "Time will tell".

Frustrated with the uselessness of her vision Morgan turned her gaze once more upon the departing legation. "Mine hope is that Arthur's mission to North Rheged bears more fruit than this worthless vision". Again Gwenhwyvar gently reassured her sister-in-law, "Give thine self, reassurance that the vision shall reveal all in time" Morgan smiled at the composure and confidence that Gwenhwyvar offered her. She nodded "Aye Gwenhwyvar". But there was more to the Queen's tone than kindly sage. Morgan could tell that there was finality to her words. It was as though a decision had been made by the monarch, but Morgan did not know exactly what. They watched the delegation in silence until they could no longer be discerned by its youthful eyesight. Amhar had fallen asleep, his head rested upon his mother's shoulder. Maternal instinct alerted Morgan that it was time to feed Mordrede; she excused herself and left the Mother and son alone on the battlements.

Chapter 5: The Queen's Antechamber, The Following Day

Gwenhwyvar and the ladies of the court were completing the latest in a long line of tapestries that they had created together. This one however was not of Caerleon Castle, but a scene of Cellewig castle. They had begun it whilst residing there and now that it was nearing completion conversation turned toward whether or not it should remain in Caerleon or be dispatched to hang in Cellewig castle instead. Elamite, Florie and Lyonors were adamant that it should remain in Caerleon to remind them of their recent sojourn in the land of Dumnonii. Gwenhwyvar was undecided and offered suggestions as to whereabouts in each castle that the hanging may serve its purpose. Morgan, initially arguing that because the tapestry had been begun in Cellewig it ought to return there to reside. eventually became detached from the conversation and fell silent.

The ladies knew the signs; Morgan was having another vision. Needlework came to a complete stop and they all watched the sorceress for signs that she would be returning to them from the otherworld realm of second-sight. The moments dragged on and on. The three sisters-in-law exchanged worried glances. This was taking too long. What was it that Morgan was seeing? Her visions never took her away from them for extended periods as was now happening. Gwenhwyvar dared to break the silence. "Dear sister, what doth thou see?" her request was hushed, not wanting to frighten Morgan's consciousness back into the room. Morgan turned her head slowly to face the Queen; slowly her eyes became focussed upon Gwenhwyvar. The air of expectation was palpable.

"A rider in the forest" came the simple explanation of what Morgan had seen. Florie interjected immediately "Was it Garlon, our lost head of stables?" Still fresh in everyone's minds was the fact that Garlon had gone missing the previous day. Nobody knew why or where. More importantly for Gwenhwyvar and Morgan, none of the court realized that he was in fact a thief and that he had stolen Excalibur. Morgan phrased her answer very carefully. "Garlon, aye; riding through a forest, where though?" she shook her head in denial of the location. Lyonors queried Morgan's vision of the servant, "Was he in distress? Perhaps a brigand carrying him away from Arthur's lands against his will?" Morgan replied but addressed her appraisal of the situation to the Queen instead of Lyonors, "No, Garlon rides alone, encumbered only by whatever he hath taken with him from Caerleon". Morgan gave Gwenhwyvar a knowing look that went unnoticed by the other three women.

Conversation turned immediately as to why he would have so suddenly departed without making known his plans for travel. Morgan and Gwenhwyvar did not offer any conjecture to the three ladies. "Perhaps he tired of his duties in service of the King and now seeks a new employer?" offered Elamite. Florie had another theory but it was offered with a caveat. "If he had received word of an ill relative and sought to be at their side, surely he would hath informed someone in the court before leaving."

Speculation continued for a while and work resumed once more upon the tapestry. Further assumptions were offered to Morgan for approval before being abandoned in favour of some newer supposition. For her part Morgan gave non-committal shrugs and small shakes of her head but did not offer any guesses of her own as to Garlon's mysterious departure. The day wore on and the final flourishes were made to the tapestry until it was done. Somehow an accord was reached during the ensuing hours that the tapestry would indeed hang in Caerleon to remind the castle dwellers of their recent stay at Cellewig castle.

Servants were called and instructed as to the exact location of the newly completed wall hanging. Florie departed to tend to little Wigaloith and Lyonors similarly went to bathe and feed young Akhera. Elamite excused herself so that she could assist in the kitchen for the forthcoming evening meal. With the last of the servants now carrying out the furled tapestry Morgan went to leave the room as well when Gwenhwyvar motioned for her to remain behind. Waiting for them to be alone the Queen was packing away her weaving instruments and when sure that she would not be overheard she looked up at Morgan. "There is another that we may consult for the whereabouts of Excalibur". Morgan was surprised. Another? Another what, sorcerer, sorceress? How could Merlin have kept another of their kind so secret from her?

Gwenhwyvar's voice put to rest Morgan's speculation. "The Lady of the Lake". Morgan was visibly shocked. "Ye know where she may be found?" "Aye". This was almost inconceivable. Merlin had told Morgan very little about the mysterious being that had fashioned Excalibur and through him entrusted it to Uther, Arthur's father. Even during the time that Morgan was Merlin's understudy and lover, he had spoken very little of this powerful woman. How could the Queen have come to know such things? Anticipating her questions Gwenhwyvar explained the situation. "Merlin hath confided in Arthur as much as he knows about the Lady of the Lake. Arthur in turn hath revealed that information to his wife". She finished explaining the situation to the sorceress with a raised eyebrow.

Morgan once more took her seat and pondered the idea. "Ye hath had two visions now of Garlon's flight with Excalibur. What if there is no other? What if ye hath more visions that do not clearly reveal his position?" Morgan saw that Gwenhwyvar was very much like her husband. She was weighing up all of the possible scenarios and determining a course of action, just as Arthur would do in similar circumstances. Morgan felt herself relenting. What the Queen was saying made good sense. If there was further help to be gained from the Lady of the Lake, how could they possibly ignore it? Morgan's ponderous expression gave way to a look of determination. Gwenhwyvar knew that she had won over her sister-in-law with the logic of her argument. "She resides in Llyn Callyfyrth" Gwenhwyvar reached out and clasped Morgan's hand into her own. "Together we shall see that Excalibur is returned to the King."

The decision made, Gwenhwyvar divulged the details of her plan. "We shall take Sirs Galahallt, Guaen and Garethe as escort and ride to Dumnonii. I shall call upon the Lady and beseech her help. If Excalibur's location is revealed, ye can call upon Merlin that Arthur may dispatch his Knights to capture Garlon." Morgan could see that Gwenhwyvar had given this plan a good deal of thought. "Aye mine Queen. When shall we leave?"

"Make preparations for us to leave in the morning. See to the provisions and the horses. I will make known our plans to the Knights." They both stood up together. A newfound sense of purpose was mixed with excitement and trepidation; they strode from the antechamber to fulfil their assignments.

Chapter 6: The Knight's Courtyard, Late Afternoon

Gwenhwyvar was an unusual sight in the small courtyard reserved for the Knight's sword practice. Most of the knights that remained in Caerleon that had not accompanied the King to North Rheged were engaged in their usual boisterous one-upmanship whilst refining their skills with their swords. The shouting cajoling and friendly mockery of each other's abilities whilst practicing subsided at the presence of the Queen. Heads turned in query as to the reason for her visit. "Sir Guaen, Sir Garethe, I wouldst speak with thee" The two brother knights engaged in friendly battle ceased their exercising and sheathed their swords. Their chainmail rustled as they made their way toward Gwenhwyvar. "Aye mine Queen" said Guaen has he approached, echoed by Garethe.

"Find Sir Galahallt and make preparations for us to leave for Cellewig in the morning. Morgan shall be accompanying us". The royal command came as somewhat of a surprise to the knights. Astonished but unsure of how to react they both looked at each other for direction. "Our party shall consist of the five of us only. Our mission should not take more than a few days, but best prepare for longer should the need arise". The news continued to astonish the knights. The Queen on a journey without her servants to attend to her, and no reference to Prince Amhar being a part of the troupe? It was possibly the most extraordinary order that either of them had received since pledging their allegiances to King Arthur years ago.

Guaen made to object in some way but, unable to find grounds to oppose a direct order from the Queen, he fell silent. Garethe, still taken aback, managed a stiff bow and confirmed his understanding of the direction with a simple "Aye mine Queen". Realising that he had not acknowledged the command, Guaen offered "Sir Galahallt is upon the battlements, I shall inform him directly Majesty". Gwenhwyvar nodded her approval and gracefully turned to leave the knights to their new errand. The knights that had overheard the exchange with a singular look of absolute amazement watched as Gwenhwyvar walked away.

Chapter 7: The Southern Coast of Sussex, Nightfall

Garlon watched the fading light over the sea. The sound of the water lapping the shore was soothing. His horse was resting after the long journey, and now it was his turn. In the morning, he would hire passage across the water to Insula Vectis so that the next part of his intricate plan could be implemented. He held Excalibur in both hands and began to go over in his mind the events that had transpired only a few nights before.

***

Walking the battlements during the night had become a known habit of his. The Knights that were supervising the soldiers were accustomed to seeing Garlon night after night. It was a little ritual of his before retiring to bed. This night there was no Gaelach in the sky to shine her light upon them. The men on watch could only see the firelight filtering through the village huts' windows at the base of the hill upon which sat Caerleon. They thought nothing of Garlon as he wandered past them one at a time. Furtively he reached for the faerie dust that he had obtained. One by one without being spotted he sprinkled the men on duty. Overcome by a sudden wave of tiredness each of them was unaware of the other slumping quietly down to sleep, until it was done. Now there was nobody watching the quiet world below.

Garlon made his way into the castle and directly toward the King and Queen's chamber. There was one more foot soldier to take care of before he could safely enter Arthur's room. Without a sound he managed to lift the latch and push the door open enough for him to slip in sideways. It was dark, lit only by the dying embers of the fire in the fireplace. He pushed the door shut and waited for his eyes to adjust to the darkness. He could make out Arthur and Gwenhwyvar in their bed. Arthur's heavy breathing dominated the room. There to his side and leaning up against a stool was his prize; Excalibur, the magical sword, and the very symbol of the King's rightful heir to the throne. He could feel his heart beating faster. He moved to stand above the sleeping couple and threw another couple of pinches of the faerie dust over them. Now there was no chance of them waking suddenly.

Brazenly he lifted Excalibur and unsheathed it. It was heavy; exactly as he had expected of such a weapon. Giving it a masterful twirl in his hands he brought it to bear a hair's breadth from Arthur's throat. He could kill this upstart right now. He contemplated the moment. He could be the man who rid the land of the would-be-King of all Briton; and he was sorely tempted. But then there would still be Merlin to deal with. Perhaps the faerie dust would work on the old sorcerer as well. He could sprinkle the old man and kill him right now. There was a long pause whilst he contemplated the move. Doubt crept into his mind. What if the faerie dust did not work on Merlin? The Wiley old conjurer was a force to be avoided. No, he would stick to his original plan and see Merlin consumed by the evil creature that he had made his deal with. Arthur, without his wizard and without his magical sword could then be defeated and expelled from Briton at the hands of the Saxons. With nobody for the natives to rally behind, the Saxons could continue to claim more and more parts of the country for themselves. It was a perfect plan. He had thought of it every day since he first heard of Arthur's defeat at the hands of Aelle. His scheming had brought him this far. Now all he had to do was complete his plan and cover himself with glory in front of his own countrymen. Lifting the sword from Arthur's neck he sheathed it. With a final curious look around the royal chamber he stealthily exited the room.

***

Pleased by his recounting of the recent events, Garlon laughed. He wrapped himself in his cloak and began to gather drift wood so that he could make a fire to warm himself against the night.

Chapter 8: Caerleon Main Courtyard, Morning

The three brother Knights had risen before sunrise to make final preparations for the journey to Cellewig castle in Dumnonii. It was obvious from the expressions on their faces when the two ladies arrived, that they did not approve of this surprise visit to Cellewig castle. Surely it would be better for them to wait for Arthur's return here at Caerleon. Why risk a journey through Saxon held lands? Although it would only be a day or two and then they would be in Arthur's south-westernmost realm once more. Nevertheless, it was a dangerous journey. None of the knights were accustomed to the Queen commanding them to do anything. She had always been the perfect ruler of the court for all things that a Queen was meant to oversee. What had changed that she would now begin to use her authority to instruct the Knights of the Round Table?

Gwenhwyvar approached the men with Morgan following closely behind. She gave a wry smile able to easily guess what the three brothers were thinking. Galahallt looked up as the Queen approached. From his peripheral vision he could see Elamite in the distance. She was coming to bid him farewell. Florie holding little Wigaloith and Lyonors cradling Akhera could be seen following Elamite out of the main door to the castle. "Sir Knights" Gwenhwyvar thought it best to offer some kind of relief for the men's troubled minds. The men stopped what they were doing and looked at her expectantly. "Although our mission to Cellewig must remain for the time being a mystery, know that it is not a flight of whimsy, but of great importance to Arthur's rule". Almost as one, the knights answered "Aye mine Queen". Both Gwenhwyvar and Morgan had chosen non-descript garments for the journey. As was common sense for such a small band, they did not need to attract attention to themselves. The two women were aided upon their mounts by the Knights nearest to them.

By this time the brother's wives had arrived and there were the expected parting kisses and embraces. Little Akhera was a particularly bright-eyed and happy child that loved to grab Guaen's short beard and eyebrows. He laughed as she did once more, never tiring of his little girl's antics. Eventually the time came for the men to take their mounts. The women stood back to allow them to do so. This gave Gwenhwyvar a chance to offer some solace to the ladies of her court. "Fear not ladies, there is no-doubt that thine husbands shall return safely to ye" Comforted by this assurance from the Queen the three sisters-in-law stepped back and with final waves and well wishes, the group began their journey.

Horse's hoofs made a soft pattering sound against the earth of the courtyard, as they ambled up to, then through the main gate. Morgan noticed that the three brothers all at some point turned around to wave yet again to their wives. It was unusual, she thought; normally once mounted they would be looking forward steadfastly. She surmised that maybe it was because they were not riding with Arthur. She continued to muse as to the possible reasons all the way down the hill and to the village. Then deciding that there was no way to resolve the uncharacteristic behaviour without asking them, Morgan decided to give it no more thought. Instead she began to wonder about the task that lay ahead and most importantly about the possibility of meeting the Lady of the Lake. It was a daunting prospect; even Merlin himself knew very little about her. That fact alone gave the mysterious figure an ominous aura. As if able to read her thoughts, Gwenhwyvar moved her horse into position beside Morgan's and began to speak at a volume that ensured that the men would be unable to hear. "Our journey shall not be wasted. Surely the Lady of the Lake will be able to aide us in our quest" Morgan wasn't sure if the Queen was asking a question or making a statement. Nevertheless she felt that some kind of response was required. "Aye mine Queen. If anyone can help us recover Excalibur, 'twill be her."

"We shall ride to Cellewig castle, as the men believe. Once there, we shall take our leave of them and head north to Llyn Callyfyrth" Gwenhwyvar outlined the coming course of action. "What if the knights insist upon accompanying us?" gently objected Morgan. "It shall be a royal command that we strike out on our own. We shall be in Arthur's territory without any Angles, Saxons or Jutes nearby. They will have no real cause to object. Furthermore, mine safety is assured." Gwenhwyvar gave Morgan a warm smile "Who better to protect the Queen that a Sorceress". The vote of confidence in Morgan's abilities warmed the Enchantress' heart. With the sun now well and truly risen, they picked up the pace of their ride and had soon left Caerleon village behind them.

Chapter 9: Wessex. Nightfall

The small party of five had made good time during the day. Unencumbered by foot soldiers slowing them down, they had entered the Angle controlled lands that Caerleon bordered and quickly left them behind. Now they were in the Saxon controlled land of Wessex. The Knights were keen to press onwards for as long as they could before setting-up camp for the night. So far they had been lucky to not encounter any hostile forces. Gwenhwyvar showed that she was more than up to the challenge of the extended ride and gave the knights leave to continue for as "long as necessary" before stopping for the day.

Gaelach was a crescent in the sky; she offered no useful light for the travellers. Eventually Galahallt signalled that they should stop for the night. They were in a small clearing in the middle of a treed area. The men dismounted first and aided the women down from their horses. Firewood was gathered and soon a small fire was ablaze and the party encircled its flickering warmth. Conversation turned to the day that had been. No encounter with the Angles bordering Caerleon. And now, so far, no encounter with the Saxons of Wessex. As if willing it into existence by talking about it, unobserved by the party of five, two sets of malevolent eyes pried upon their campfire conversation. They were Saxons, loyal to Aelle, yet far west of his kingdom. The firelight had attracted them to the clearing. Surreptitiously they made their way to a vantage point where they could observe the quintet.

"We should report back to Aelle" said one to the other. Nodding in agreement the other replied in an equally hushed tone "Clearly ladies of distinction to be accompanied by three Knights". No detail was missed by the two prying Saxons. The bland clothing did not disguise the relevance of the party. Creeping backwards the way that they came, the two Saxons almost made good there retreat. It was a bird that they disturbed, one that had settled upon the ground for the evening. The pheasant noisily fluttered up and away from the intruding men. As one, the party from Caerleon looked toward the disturbance. "What was that?" queried Morgan. The brothers, more paranoid than the women, gave each other a grave look. "Seek, find' Gwenhwyvar's instructions were clear and succinct. Without another word of exchange between them, Galahallt and Guaen moved off in the direction of the sound to investigate whilst Garethe remained to guard the two women. Nervous looks were exchanged between the three around the campfire. What if.....the possibilities all revolved around Saxons discovering that Knights and Women of Arthur's court were discovered in a hostile land?

The two Knights moved as quietly as the undergrowth would allow. It was clear now that somebody was moving ahead of them. Quickening their pace Guaen and Galahallt moved to within arrow shot of the strangers that had so abruptly intruded upon them. By then it was too late. The suspected Saxons had reached their horses and taken their mounts. There would be no chance now to catch them on foot. With a cry of angst, Galahallt cursed the escapees as one the brothers turned to run back the way they had come. There was a vein of hope in preparing their horses in time for a pursuit. The two burley

Knights crashed their way back into the clearing. Garethe, Gwenhwyvar and Morgan stood up as they approached. "What was it?" queried Gwenhwyvar. "Saxons mine Queen?" replied the exasperated Galahallt. It was clearly a guess, he did not know for sure. The two brothers were heading in the direction of the horses. Guessing that they intended pursuit, Gwenhwyvar turned to Morgan for assistance. "Is there something that can be done?" she bid. Morgan's mind raced, perhaps she could project herself ahead of the marauders, but that would only be a dream-like vision. It was nothing that could interact with real people that were now on horse and in flight. Morgan felt completely helpless. If these intruders turned out to indeed be Saxons, then their presence in the land would surely be found out. They may have to contend with a large force of Saxons hunting them down after all.

In the distance there was a twin neigh of alarm from two horses, followed by the shout and sound of distressed men falling from their horses. The quintet all looked at each other for direction. It was the Queen that set the course of action by running toward the the commotion. With no other choice than to accompany the Monarch, the remaining party of four followed in rapid succession. It was as though the undergrowth and low-lying branches of the trees we collaborating to impede the progress of the ladies and knights. Twice Gwenhwyvar stumbled over a branch in the darkness but managed to keep her balance and continue the dash forwards. Blood-curdling cries from just ahead stopped the queen dead in her tracks.

A man's death knell could be heard; it sounded like blood choking his throat as he gasped his final breath. A second man's unbridled scream of absolute terror was similarly cut-off with a shriek that sent a shiver through Gwenhwyvar. By this time the other four had caught up to the Queen. Eyes wide with terror at the unseen calamity that had befallen the men, the three knights drew their swords as one. Taking the lead the three brothers formed a line ahead of the two ladies, determined to protect them with their lives. A female voice hailed to them from the darkness ahead. Morgan recognised it instantly, Nimue. "Queen Gwenhwyvar, Morgan Le Fay, come forth". The two women looked at each other. Morgan leaned forward and urgently whispered, "Tis Nimue for sure". Gwenhwyvar's look of horror turned to one of distain in an instant. The malevolent faerie that had been the cause of so much misery at Caerleon only a few short years ago; Morgan had told her all about the vile creature. This was the other-worldly being responsible for beguiling Arthur and Morgan into sleeping with each other.

"Stand aside", Gwenhwyvar's voice pierced the darkness. For a moment the three brothers did not realise that it was them she was addressing. Guaen was appalled, "Mine Queen, let us go and slay this threat whatever it may be". But Gwenhwyvar was in no mood to be told what to do. Pushing her way past the shocked knights she strode forward, her resolve fixed upon her beautiful features. With the dismayed knights following closely behind, Gwenhwyvar made her way towards the voice. "No harm shall befall ye" comforted the disembodied voice. Taking a small white stone from her robes, Morgan spoke a few words in the old Galatian language and the stone became impossibly bright. Holding it high above her head, the stone spread its revealing light across the scene that befell them.

Nimue was standing before the bodies of the two men that the party had made a futile effort to pursue. Their horses were nowhere to be seen. Gwenhwyvar walked purposefully up to Nimue stopping only because the bodies blocked her path. "Saxons Queen Gwenhwyvar, in the service of Aelle; surveying this land for his benefit." Nimue offered them the identities of the now deceased spies. There was a cold silence that lingered and became awkward. Gwenhwyvar held Nimue's gaze without flinching. The faerie could see the determination in the Queen's eyes. Gwenhwyvar looked down at the hapless victims of the faerie. They had been speared with something sharp. Blood still oozed from the open wounds. Slowly circling the fallen men Gwenhwyvar lifted her stoic stare once more to Nimue and queried with commanding conviction "How did ye kill them?"

Nimue took a few steps backwards. Her form shimmered and she became a twelve pointer stag; a huge deer with antlers as sharp as any arrow and clearly, just as deadly. Galahallt let out a small yelp and made to intervene, fearing for the Queen's life so close to such a fearsome creature. In a moment of time, Nimue had transformed back to her human form. Gwenhwyvar seeing the motion from her peripheral vision raised a hand to bid the knight to stay put. Morgan was amazed at the sight. Nimue had taken the male form of an animal. Her mind tried to quickly review all of the words that she had read in Merlin's scroll on the faerie people. Was it possible for the faerie to spontaneously change gender? She was sure that it was not. What could it mean? Had Nimue's powers somehow developed since their last encounter with her?

"Why wouldst ye assist us Nimue?" Gwenhwyvar's question was direct and laced with a tone that hinted she would not tolerate anything less than a truthful answer. Nimue drew a breath in preparation to answer and sighed, shaking her head, clearly annoyed at herself for some reason. "Let us talk Queen Gwenhwyvar, but not here". She motioned to the corpses lying motionless on the ground. In a move that shocked Morgan and the Knights, and clearly startled Nimue, Gwenhwyvar motioned with her left hand, "Accompany us back to our campfire so that we may talk in comfort". Alarmed at the possibility of hosting the eerie creature, the three brothers all stifled objections that made to emanate from their throats. Morgan too had to catch herself rather than directly contradict an offer from the Monarch. This was a terrifying prospect. The very faerie that had caused so much heartache in Caerleon, now an invited guest to their campsite. What was Gwenhwyvar thinking?

They made to move toward the site of their still-lit fire; Morgan leading the way with her amazingly bright stone. The journey was undertaken in complete silence. Pushing their way through the undergrowth the six reached their campsite after what seemed like an age. Gwenhwyvar once more surprised all with her next words. "Come Nimue, sit by the fire". The light emanating from Morgan's small stone faded and she buried it in her robes once more. The faerie, now on-guard and fearing some subterfuge, moved to a position near the fire and sat on one of the logs that had been moved into position surrounding the flickering and now much smaller blaze. With a motion from the Queen, Guaen moved in to stoke the fire with more recently gathered dry wood. It hissed and crackled as he did so. Now only lit by the flames, starting with Gwenhwyvar and Morgan, the remaining party took their seats.

There was no fear of another awkward silence; Gwenhwyvar ensured that, "Aelle's men may hath made our travel more difficult were it not for thine intervention Nimue. Once more, why wouldst ye assist us?" The question was direct and asked in a demanding tone. Nimue seemed to be gathering herself, she looked directly at Gwenhwyvar and answered, "Mine people are in danger." Without a second of hesitation the Queen continued her questioning "In danger of what?" Nimue looked at Gwenhwyvar and then at Morgan before replying in a single word, "Extinction".

"Tell us everything Nimue". The Queen's tone had not softened, she was clearly not easily given to sympathy at such a dramatic announcement. And so Nimue opened up and told the small group of the events that had transpired after her expulsion from Caerleon by Merlin. "Arthur's defeat at the hands on Aelle was because he had help from renegade faeries not of this land, we suspect from Aelle's own; at least that is what King Hellekin hath told our people. Hellekin made a pledge to offer his assistance to Arthur should they continue to aid the Saxons or any others in their conquest of our lands. But for some reason they hath not revealed themselves at any of Aelle's other battles. Nor hath we heard word of their intervention with the Angles, Jutes.... " she trailed off before beginning again, "It is as though they hath disappeared without trace. Hellekin ordered a search for these renegades be made, but his guards found no intruders anywhere". Her expression changed to a frown, she brought her hand up to her temples to rub them gently before continuing. "As ye knows" she addressed Morgan now, "part of King Hellekin's duty as ruler is to uncover the lost spell of fertility for the faerie people. With our entire body of knowledge available to him, the King thought that there was a spell that could make individual faeries fertile, but it failed". A look of dejection covered her features.

She paused briefly to gather her thoughts, "There hath been no births to any of the faeries this past year. My plea is a simple one.." Nimue looked directly into Gwenhwyvar's eyes. "We ask for Merlin's intervention to save us. To forgive mine past transgressions and locate the spell that will allow us to bear children once more". Morgan interjected, "What of faeries born to simple folk, conceived at the height of Belewe Gaelach?" Morgan was referring to the conception of a faerie by humans who copulated during the rare instance of a fourth full moon within a season. The three brothers were wide-eyed over the entire proceedings, but Morgan's intimate knowledge of such things was unnerving for them. They traded concerned looks through the firelight. Nimue for her part showed no surprise at Morgan's familiarity with the circumstances surrounding the conception of faeries. "None have eventuated for the past seven years".

Gwenhwyvar contemplated her next question. "Ye say that Aelle's victory was aided by faeries that cannot be located. What say ye of this?" Nimue began to recount Hellekin's summary of the events but the Queen cut her off, "No Nimue, what say ye of these events? We hath heard ye relate Hellekin's opinion already". Gwenhwyvar was searching for more information than Nimue had given about the situation that could have seen the end of Arthur's life at the hands of the Saxon. Nimue turned and tilted her head slightly. She was perplexed at Gwenhwyvar's question, but it had also clearly struck a chord with the faerie. "None hath questioned the wisdom of the King." There was pause, "But surely one of his subjects wouldst hath seen something of these renegades and brought it to the attention of his court". Nimue looked as though she had finished her reply, but then a flash of something crossed her face, as though she had contemplated something and then failed to divulge it. Prompted by a look from the Queen, Nimue cautiously ventured her own opinion on the matter. "It is difficult to conceive that renegades could hide amongst us and then completely disappear. Hellekin's search for them was abandoned too easily". She seemed to be lost in that train of thought for a moment, but did not elaborate upon it.

Gwenhwyvar offered to everybody her summation of the situation. "Ye wouldst hath us forgive ye, and offer Merlin's services to aid thine people; yet no account can be given for the faerie involvement in Arthur's defeat at Anderitum. And now Anderidae lies within the clutches of a murderous Saxon." The problematic nature of Nimue's appeal was laid out before all of them. Guaen spoke up "Mine Queen, ye should not trust this creature". Nimue stood up in objection at being referred to as a creature. This sparked the three men to once more reach quickly for their swords, highlighting the fragile nature of the truce they were holding. Gwenhwyvar motioned for them to keep their swords sheathed. Gwenhwyvar presented the question that her party were all thinking. Standing to face Nimue she said, "Why wouldst we help thine kind

Nimue? What do ye offer us in return? Not the faerie renegades that allied themselves with Aelle. What then?"

Nimue was crestfallen. She had given herself to Hellekin and allowed him to take his lustful fill of her body time and again in the hope of conceiving a child once more; a child to help fill the vacuum within her heart that she had felt since she had miscarried Ellergia. It was at her insistence that he finally relented and gave her permission to seek Merlin's intervention. She had offered Gwenhwyvar the truth of her people's situation, but deep down she realised that she could give the Queen nothing in return; certainly nothing that she would value. Tears began to well up in her large brown eyes. "Hath pity Majesty. Ye art mother to a baby boy, as are ye Morgan. What I want is the privilege of motherhood". Morgan's eyes flashed with anger at the very thought of how Mordrede was conceived at the devious hands of this selfish faerie. She could contain herself no longer. "Ye wants motherhood", Morgan's tone was as cold as the winter winds. "What kind of mother could ye make to a helpless child? Ye cannot see past thine own venal desires!" Morgan was now shouting. Nimue made to defend herself from the verbal onslaught. But Morgan had reverted to the old Galatian tongue and was now reciting the spell of beguilement.

Before all of their amazed eyes Morgan projected an exact likeness of Nimue an arm's length in front of herself. Stepping into the shimmering form it enveloped her and Morgan became the exact likeness of Nimue. Marching defiantly forward, Morgan stood in front of the shocked faerie. "Go, Nimue, tell Hellekin if he wishes Merlin's help then he shall have to deliver to us all of those involved in Arthur's defeat at Anderidae." Gwenhwyvar was quick to add a caveat to the offer made by Morgan. "Even then ‘twill be at the grace of the King if any help is offered to thine people". The Queen was thinking on her feet. It would be best not to commit to any offer of assistance to these untrustworthy beings. However, it would also not help matters to reject them completely and give them reason to turn against Arthur. "Leave us Nimue," Gwenhwyvar's command was resolute.

Nimue made to object once more, but Gwenhwyvar was not prepared to negotiate any further. She motioned to Morgan with a flick of her hand to see to Nimue's immediate departure from their campsite. Morgan once more began to speak the old Galatian language, but this time it was the spell of faerie expulsion. Realising what was happening, Nimue's tear-filled eyes narrowed to dark slits on her face as it tensed up and took on an almost manic expression. Her hands imitating the claws from a bird of prey, she looked as though she was about to pounce upon Morgan and savage her. The three Knights simultaneously stood up and drew their swords. However it was too late, the spell had begun to take effect, Nimue could feel it crushing her from every direction. It was excruciating. With a final cat-like hiss at Morgan she turned into a falcon and flapped noisily away into the darkness.

The Knights all took up position, one near to Morgan, and two to protect the Queen. With a dramatic wave of her hand, Morgan disposed of the disguise that she was wearing. It crackled away and disappeared into nothing. Gwenhwyvar turned to Morgan. "Will ye be able to ensure our travel to Cellewig is free from faerie spies?"

Morgan gave a definitive nod of her head. "Aye mine Queen. The spell of expulsion can be cast at random intervals to ensure that it is". "Excellent. We shall resume our journey at first light". As practical as ever, Gwenhwyvar finalised her orders to the group. "We shall eat and then retire for the night". The knights were still reticent to leave their protective positions so they organised amongst themselves for Garethe to fetch supplies from the horses, whilst the other two remained to continue their vigilance. Each of them however, now felt that their services were somehow diminished. It was clear that Gwenhwyvar had no fear of other-worldly creatures, and Morgan was more than capable of looking after herself. Nevertheless, they may encounter more Saxons in this land, and then they would be able to show their mettle.

Chapter 10: The Outskirts of North Rheged, Mid-Afternoon

Arthur's party had made good time in their journey northwards. They had stopped briefly at various Noblemen's homes in North Wales and Northumbria. It was all part of Arthur, showing that he was still a strong and vital King, capable of uniting the land, in spite of his defeat at Anderidae. It had been worth it. Some of the houses that had fallen away from Arthur had now re-pledged their loyalty to the young King. The delineation of Northumbria and North Rheged was the river Dudyn; it lay before the men now. "We shall cross at the narrowest and most shallow point" Arthur was pointing in the direction of their goal. Expert direction-finding from Merlin had led them to the exact place. The trees were not as thick in this area for some reason that nobody knew or even guessed at. It was convenient though not to have to traverse thick forest in order to get to the area where they would cross the water.

With a swift action the King dismounted his mare. The other knights followed his lead and as one they began to walk forward with the small contingent of foot soldiers that had accompanied them. "Shall ye not levitate us across the water Merlin" Sir Brumean playfully taunted the old sorcerer; knowing full-well that Merlin would do no such thing. Merlin gave a loud grunt of amusement. "Tis time that we all bathed after our long journey" he mockingly scorned the knight in return. This elicited laughter from those that had heard the exchange. One by one they waded into the water. It was cold. Thankfully the weather was warm and they knew that the discomfort would be short lived. Although this was the easiest point to cross the river, it still held some amount of treachery. At its deepest point the men would be up to their necks in water. The very thought would normally frighten most of the foot soldiers, none of whom had a horse to hold on to for assurance. The presence of Merlin however, was a guarantee of rescue should any of them get into difficulty.

The crossing proceeded in single file without incident, and soon the men were on land in North Rheged shaking themselves dry and squeezing the water from their tunics. "Let us make King Rhydderch's castle before nightfall", commanded Arthur. The order was not out of the question, but it would mean that they would have to proceed with some haste if they were to reach their destination before the daylight disappeared altogether. Rather than taking his mount once more, Arthur led the way on foot with his mare in tow. Some of the foot soldiers could be seen visibly sighing with relief. Now at least they did not have to try and keep pace with the horses for the final stage of their journey.

Chapter 11: The Village Outside of King Rhydderch's Castle, Dusk

The arrival of King Arthur and his men roused the villagers from their huts. Word spread faster than a bird can fly and soon they found themselves surrounded with the smiling faces of peasants all wanting to once again get a look at the legendary young King Arthur Pendragon. People cheered at the sight of him and then "ooo'd" and “awed” at the sight of the mysterious Merlin by his side. Individual calls of "Welcome" could be heard above the ruckus. Arthur smiled and greeted the people. His lack of pretentiousness had always pleased Merlin. It was something that he had tried to instil into the boy whilst raising him, however he knew that Arthur was genuine with his modesty, and it came deep from within and not just from being raised to be so.

The village was well laid-out and the roads were wide, which allowed many people to gather around his small troupe of knights and soldiers. Recent rain had made the ground muddy. The light of dusk was gentle and helped to enhance the moment in Merlin's mind. However, it would not last forever and he was keen to get to King Hael's castle to settle in for the night. "Come mine King, so that we shall not intrude upon the evening meal in the castle" It was a timely reminder from Merlin that he was eager to once more be with his twin sister. Progress to the main gate of the castle was slower than the old sorcerer would have liked but it was unavoidable given the conditions. After what seemed an age they made their way into the expansive main courtyard of the castle. Servants scurried forward to take charge of the horses from the knights, the wizard and the visiting King. Forming a line behind Arthur, the delegation marched into the great hall. A huge vaulted ceiling covered the expanse of the long rectangular room. This was both Rhydderch's throne room and banquet hall.

Two extensive tables flanked either side of the room. Ahead of them King Hael could be seen seated upon his throne, with Queen Ganieda seated at his side. There were various members of the court in small gatherings here and there. All faces turned to watch as Arthur approached to appropriately greet the King of North Rheged. "It hath been too long since mine last visitation King Hael. Good tidings. Rather than go through the usual formalities King Hael stood up from his throne and walked down the two steps of the raised throne section to the hall floor. He embraced the young King with genuine warmth. "Tis good to see ye King Arthur". Ganieda too, unwilling to endure the expected conventions of a royal greeting, left her throne to embrace Arthur and then Merlin. Further greetings and acknowledgements were exchanged between the monarchs and the knights one by one until finally they could talk about the reason for Arthur's journey to North Rheged.

King Hael was a once fearsome but honourable King that had mellowed with age. His quandary for these past few years had vexed him and defeated all of his advisors. "The people of Galloway, most notably at the township of Pen Rhionydd, busy themselves with the dismantling of Vallum Hadriani. Despised though it is for its Roman origins, it is a symbol of security for mine land from any potential threat from the Gael and Scoti from the north. News hath now reached us, confirmed by mine own men that Vallum Antonini is now all but gone. The Picts hath used the stone in construction of their villages. With no wall further to the north, Hadriani is the only thing that secures mine land and yours Arthur", he motioned to the young king, referring to the northern most border of Northumbria. "And ye cannot lift a sword to the people of Galloway because they are not invaders like the Saxons or Angles", Arthur completed the conundrum that faced King Hael. Merlin took up the summation of the situation that they now faced. "The Picts are of this land too. Should they wish to build villages from the Roman wall ordered by the Emperor Antonini, how can we refuse them or even negotiate with them to not do so? They recognise no King. Disparate feudal tribes, they want for their own company only. Do not the people of Galloway fear invasion from the Gael or Scoti?"

King Hael shook his head, but it was Ganieda that offered the answer. "As one, the entire township now worships the Christian God. Love thine brother they preach. They seem to fear no expansion of the Picts into their territory; indeed they would welcome it, if only to advocate their religion to the Picts as well." Arthur and Merlin could see the complexity of the problem. It was not as if Hael and his knights could wage war upon the people of Pen Rhionydd to prevent them from dismantling a valuable strategic asset to both Northumbria and North Rheged. It was a much maligned wall during the days of Roman occupation, designed to control trade between the northern regions and those to the south. However, now that the Roman occupation was well and truly over, it served a new purpose: security from the incessant raiders called the Gael and Scoti from across the water. Galloway was the closest point to the raider's island to the west. They could land upon the shores of Galloway and easily attack either North Rheged or Northumbrian settlements.

The dismantling of the wall was of less worry to all of them. Keeping the Picts in their own territories was a primary concern of the then Emperor. The Picts had proven themselves to be unconquerable because of their perceived barbaric natures. If they now chose to use the wall for their own ends, what harm could there be? However, it was curious that they did not feel that Antonini's wall offered them some small protection from the raiders that terrorised them at regular intervals. There followed a general agreement that it was pointless to offer conjecture on the reasoning behind the Pict's way of thinking. The real case at hand was Hadriani's wall. Something had to be done to convince the people of Galloway to leave it intact, but what?

Even though this situation had been brought to Arthur's attention shortly before his now infamous battle with Aelle, it could not be addressed until now. The damage that Arthur's defeat had caused was that many of his supporters turned their backs upon him. Arthur had spent the ensuing two and a half years travelling throughout Dumnonii, Wales and the southern-most realms of Northumbria reinstating his rule. This was how he had grown the number of Knights that were now in his service. Arthur found that his musings about the events since the battle for Anderidae were not helping him come to any decision. He was no closer to offering a solution to the problem than was King Rhydderch.

Merlin interrupted his train of thought. "Who is their leader?" the wily old sorcerer looked from his Sister to Rhydderch expecting one of them to answer. Instead they both just looked at each other then back at Merlin. "They have no leader Merlin", Ganieda replied. "No King?" Merlin was astounded. Both Ganieda and Rhydderch shook their heads. This was an unusual situation. Who would they then need to negotiate with in order to have the people of Galloway stop their pillaging of Vallum Hadriani? The unasked question was answered by Rhydderch. "Word hath only recently reached me of a man that is well respected in the township of Pen Rhionydd. He is the one we should seek out; Maelgyn". Arthur was pleased; the name of a true Briton. Now with a purpose for their mission to Galloway, he started to think through the finer details.

"Let us speak with this Maelgyn and find out where his loyalties rest. If he hath influence within Galloway then it is he we shall bargain with. If not, we shall find those that do." It all seemed so simple. The knights murmured in agreement, but Rhydderch was not so easily convinced. He looked a little disappointed with the over simplified direction that Arthur offered to resolve the situation. But he was happy to have assistance from the young king and his knights. A show of unity from the two Kings could make all of the difference to the state of affairs that had so far befuddled him. "Aye King Arthur", he began and then motioned for the servants to begin serving the evening meal. The room became full of servants hurrying to set up the tables ready for the welcome repast. Ganieda and Merlin moved to be closer together so that they could catch up on all of the news that each had to tell the other since their last meeting.

Rhydderch motioned to Arthur, "Shall ye rest here for a day or two before setting out for Galloway?" Arthur shook his head. "Make provisions for our departure tomorrow". He felt that there was simply no need to wait any longer to investigate the damage to the wall and the actions of the people of Galloway. The resolve of the young King was heartening. Rhydderch beckoned for Sir Brastias and bade him to make the necessary arrangements.

Food began to appear on the tables. At the presiding King's indication, the assembled members of the court and the visitors were shown to their seats and the banquet horn was sounded, heralding the beginning of the meal. Rhydderch gave a traditional blessing for the harvest and thanks for the safe arrival of King Arthur and his delegation. This delighted Arthur; any recitation of the old ways always warmed his heart. The meal commenced and the men and women spent the next few hours taking their fill of the best of North Rheged's bounty, expertly prepared by the kitchen servants.

Chapter 12: The Border of Dumnonii, The Following Afternoon

Gwenhwyvar's ensemble had made good time during the day. They were at the Border of Dumnonii, Arthur's southern-most realm. Now at least the knights could breathe a little easier. This far west there would be almost no chance of running across any Saxons. The river Taemer was before them. On the far shore, almost out of sight, was the safety of Dumnonii. They made their way towards the point where they would be ferried across the river. As ever, it had been attended to with great care by the ferrymen that made their living from hauling people across the river. There would be no payment to be made though. Arthur and his entire court had used the longboat ferry, the largest of them all, to transport the horses and themselves to and from his recognised land. Gwenhwyvar smiled to herself. When they lit the signal fire to summon the longboat, the ferrymen would be pleased to have what they assumed would be paying customers. They would be somewhat disappointed to find out this it was the Queen, her sister-in-law and three of Arthur's knights.

They stopped at the river's edge. The wood for the signal fire was neatly arranged beneath its crude mud and straw roof; ensuring that it would always be dry enough to ignite. Without realising it all eyes had turned to Morgan. Although the knights were more than capable of beginning the blaze with the supplied pieces of flint, it was somehow just expected that Morgan would user her sorcery to make fast work of it. Realising what her fellow travelling companions must be thinking, Morgan dutifully stretched out her hand to make the spell of fire. It reminded her of the first time that she had done it in Merlin's chamber. She had been so excited to accomplish such an amazing and practical piece of conjuring. At the time as she recalled it had come more easily than she would have thought. Perhaps it was Merlin's tutelage, or maybe her eagerness to please him. Nowadays such an undertaking barely consumed any of her concentration or strength.

With a loud crack the carefully assembled branches and twigs erupted into a blazing fire. One by one they party dismounted to await the arrival of the longboat. A large boat, it was capable of handling passage for all five of their horses and themselves at once. The horses would need to be positioned in the centre of the boat facing sideways and tied together to prevent them from moving too much and potentially tipping the boat. Gwenhwyvar spoke, "To make Cellewig by nightfall we shall need to ride hard." It was a keen observation on her part. Because the days were longer than the colder months, it would indeed be possible to reach the Castle in the time that they had left. Sir Galahallt confirmed her summation of the timing. He took into consideration the time that it would take for the ferry to arrive, load the horses and then cross to the other side and disembark. "Aye mine Queen. The horses hath not been too hard pushed this day. With a good rest during the river crossing, they should see us through".

It had been some time since Morgan had recited the faerie expulsion spell. Whilst there was nothing else better to do except wait for the ferry, she began to recite the spell. She was most of the way through when the sound of not one but a flock of birds erupted from the bushes close to the tree line from whence they had come. The party all turned to see the commotion. Birds, about ten or twelve, beat their wings and took flight. The knights having observed Morgan once more casting the expulsion spell all took up their defensive positions near to the two women, fearing the worst. Swords drawn, the men looked like they were set to charge forward should the need arise. "Faeries?" Gwenhwyvar ventured to Morgan. "Perhaps 'twas just a coincidence." Replied Morgan in a tone that indicated she was not at all convinced by her own argument.. She continued "If 'twer faeries; so many!" She gave a worried look to Gwenhwyvar. It was a bad situation. Maybe they were just being paranoid about being watched by faeries. Or worse still, their suspicions were indeed correct and the number of faeries now observing them had increased enormously.

"Could Nimue hath returned to her King with thine message and this is the result, more faerie spies?" Gwenhwyvar's question was unnervingly direct. But it could only be answered with speculation. Morgan shrugged in almost exasperated way. She simply did not know. Guaen could not contain himself any longer. "Mine Queen, what is the nature of thine mission to Cellewig? Are these events connected?" It was a query that Gwenhwyvar did not feel disposed to discuss; especially now that they may have picked up a number of faerie spies. But it did not seem fair to brush aside the supposition that the happenings may be somehow connected. He was a good man, clearly concerned at the events that had unfolded and fiercely loyal to Arthur and his reign. By this time his two brothers satisfied that there was nothing about to burst forth from the undergrowth, turned their attention to Gwenhwyvar, hoping that she would answer Guaen's query.

"Brave Knights" she began, "Secrecy is now more important than ever. The risk of the faerie people discovering the reason behind our mission to Cellewig could undermine Arthur's rule." Turning to Morgan she continued "Morgan, from this point onwards cast thine spell more often, just to be certain". With an assurance from the Queen as well as a plan of action the knights were somewhat comforted, but still apprehensive about the clandestine nature of their undertaking. Garethe showed more frustration than the other two but tried to contain himself. He looked across the river. "There!" he pointed "The ferry approaches". They all turned to see where he was indicating. The ferry was on its way. The sight of it, even though still quite distant, gave them all a sense of relief.

Chapter 13: The Island of Vectis, The Same Afternoon

Garlon was once again waiting. He had crossed the water to Insula Vectis and was waiting for a creature that would assist him in the next phase of his intricate plan. The timing of his plan was very important. She would have observed him arriving on the island. But it suited her vanity to make him wait. If there was one step of his overall plan that he was looking forward to the most, it was this one.

He drew Excalibur from its sheath. Lifting it high as he liked to do, the amazingly smooth surface picked up the blue of the sky and made it almost disappear in an optical illusion. It was difficult to focus upon the blade at this angle. He was completely besmirched with the sword. It was not something that he had expected would happen. Never in all of his life had he seen such a perfect edge to a blade. He would have quite happily brandished it about for a long time more, but the hairs on the back of his neck pricked up. He was not alone. There was someone standing behind him, he could feel it. Startled, he spun around. "Usla" he greeted the beautiful woman who had appeared. She responded first in the language that she was apt to speak. It meant nothing to him. In all his travels he had not heard this language before. Then at last she said something that he could understand, "Come to seek passage across the sea once more?" He sheathed the sword and took one step closer to her. "Aye". He replied. She yawned and stretched as though she had just awoken from a slumber. Bringing her hands down she ran her fingers through her long brown hair. Then following the form of her body she seductively caressed the soft gown that hugged her body.

"Ye knows the price to pay". Her voice was sensual. He closed the remaining distance between them and grabbed her around the waist pulling her forcefully against his body. "Aye" he said once more before kissing her expectant lips. Garlon knew what would happen next. This magical creature had worked her sorcery on him before. There was no sensation of his clothing being removed, or hers. When he eventually had taken his fill of kissing her succulent lips he pulled his face back and looked down. They were both completely naked. Garlon could feel the lust grow within him. He did not know if this was part of her magic or if it was because she was such a striking woman. At this moment he did not care. The fee that Ulsa demanded for safe and fast passage to Gaul was extended rambunctious sex and he was more than prepared to pay the price.

He could feel his penis become erect against the soft skin of her body. The quell of passion began to rise making him light headed at first, then as though somebody had lit a bonfire in a dark cave, he became resolutely focussed upon sating his lustful desires. He threw Ulsa to the ground. There was a soft thunk as she hit the clover covered ground. She laughed a little and with a look of pure amorous hunger on her face, she began to spread her legs slowly and provocatively. Unable to resist the urge to mate with her any more, Garlon dove on top of her and pushed himself deep into her vagina. This was the beginning of a mating that he knew she would extend, at least until morning, or maybe longer if she so desired.

Chapter 14: Cellewig Castle, Dusk

Gwenhwyvar's prediction that they would reach the castle by nightfall had proven to be accurate. The steward of the castle, who must have observed the approaching party from high atop the single turret that was the castle, was at the closed gate to meet them. He was not expecting to see the Queen, three of Arthur's knights and Morgan Le Fay. It showed in his face. "Mine Queen.. " he stumbled, flummoxed by the sudden appearance of Gwenhwyvar. He turned and hurried back through the still open hatchway so that he could unlock the gate and allow the royal party to enter.

With a series of resounding thumps as large beams were pulled back, the gate was pushed open one site at a time; the steward pressing his entire body weight against each half of the gate in turn. "Please majesty enter, enter" the caretaker said beckoning with his hands. Lead by the Queen, the five riders ambled their way into the courtyard of the castle. It was smaller than the main entrance area of Caerleon. But nevertheless it had held Arthur's entire court recently for the winter months. Looking around to see that everything was in place, Gwenhwyvar dismounted before the steward could offer his assistance. He scurried up to her and gave a courteous bow. It was clear that he too was surprised her unexpected presence, and wondered at Arthur's absence. Almost fearing to ask either he rose from his bow and stammered through a few "Umms" and "Ahhhhs" before Gwenhwyvar, smiling, took pity upon him and explained the reason for their unheralded visitation. "Faithful Steward of Cellewig, there is a matter of some importance that must be attended to. Our stay shall be brief. Prepare rooms for us, our journey was wearisome." With his unasked questions unanswered, the caretaker bowed once more and replied "Immediately mine Queen", before hurrying away to do as he was bid.

Morgan and the knights had dismounted by this time and they all assembled around Gwenhwyvar. Morgan offered "Shall I begin preparing the evening meal?" This was a trait of Morgan's that Gwenhwyvar liked about her sister-in-law. She was always willing to take on duties that would usually be left to the servants. "Thank you Morgan, that would be lovely" responded the Queen. "Stoke the fires in the main room" Gwenhwyvar assigned the task to Sir Guaen. "Close the gate and see to the horses" she commanded Sirs Galahallt and Garethe. With everybody duly assigned to a task, suddenly Gwenhwyvar felt at a loose end. This entire journey was based upon an assumption that the mystical Lady of the Lake would appear to her and somehow know the whereabouts of Excalibur. What if all of her assumptions were incorrect? What if the Lady would not respond to her plea? Even if she did, what if it was beyond her powers to locate the magical sword? Self-doubt began to fill every part of her heart. She could not let anyone see her so obviously worrying about things that could simply not be discussed. Gwenhwyvar looked up to the top of the turret. Perhaps high atop the castle would be a better place to allow these concerns to surface.

It took some-time to climb the multitude of stairs that lead to the top of the castle. When she finally arrived, the remaining light was diminishing quickly. There would soon not even be the distraction of the view to help put her mind at rest. "Will thee speak with me Lady of the Lake?" she said, throwing the words softly into the air. A small brown sparrow landed upon the stone turret near to her. Regarding it with some suspicion, Gwenhwyvar moved forward to shoo it away. The bird tweeted and took flight. Perhaps it was time to have Morgan recite the faerie expulsion spell once more thought Gwenhwyvar. She made her way back into the castle to do just that.

***

Morgan was with the Steward in the kitchen when Gwenhwyvar arrived. He must have finished preparing the rooms in a very short timeframe and then come to the kitchen to see to the evening meal. They were working well in unison. A large iron pot was hanging over the main fire heating a stew of some sort that had an appetising aroma. They both looked up from their tasks-at-hand when Gwenhwyvar entered the kitchen. "Morgan could you please ensure that we have no unwelcome visitors," it was a message that did not make any sense to the caretaker, but Morgan acted upon it immediately. "In the courtyard, in the main hall and from the look-out; that should be enough to ensure our privacy," assured the sorceress. She was referring to the number of times and the places that she would need to recite the faerie expulsion spell. This only mystified the hapless curator even more, but too anxious to question the unusual exchange between the women, he elected instead to shake his head and return to cutting up some root vegetables.

To his surprise Gwenhwyvar took over the chore that Morgan was performing. "At first light tomorrow, prepare horses for Morgan and me." She stated with a casual tenor. He responded a little vexed, "And the Knights to accompany ye?" Gwenhwyvar looked up from her task of crushing some dried herbs together and stared directly into the Steward's eyes so that there would be no misinterpretation. "We shall ride out tomorrow without the Knights as escort." He was absolutely astonished. So much that he almost objected before catching himself and humbly responding in the affirmative. "Aye mine Queen".

One down, and three more to go, thought Gwenhwyvar. This would be a test of her abilities to command the knights. It was up to her to stop them from accompanying Morgan and herself on the journey tomorrow. She was determined to keep her final destination a secret, not just because the dwelling place of the Lady of the Lake was told to her in confidence, but because she feared that the knights' presence may contribute to the Lady not wanting to show herself. Gwenhwyvar wanted to give her plan the best chance of success. This, she hoped, would contribute in some small way to a fruitful result.

***

It was a further half an hour before the meal was ready to be served in the main hall. It was only about one quarter the size of the banquet hall in Caerleon. But that meant that it was much easier to heat. It felt warmer than Arthur's main castle's equivalent room. The steward finished carrying the last of the implements into the room and deposited them on the table before disappearing, no-doubt to the kitchen to have his evening meal as well. Gwenhwyvar said a traditional blessing over the meal to the surprise of the knights. It was a tactical decision on her part though. By taking over the duty that would normally be assumed by the King she was stating that she was the one in charge in his absence. It was not something that the men had never doubted, but somehow the Queen was being much more forceful than she had ever been before.

They were eating for a short time before Gwenhwyvar introduced the topic of tomorrow's ride. "We are safely within Arthur's borders here at Cellewig", she began. Any conversation that had been underway stopped to listen to the Queen. "Thou hath seen the abilities of Morgan to vanquish those pestilent faeries." The three brothers all began to look quizzically at each other. This was leading to something. "Aye mine Queen", ventured Galahallt cautiously. "The reason that we have come to Dumnonii is to aide Arthur. However, the exact nature of mine mission must continue to remain concealed from ye. Tomorrow Morgan and I shall ride out to complete that duty." This was a horrifying situation. The two most important women in Arthur's court riding anywhere unescorted did not bear thinking about. As one, the shocked knights objected with various protestations. Each of the three brothers ended up talking-over the other in an undignified manner. Concerns for their safety were mixed with anxieties about the women finding their way back from wherever it was they were going. Trepidations about marauding Saxons within the border, and further disquiet about the manifestation of faeries or any other form of other-worldly apparition that may intercept the ladies on their journey.

Much like Arthur, Gwenhwyvar listened patiently to all of the doubts and worried scenarios and allowed them to come to their own conclusion before answering them in total. Rather than simply putting her foot down and making this a royal command, the Queen thought it best to offer some consolation to the well-meaning Knights. "Thine bravery and skill in battle is not in question dear Knights. We ride north, that is all I shall say. And we shall return by mid-afternoon. If not, then ye may ride out to find and return us safely to Cellewig". Somehow comforted but at the same time unsatisfied with the outcome, the Knights politely but begrudgingly bowed to the Queen's instructions. One by one they gave their acknowledgement and obedience to Gwenhwyvar. Without showing it, Gwenhwyvar breathed a sigh of relief. They all returned to consuming their tasty meals.

Chapter 15: Cellewig Castle, Sunrise of The Following Day

Morgan could tell that Gwenhwyvar had not slept well. There were dark rings beneath her eyes. As perceptive as ever Gwenhwyvar noticed that Morgan too had similar tell-tale signs of a restless sleep. Clearly they were both nervous about the task ahead, but neither spoke of it openly whilst in the company of the men. The steward was holding the reigns of both horses when the two women appeared through the doorway and entered the courtyard. All three knights were awaiting them as well. With a signal from Galahallt, Guaen and Garethe made their way to unlock and open the gate.

As the two women approached, the Steward and Sir Galahallt took positions to assist them onto their mounts. Certain that he should not say anything more on the subject of accompanying them, the Knight bade them simply, a good morning. The greeting was returned followed by a short silence. It was almost as if the menfolk were expecting the Queen to say something further. Sensing that they needed additional reassurance Gwenhwyvar said, "Tis a fine day for riding; we shall not be hampered by inclement weather."

After assisting her on to her steed, Galahallt gave a simple but effective goodbye to the both of them "Travel safely mine Queen; mine Lady." Not wanting to prolong the moment any more than necessary, Gwenhwyvar gave an almost imperceptible tug on the reigns and her horse sauntered forward. Morgan smiled her thanks to Galahallt and goaded her horse into motion to follow the Queen. Passing the two brothers at the gate further farewells were exchanged and the four men watched as the women expertly guided their horses northwards.

In an unspoken agreement both women did not look back as they distanced themselves from the castle. A large part of the journey was undertaken in silence. The miles moved past as gently as the occasional clouds overhead. This part of the land was beautiful thought Morgan. Her first time in Dumnonii was when Arthur moved his court here temporarily before returning to Caerleon. Although cramped compared to Caerleon, Cellewig was nevertheless cosy. The landscape in which it sat was worthy of being captured in a tapestry. The orchard that began at the bottom of the hill from Cellewig eventually gave way to a dense forest. By riding northwards they had bypassed Cellewig village. It too was smaller than Caerleon village, but Morgan thought that it had more character. The mixture of very old and more recent dwellings had taken her fancy. It was surely another tapestry scene to be woven at some future date.

The two women moved closer together to afford some comfort to each other now that they were so far from Cellewig. "Arthur hath shown me Llyn Callyfyrth but once" stated Gwenhwyvar. This gave Morgan some small concern. "Ye shall be able to guide us there and back though?" queried the sorceress. Rather than answering; Gwenhwyvar changed the topic of conversation temporarily. "Recite the faerie expulsion spell once more Morgan to ensure we hath no unwanted company." Then she put Morgan's mind at rest, "Aye Morgan; I shall guide us to the lake and back without error." Morgan spake the words to the spell once more; when finished both women looked around for signs of disturbed wildlife. Birds continued to chirp in the trees, there was no obvious result from the spell. This was a good result. Maybe Morgan's regular incantation had driven them off once and for all. It was wishful thinking on both their parts, but comforting nonetheless.

It was a two and a half hour horse ride to the lake. The women engaged in speculation as to whether or not the Lady would appear to them. In fact all of the concerns that Gwenhwyvar had pondered recently were brought back to light. Normally not having anything but conjecture to talk about would have irritated Gwenhwyvar, but this was almost therapeutic. It was good to know that Morgan, a powerful sorceress, had the same apprehensions as her own.

In time the dense forest gave way to a landscape with occasional trees. Then after riding over a gentle slope the lake could be seen through the shrubbery in the distance. It was beautiful but unnerving. This was it, soon now the reason for their flight from Caerleon would either be answered or not.

Chapter 16: Llyn Callyfyrth, Mid-Morning

The trees had given way to a gentle green slope leading all the way down to the shore of the lake. Gwenhwyvar and Morgan sat atop their horses and beheld the beauty of the large body of water. It was impossibly smooth. No ripple could be seen on its mirrored surface. They had reached the shore in complete silence; filled with the awe of what they were attempting to do. Looking at each other for reassurance, there was a brief pause, Gwenhwyvar dismounted and asked Morgan to hold the reigns of her horse. She moved forward until her feet were almost in the water, and then forcefully and loudly Gwenhwyvar threw her voice over the lake as far as she was able. "Lady of the Lake, I am Queen Gwenhwyvar, wife to King Arthur Pendragon. I beseech thee to speak with me." The sudden noise startled both horses, but they were easily quelled by Morgan's firm hand. They both looked over the surface of the lake for some sign of life, or response. Morgan could feel something; it was like a tingle throughout her entire body. She recognised it as a magical presence, and it was close.

Silence hung in the air like a thick fog. Steeling herself once more Gwenhwyvar continued her plea, "Thine sword Excalibur hath been stolen, we know not where to find it, please help us Lady, I beg thee." Realising that in her nervousness, she had shouted forth the crime that she had tried so carefully to conceal; a sudden wave of panic gripped her. What if there were faeries within hearing distance? Gwenhwyvar had meant to have Morgan recite the faerie expulsion spell upon their arrival but had forgotten to in the heat of the moment. Turning back she articulated her fear, "Quickly Morgan the incantation once more."

Morgan realising what must have gone through the Queen's mind drew a breath and uttered the first few words of the invocation. Then from all around them there came a voice. "Wouldst thee seek to expel me Morgan?" It was full of reprimand, but gentle at the same time. Almost like a mother scorning the attempts of her child to pit its strength against her own. Morgan and Gwenhwyvar looked around them to find the source of the admonishment. No matter which way they looked there was no sign of anyone. Then a sound of bubbling water attracted their gaze once more toward the lake. Ripples were emanating from a point that would have been a far stone's throw from where Gwenhwyvar now stood. Morgan and Gwenhwyvar could both feel their hearts skip a beat.

The surface of the water was broken by the head of a woman. Slowly she rose out of the water. It was difficult to tell if she was old or young looking, the water fell away from her face and intricately braided dark hair. Bit by bit more of her form was revealed. She wore a white shiny garment that looked to be made of the same material that Nimue wore. But it was still too distant to be sure. Her skin was pale, even more so than Gwenhwyvar's. She was slender and sensuous with full buxom breasts and shapely thighs. Her wet clinging garment revealed every line and curve of her form. Gwenhwyvar and Morgan were mesmerised by her. It took a moment to realise that the Lady was now standing upon the water, or at least she seemed to be. A closer inspection revealed that the woman was floating just above the surface which was sending out ripples in all directions as the water continued to fall from her figure.

"Ye art a wise Queen indeed to seek mine sage in this matter Gwenhwyvar." Once more they heard that amazing voice, yet it could not have been spoken by the woman; her lips did not move. The Lady began to float towards the shore. Omnisciently hearing both of their thoughts she responded, "Ye art privy to mine thoughts because ye wish for it to be so" Gwenhwyvar had to fight the urge to take a step backwards at the approaching woman. She offered her interpretation of what she had just heard, "We hear thee because we want to?" The Lady smiled a warm smile of affirmation. She had now reached position in front of Gwenhwyvar. "Mine sword is now in the hands of one who wouldst use it to trap Merlin and end Arthur's reign." Gwenhwyvar seized upon the words, "Ye know the location of this brigand?" The Lady nodded once. "The island of Vectis off the coast of Sussex; Garlon hath arranged for a water horse to take him to Gaul."

Gwenhwyvar was perplexed, "A water horse?" she began. The Lady answered before the rest of the question was asked. "They are rare creatures that can take human form but live for the most part in the sea. Garlon knows that the journey to the mainland can be made in a short time with the help of such a being." Matters were worse than Gwenhwyvar had imagined. Excalibur was being taken from the land and there was the involvement of enchanted creatures to assist him. The Lady cut across Gwenhwyvar's worrying, "Have no fear Gwenhwyvar; travel to Insula Vectis and seek out such a creature by the name of Alus. He can carry ye both to pursue Garlon. Act quickly Garlon rides his water horse, Ulsa to Gaul." This was both terrifying news and welcome information at the same time. Now they knew for certain where the sword was and where it was headed.

Further enlightenment on the situation they faced was forthcoming from the Lady. "Garlon intends to leave the sword in the keep of a foul creature in the hopes that Merlin will come in search of the sword. He erroneously believes that Merlin will know the location of Excalibur and seek to recover it. Try thine hardest to intercept Garlon before he reaches the Minotaur." Morgan could feel her body become cold. "A Minotaur from Greek mythology?" she exclaimed. "Once a faerie that had taken the form of a bull and was then unable to transform himself back completely. He is an ancient being that hath found the way to drain life itself from his victims. It extends his own life; he hath lived for almost as long as I. Garlon's bargain with the beast was to set a trap for Merlin. The Minotaur hopes that by taking the life of a powerful sorcerer he will inherit Merlin's powers."

There were so many questions going around in Morgan's head that it was difficult to know which to ask first. The very mention though of a faerie had brought back her earlier suspicion about the Lady of the Lake's clothing. She was certain now that she could study it more closely that it was made of faerie silk. She must be a faerie. "Aye Morgan, I am a faerie; the oldest and wisest of them all." This shed an entirely different light upon the proceedings. Could this woman be trusted, or was she like Nimue, a deceitful and treacherous being? How could she be sure of anything that this woman was saying? "Calm thine self Morgan. I am not like the faeries that ye have thus far encountered. I hath no part in the society that ye knows of. Indeed the faeries do not know of mine existence. Mine sword was lent to Merlin in order that men should be united by a symbol and cease their petty squabbles so that a new age of peace and harmony may begin. Excalibur was in turn offered to Uther in the hopes of achieving that end. Alas", she looked forlorn, "It was not to be. And now Arthur hath taken up his father's mantle."

Gwenhwyvar offered the Lady her own summation of Arthur's achievements. "Arthur hath united a great many noble houses throughout Dumnonii, Wales, Northumbria and North Rheged. Even now he rides to Galloway..." she began to spruik Arthur's current mission north but the Lady held up her hand in a gesture to stop the Queen. "Tis mine wish that Arthur remain in possession of Excalibur to compete his work. It will continue to serve the authority for which it was meant." This was nothing short of revolutionary thinking for Morgan and Gwenhwyvar; a faerie that wants to assist the spread of a unified rule across the land; the rule of King Arthur. It was Morgan that asked the question that would see the both of them become privy to a piece of information that nobody had known for over three thousand years. "What is thine name Lady?"

Even as the question came out of her mouth, Morgan was not quite sure why that was the next query in a plethora of questions that filled her mind. "I used to have a name long ago." There was a dramatic pause and then she said, "Matrona." Although the name meant nothing to Gwenhwyvar, Morgan reacted strongly, she gasped loudly. "Matrona" she repeated the name in a reverend hush. Gwenhwyvar looked up to Morgan, "The name means something to thee?" Morgan was looking directly at Matrona when she answered the Queen. The faerie Queen that presided over the first casting of the fertility spell for the faerie people. It was in an age when the stone circle was new." To punctuate exactly how long ago that was and how old Matrona was, Morgan turned her focus to Gwenhwyvar "Three thousand five hundred years ago." By the look of absolute amazement upon Morgan's face, Gwenhwyvar did not question the impossible figure that was offered.

"How is this possible?" Gwenhwyvar looked from Morgan to Matrona, her voice shaking slightly. Matrona's voice filled their heads with her reply. "I hath read Nimue's account to Merlin's in one of his scrolls in which he keeps his acquired knowledge of the faerie people." Matrona bade Morgan to tell the story that she had read. There it was again an almost motherly tone that was reassuring. Morgan took up the narrative. "A sorcerer in those days was found by the faerie people to make them fertile and able to produce their own offspring. A deal was struck. The presiding king of the faerie people was succeeded by Matrona who sacrificed the king so that the sorcerer may have the materials from his body to cast a spell of eternal life, as payment for his spell of fertility. The spell itself hidden somewhere in the stone circle but the faeries hath been unable to recover it. But in Merlin's scroll it says that the spell of eternal life was a failure." Morgan finished her summation of the story as she had understood it.

"The spell did indeed fail for the Sorcerer, but not for me. The next night after the fertility spell was successfully cast for mine people I sought out the sorcerer and asked to be included in his immortality spell. There was enough of the potion that he had made with the parts of the king's body needed to cast the enchantment. He invoked the spell I knew that I had accomplished immortality. Time would tell that it had not worked for the Sorcerer. I ruled for a further hundred years and then abdicated and bade mine people farewell, telling them that I would return in the future. I left to travel to the farthest lands and increase mine knowledge of all things. Over the next thousand years I saw many lands and countless enchanted beings. Mine experience encompassed the world as it was known then and more." Matrona's eyes were no longer focussed upon the two women. Instead they could see that she was reliving the chronicle of her journey through immortality.

"I watched as the empires of men were made and surpassed; Egypt, Greece and Rome. I was there during them all. That is why I know that the time of the faerie people is coming to a close. I hath seen the ingenuity of men and the hedonistic civilisation of the faeries that never evolves, does not innovate or create new ways. Great cities, art, learning; these things are not fashioned by faeries." The depth of Matrona's experience was awe inspiring. She seemed to come back from her enraptured state. "Returning to mine home, here" she indicated the lake and its surroundings, "I hath lived in peace and solitude for these past forty years."

"Ye do not wish to return to rule the faerie people? Change their society into something more?" The observation from Morgan looked as though it pinched a nerve with Matrona. "I can hear the thoughts of all faeries, everywhere. That is how I know of Garlon's agreement with the Minotaur in Gaul; a sad creature that hath begged me for help in the past. Why would I?." Gwenhwyvar was quick to exploit this new-found source of information. If Matrona could indeed hear the thoughts of all faeries then she would know the answer to a question that had consumed the young Queen. "Please Matrona, tell me; did the faeries cause Arthur to lose his battle at Anderidae?" The instant of silence before her question was answered seemed to suspend itself in time. Matrona's expression turned sullen. "King Hellekin in collusion with King Aelle, engineered the defeat of Arthur at Anderidae, using his own personal guards to substitute Arthur's horses on the night before battle. The ruler hath convinced his people that it was the interference of outsiders. But there are many now that question his veracity." The news felt like it ripped through Gwenhwyvar. They were betrayed by an evil ruler of a furtive race to a Saxon!

Morgan clutched at a single thought that now enveloped her consciousness, "Did Nimue hath any part in this foul scheme?" Her eyes narrowed; she could no longer see the picturesque lake that surrounded them. Morgan's entire attention was focussed upon Matrona and the answer to her question. "No" came the simple reply. "Nimue was fooled by Hellekin as were all of the faeries." The knowledge came as a relief to Morgan. She felt vindicated from being Nimue's friend for the time that they were. There was a pause and Matrona continued, "Indeed her unborn child was aborted by Hellekin in fear of what the future held for the baby. He had a vision that the girl would grow into a powerful sorceress that recovered the spell of fertility and sacrificed his body to ensure its success. It was a display of degenerated selfishness that strengthens my resolve to no longer give assistance to the faeries." The words were not spoken with particular anger, but the underlying message was one of cold detachment. This helped solidify in the minds of Morgan and Gwenhwyvar that Matrona had truly abandoned her former people. But there was one more thing; it felt like a seed of doubt in Morgan's mind.

"Do ye know the location of the fertility spell?" Morgan asked. "It is exactly where I left it" she replied mysteriously. But the incompleteness of the answer only raised more concerns with the two women. What if it were to be found by the faeries? Could it be successfully cast again? If it could be, who would be able to achieve this? Both Gwenhwyvar and Morgan were lost in a sea of further supposition and conjecture. But before either of them could formulate their next question Matrona began to drift backwards away from them and into the lake. "Wait Matrona, there is more that we need to know" pleaded Gwenhwyvar. She stretched out her hand and even took a couple of steps forward into the water. But it was no good. Matrona was turning the same silver blue colour as the water. Before their eyes her body first became a pillar of water and then it receded into the lake. She was gone.

Gwenhwyvar breathed deeply in and out and composed herself. Looking up she could see that Morgan was doing the same thing. "It appears that our audience is at an end" said the Queen. Morgan felt a mixture of emotions that she was sure Gwenhwyvar was also experiencing. Primarily there was elation at having met such a fantastic being; relief that there was no overall faerie conspiracy to topple Arthur and exasperation at the task that lay before them.

Gwenhwyvar put all of her emotions to one side though and concentrated on formulating a plan of action. "We return to Cellewig. Then onward to Insula Vectis" Morgan knew that this meant entering King Aelle's domain of Sussex. "If Aelle captures us he could demand Arthur's kingdom as ransom." But Gwenhwyvar was resolute "Aye. We shall rely upon thine sorcery to prevent such an occurrence Morgan; tis more important now to intercept Garlon before he reaches the beast in Gaul, and baits his trap." Morgan was dogged with doubt. But she believed that in Arthur's hands Excalibur could achieve what they all wanted for Briton; unity. "Aye mine Queen." She vowed her commitment to Gwenhwyvar's strategy.

Handing down the reigns to the Queen, Morgan steadied the horse whilst Gwenhwyvar took her mount. With a final look back at the shimmering blue lake, they turned their horses toward Cellewig and began the return journey.

Chapter 17: Cellewig Castle, Midday

Sir Guaen was atop the castle on look-out duty. He easily spotted the two riders that were entering the orchard to the north of the castle at the bottom of the hill. He shouted down to the courtyard. "The Queen and Morgan return." In the courtyard Galahallt and Garethe were with the steward sorting out supplies should the need arise for them to venture out on a rescue mission. Galahallt was overjoyed at the news he heartily slapped his brother on the shoulders and exclaimed "See, told ye, the Queen can look after herself, Ha!" Garethe was having none of his brother's interpretation of their previous conversation. "Hold thine tongue Galahallt. Was it not I that told ye of the Queen's extraordinary adeptness to…." He did not get the chance to defend himself from the jibe. Galahallt was already making his way to the gate to unlock it in preparation to receive the Royal party of two, returned safely to the castle.

Gwenhwyvar and Morgan's progress was followed closely by Guaen. He periodically shouted updates down to the three men below. Galahallt and Garethe were impatient to get the two ladies safely back inside the castle walls. It seemed like an age before Guaen shouted down that the women were rounding the castle to enter through the main gate. Gwenhwyvar and Morgan were a welcome sight to the brothers when they finally appeared at the entrance. They raced up to take hold of the horses as the women brought them to a stop in the middle of the courtyard. Dismounting gracefully, aided by the men the Queen and Sorceress exchanged a look that was not unobserved by the Knights. "Mine Queen", said

Galahallt, "tis good to have thee and Morgan safely back inside the walls of Cellewig. Was thine mission successful?" This was a conversation that Gwenhwyvar had not looked forward to. "Call down Sir Guaen and have the steward tend to the horses. Then come inside."

The two Knights hastened to carry-out the instructions from the Queen. Morgan approached Gwenhwyvar and leant in closely so that she would not be overheard. "There are enchantments that may assist the next leg of our journey. Outside grows a willow tree; some bark must be harvested. Then various herbs from the garden…." Nodding her approval, Morgan made her way past Gwenhwyvar and once more toward the castle gate. By this time the steward had appeared. The two knights handed over the reins of the horses to him and looked over at Morgan exiting the castle with a mixture of concern and question. Unwilling to disobey the Queens orders they followed Gwenhwyvar into the main hall.

By the time they had reached it, Gwenhwyvar was sitting in the chair that would normally be reserved for Arthur. Unlike Caerleon, this was a more traditional main hall with two thrones for the presiding King and Queen. To the right and left were a number of smaller and less ornate chairs that were meant for other courtly dignitaries. It was a small tactic by the young Queen to once more reinstate that she was in charge whilst her husband was in absentia. Noting their vexed looks with hidden amusement Gwenhwyvar bade the brothers to be seated. They waited in silence until the puffing and panting of Guaen could be heard approaching the door to the main hall. When he walked in and took in the sight of Gwenhwyvar in

Arthur's throne and his two brothers in chairs to her left he stopped dead in his tracks. "Come forward Sir Guaen we hath much to discuss." Not needing any further encouragement Guaen hastened forward and seeing that the Queen was motioning to the final remaining chair to her left, he quickly took his seat.

"Dear Knights. Ye must be puzzled by the sudden departure from Caerleon and urgent journey to Cellewig. But 'twas taken in desperate need; the night before King Arthur left for North Rheged, Garlon stole Excalibur." The three brothers were visibly shocked. "Garlon!?" Garethe exclaimed. "We know this to be true, Morgan and I sought the counsel of….a seer that lives nearby. She hath confirmed our suspicions." "But saw Excalibur, I did. At Arthur's side as he rode out of Caerleon." Galahallt offered his disbelief before realising that he was directly contradicting what Gwenhwyvar had just said. "Merlin fashioned a replacement, which mimicked the look of Excalibur. Had Arthur found cause to use the forgery, then the deception would hath been revealed." The three brothers were in a mild state of shock. Gwenhwyvar could see a torrent of questions about to erupt from their mouths and although she would normally have listened to each one as patiently as Arthur would have, there simply was not enough time. Holding up her hand to placate them a short while longer, she continued. "Garlon seeks to present the sword to a gathering of Saxon warlords as a symbol of Arthur's weakness and ripeness to be conquered." This was too much for the knights; they all stood up in objection. "Never!" shouted Guaen. "Not whilst there is breath in mine body!" asserted Garethe. "We shall die before allowing those Saxon…." Galahallt was in full diatribe when he cut himself off. The sudden lack of a completed sentence caught everybody's attention. A dawning of realisation came over Galahallt's face. "Mine Queen" he said. "Garlon stole Excalibur from thine chamber whilst thee slept?"

The reality of the situation that Arthur and Gwenhwyvar had faced within the walls of their fortress and inside the boundaries of their monarchy was made perfectly clear by Galahallt. The brother's minds immediately turned to the possible outcome of such an appalling failure in their duty to protect the King and Queen. She could see it written over the Knight's faces. It was a mixture of shocked realisation and abject failure. "Thee could hath been slayed in thine bed" Guaen stated the very obvious, but is struck at the heart of them all to hear it spoken. There was a long moment of horror-struck silence. "Please sit" said Gwenhwyvar. Her voice was even and soft. It showed no sign that she was perturbed by the situation that had passed so closely to her and Arthur. "Garlon knows of Merlin's ability to see the future. Should he hath planned to murder us in our bed, then he risked Merlin's intercession and wrath. Something the brigand could not hope to stand against. No, Sir Knight's I do not believe that our lives were in danger when Excalibur was taken. 'twill serve Garlon far better to brand Arthur as pitiful and unable to hold on to his own symbol of power within his own walls."

Taking a short moment to consider her next words, Gwenhwyvar leant toward them as though about to impart something of great importance. "The seer that Morgan and I consulted told us his whereabouts." The three brothers too leant toward the Queen eager to hear what she said. "There is still a chance to intercept him before he leaves our shores." Guaen all but fell out of his chair he was leaning forward so much. "Say thine word mine Queen and I shall ride like no other man hath before, so that I may catch the swine." This made Gwenhwyvar inadvertently smile. Referring to somebody, even this thief, as a swine would have normally been kept for male company alone. This was perfect, she thought, the acceptance as one of the men would serve her well in the time that was to come.

"He leaves Briton with Excalibur to journey to this meeting of Saxons?" as ever Sir Galahallt was busy trying to think things through. This was when Gwenhwyvar realised that she had become trapped in, not telling the Knights a lie, but omitting to tell them all of the facts. Sir Galahallt had supposed that the meeting would be in a neighbouring land. In fact the meeting place for the Saxons was unknown to her. The journey to Gaul was as far as she knew, to lay a trap for Merlin to walk into. Thinking quickly, Gwenhwyvar decided that it was best that the men did not know the full story unless circumstances changed. They would surely object to escorting Morgan and herself to the island only to be abandoned by them and continue the pursuit without their Knightly protectors.

"We should leave at once mine Queen" volunteered Garethe. "Aye Sir Knight that we should. Make preparations for our immediate departure. We ride for Insula Vectis." She dropped the name of their destination like a stone into a smooth pond. Hearing this, the three brothers objected as one. "Vectis is off the coast of Sussex." "That is Aelle's territory." "Mine Queen we cannot venture willingly into the land of such a deadly enemy, not with thine royal presence." The three protestations came over the top of each other and quite loudly. Gwenhwyvar surveyed their concerned expressions. What could she say now that would convince the Knights to race through Sussex and then cross the sea to the nearby island. Gwenhwyvar was torn between directly commanding them and trying to reason with her protectors. The decision was taken away from her with the entrance of Morgan.

"The enchantments are ready mine Queen" she announced from the far end of the hall, whilst walking purposefully toward them. "Enchantments?" queried Guaen. Gwenhwyvar seized upon the serendipitous moment. "Aye Sir Knights; apart from thine good selves to protect us, Morgan will be using all of her abilities to ensure our journey is free from trouble." It was a vague promise at best. Morgan heard it and immediately guessed what had been happening. The Queen would have been having a difficult time convincing the Knights to escort them through enemy territory and onward to Insula Vectis. Picking up from where Gwenhwyvar left off, Morgan continued, "It would be a foolish Saxon that would seek to impede our progress." The reality was far removed from that. Morgan had prepared two spells, one for the riders and the other for the horses, nothing more.

The Knights were at a disadvantage now. Morgan was in many ways even more mysterious than Merlin. They had witnessed Merlin's amazing magic, and knowing that Morgan studied beneath his tutelage, could only guess at what she was capable of. A surreptitious look passed between the Queen and the Sorceress.

Would the Knights mistakenly believe that Morgan could assist them in fending off hoards of Saxons should the need arise? It was a clever strategy which after some brooding silence from the brothers, proved to be very effective. It was Sir Galahallt that led the Knights in their re-gathered support for the pursuit of Excalibur. "Let us leave immediately mine Queen." Gwenhwyvar, unobserved, let out a sigh of relief. She stood up, nodded her approval at Galahallt and strode toward the exit with her entourage in tow.

***

When they had gathered their belongings together, they met in the stables. The steward was busy feeding the horses a concoction mixed with straw and oats that Morgan had given him earlier. Morgan let the others in on what was taking place. "The feed hath been mixed with certain herbs and a spell cast upon it. The horses will be able to ride for much further than normal without tiring or sweating." Garethe was the first to see the disadvantage in that situation. "What of our ability to endure….." Morgan did not let him finish the question before answering. "When the pain becomes too much to bear; chew on this bark, swallow the juices that your mouth makes with it, but not the bark itself; it will quell the pain." She handed out similar sized pieces of Willow bark to them one at a time. The Knights looked at it with some trepidation, but accepted it with gratitude.

They tied their bags to their horses and the two women were assisted onto their mounts. When the men had joined them the group cantered toward the gate that the Steward had opened to allow them exit from the castle. He waved his farewell to them and watched them for a while wondering where they were heading off to now. He assumed back to Caerleon, but it was not his place to know these things. Shaking his head in resignation he closed the gate to once more take up his duties tending to the castle in the King's absence.

Chapter 18: The Outskirts of Pen Rhionydd - An hour past noon

King Arthur and Merlin had stopped at Vallum Hadriani to survey the amount of damage that had been done. The wall was a shadow of its former self. They had been anticipating that it would have been diminished by the continual ravaging, but did not grasp the full extent of the decimation until they had seen it with their own eyes. Its purpose for the Roman Empire, to restrict the trade between the northern most parts of the island and the rest was all but forgotten. The wall would be unable to stop a mildly determined person from climbing it's now diminutive stature. Nevertheless, Arthur's band of men made their way toward one of the huge gates that had long since been battered down and now offered no obstacle for them.

Since then, the group had been quiet. Merlin thought that the men would have been more vocal in their disbelief that such a formerly towering and imposing structure had succumbed to such thievery. But instead the sight of the wall that each of them had either seen with their own eyes as younger men, or heard stories of throughout their lives, was imparting a mood of sombre reflection. It had stayed with them when they set up camp the evening after journeying through the stone border. Then even the next morning as they made their way through the hilly and beautiful terrain of Galloway, it hung over the men like a cloud. Now that they were approaching their destination Arthur was sensing a foreboding amongst the party.

"Merlin", he called back to his sage. Dutifully Merlin goaded his mount to catch up with the King's mare. Taking up a place in parallel to the King he said, "Aye Arthur." "Can ye feel a mood amongst the men of anxiety about our arrival at Pen Rhionydd?" To his surprise Merlin shook his head, perhaps a little to furiously. Arthur was sure that Merlin would have been able to sense the sullen mood of the Knights and foot soldiers. "Arthur, I feel a magical presence. It overwhelms everything else." The King was taken aback. "Magical presence; another Sorcerer?" he enquired. For his part Merlin closed his eyes and leant back with is face pointing skywards. He turned his head right and left before opening his eyes and once more facing Arthur. "No. Not one Sorcerer. Many. More that I hath ever encountered in mine entire life. Sorcerers, Sorceresses. Some of great age and others still quite young."

This changed everything. Arthur thought that the was going to meet with a fledgling community of men and women. King Rhydderch and Queen Ganieda had not mentioned anything about sorcery being practiced in the township. "Will they welcome us?" Arthur was concerned with the all too immediate future. "Aye, mine King. I sense a great love and peacefulness in this place." Arthur was relieved. Turning his attention back to strategy he supposed that they could be a great asset for them both. "Could they be convinced to use their powers to aide is in our quest to expel the Saxons, Jutes and Angles?" Arthur could feel the excitement within his stomach. Think of it; a town full of conjurers all assisting them to unite the country and dispatch with the foreigners; it was a satisfying thought. Merlin had contemplated it already. "Aye Arthur, with such a force behind us, none could stand in our way."

Cheered by their collective vision for the community, they had unknowingly gathered up their pace. Merlin was the first to notice that the foot soldiers were now having trouble keeping up with them. He signalled to Arthur to look at the situation. Realising what he must have done and wanting to display an act of contrition he ordered the horses to be rested and the Knights to walk the remaining part of the journey.

Pen Rhionydd lay before them. They could see it clearly in the valley below. A small river ran through the centre of the township, curving slightly near the centre. There were two visible bridges over the small body of running water. Even from this distance, they could make out that a large number of the structures were built from stone, including the bridges. Stone that was taken from the structure of Vallum Hadriani. "They must hath used sorcery to move the stone to their township." Arthur's conjecture was acknowledged by Merlin with a simple nod. "We shall pose less of a threat by walking into the village" observed Merlin. It would not do to surprise such a large number of magically inclined people. There would be no telling how they may react. And in such great numbers Merlin knew he would be unable to stand against them with his own magic. It felt humbling. Shaking off his minor concerns, Merlin once more opened himself up to the overpowering feeling of love and unity that he could feel emanating from them. Yes, he was being silly he told himself. There was no threat from these people, he was sure of it now. And that too gave him further pause for thought. Maybe putting them to work to aide Arthur and him in their quest was impossible?

Whatever the village held, he was sure of one thing. It was going to be something that he had never before considered in his life, nor encountered in his own experience or any of the gathered scrolls of knowledge that he treasured so much.

Chapter 19: Pen Rhionydd - Two hours' past noon

The approaching band of foot soldiers and knights leading their horses did indeed cause a bit of a stir at first. However the slow march into the centre of the township rather than a charging advance went a long way to settling the initial concerns that were expressed by the villagers after the men were first spied. Arthur made sure that he smiled and motioned for his knights to do the same. They picked up a following of the villagers as they made their way towards the most imposing of the township structures. It was a tall turret of some description, yet without battlements, and what appeared to be a great hall with equally great doors leading into it. There was a man standing at the entrance, he was flanked by two others to his right and left. All three wore simple one piece garments with hoods that were at some point thrown back potentially so that they may more keenly observe the arriving delegation.

As Arthur, Merlin and his men approached, the three seemed to be in conference about something, that was eventually resolved and with nods of agreement they once more stood steadfastly awaiting the visitors. Some of the villagers had begun to form a party around the three men, in an almost protective manner. When they were all within hearing distance, Arthur was surprised to hear his name called by the man in the centre of the three. "King Arthur Pendragon, welcome to Pen Rhionydd." Merlin and Arthur looked at each other. Thankfully Arthur's reputation had preceded him and the welcoming party had accurately assumed exactly who he was. Arthur pulled up his mare and signalled for one of the Knights to take hold of the reins. Merlin and Arthur approached the man who had greeted the young King. He spoke once more as they closed the distance between them. "Mine name is Maelgyn."

This was perfect thought Arthur, the exact person that they had hoped to make contact with. Arthur responded, "Greetings Maelgyn, mine thanks for thine welcome." What followed next was a cleverly disguised battle of words by each of the men hoping to understand what the others intentions were, without making it look too obvious. Maelgyn led the verbal charge, "Thine reputation as a benevolent yet unyielding King hath spread throughout the country."

"The repute of thine township hath reached mine ears through mine friend King Rhydderch of North Rheged."

"Our closest neighbour and the northernmost part of thine Kingdom Arthur; what does King Rhydderch say of us that thee should travel so far to see with thine own eyes?"

"A township that seems to not fear raids from the Picts to the north of thine borders; mine journey was to find out how ye hath accomplished such security?"

Maelgyn would not so easily be drawn into a dissemination of their military prowess and deflected the query with a good deal of aplomb, "Only the Romans need fear the Picts and they hath all long since departed these shores." It was then clear to Arthur that this was a clever and well educated man that may be happy to joust with words until the day was done. Better to switch tact and be more forthright. He took a further two steps toward Maelgyn and lowered the volume of his voice so as to appear that their conversation was more intimate. "Fear of what is happening to Vallum Hadriani hath brought me to thine land, Maelgyn." There was a dawning of realisation upon Maelgyn's face. "King Rhydderch need not fear the dismantling of the Roman wall Arthur. T'was a symbol of a foreign empire whose time hath passed; better that it be used more fruitfully than divide Briton's from one another." There was an unmistakable sincerity that Arthur felt through the words. It caught him a little unaware. Arthur looked at Merlin for some direction.

Merlin took up the argument, "Aye, the wall represented the oppression of our people beneath the Roman occupation, but it also ensures that the Gales and Scoti do not venture into the more populous regions of Briton. Should Vallum Antonini be similarly treated, then Hadriani is the only barrier keeping them at bay." Maelgyn nodded as though in sympathy. His next words however, shocked Merlin and Arthur completely. "Antonini is long since demolished; used now to make Pictish settlements of stone that cannot be burnt to the ground by the raiders." This was completely unexpected news and it represented an alarming turn of events that neither Merlin nor Arthur had considered. The strategy meetings that they had held in both Cellewig and Caerleon about offering the Picts protection from the raiders in return for their loyalty to the Kingdom evaporated before them like mist coming of a lake in the early hours of the morning.

Thinking quickly, and trying to not show how the news had affected him, Arthur took up the argument. "Surely then King Rhydderch is right to fear incursion to his realm…" He was about to go on to state that the wall should therefore be put back to rights to prevent such an occurrence, when Maelgyn once more made a statement that was completely unexpected. "To put minds and hearts of the rulers and people of North Rheged at ease then, post thine Knights here at Pen Rhionydd to better protect thine borders Arthur." This caused a stir not from the people of the township but from Arthur's own force. They simply could not believe what they were hearing. The leader or what appeared to be the ruler of Pen Rhionydd was handing over occupation rights to Arthur and his men. "Thee accede to mine rule?" Arthur was aghast. Maelgyn gave a wry smile and responded furtively "Was unaware that we were in battle Arthur. How can one accede without first engaging in conflict? And I cannot believe that ye would wield the fabled Excalibur against thine own countrymen." Arthur was once more put on the defensive by the shrewd orator.

Merlin, who all of this time was almost bursting to ask about the magical powers that these people all seemed to possess, could contain himself no longer. He used this opportunity to both save Arthur from responding to such an assertion and bring up the subject about which he was so eager to discuss. "Wouldst thee be able to repel such a magical weapon with a hex of thine own?" he motioned to the sheathed forgery of Excalibur that hung at Arthurs waist. There was an awkward silence before Maelgyn gathered his thoughts and answered evenly. "Such miracles are the work of our Father in heaven Merlin. All that I could do is pray for his intervention and assure thee that we are a peaceful people." This was not the answer the old Sorcerer was expecting. It was entirely unsatisfactory. There was no mention of the use of his abilities, much less those of the other townsfolk. Merlin was about to change tact and ask a more direct question about the source of their powers when all conversation was interrupted by unmistakable scream of alarm from a woman.

It emanated from the area of the closest stone bridge. There was a general confusion as to what had happened, but through the murmuring of knights, soldiers and villagers alike there came a desperate plea for help, and summation of what had just occurred. "Mine son hath fallen from the bridge into the river!" cried the hysterical woman pointing from the bridge into the river below. "Save him!" she further pleaded with anybody that would hear. People ran this way and that to try and gain a vantage point to see where the youngster had fallen. En-mass the crowd surged toward the riverbank and the bridge. Somebody shouted "There!" Merlin and Arthur led the charge to the river bank in hopes of spotting the wayward child. The river although narrowest at this point was still too wide to simply reach out and grab the boy. The current was dragging him slowly away from the bridge and further, to a much wider part of the river. He thrashed about, unable to keep his head above water for more than a breath before disappearing again in a splash of flailing arms.

Arthur grabbed Merlin's elbow. "Quickly Merlin, levitate the boy to safety." "Aye Arthur" the old man responded and stretched out his arm to do as he was bid. By this time two of Arthurs Knights were busy discarding whatever small amounts of chainmail they had worn in preparation to enter the water and rescue the boy. Some of the younger men of the town were similarly attempting a rescue of their own by linking hands and forming a human chain to try and reach the hapless victim. "Quickly Merlin" Arthur was impatient at the length of time that the soothsayer was taking to perform such a simple act of magic. After a further moment had passed without any sign of the boy rising up from the water Arthur angrily turned back to face the old man. He was about to admonish the singular lack of effort from the Sorcerer, when he saw the expression on Merlin's face. "What?" he asked impatiently. "Nothing is happening!" came the reply awash with a tone of disbelief. Merlins arms were stretched out and he was physically shaking from the exertion that he was putting into the spell but it was having absolutely no effect.

The human chain by this time was more than half way toward reaching the distressed child. Arthur goaded Merlin once more "Merlin use thine powers to rescue the child." The look of anguish upon Merlin's face made Arthur soften his tone somewhat. "Mine magic doth not work!" he practically shouted back to the King. Arthur looked over to the rescue effort. Three of Arthur's knights had taken up the outer most positions of the chain. Sir Bedwere was within an arms-reach of the child and with a heave of effort he was able to grab onto the tunic that the boy was wearing. "Got him!" came the signal from the brave Knight. "Pull them back!" somebody behind Arthur and Merlin shouted. There was a moan of effort from the men making up the human chain as they strained and pulled one another back toward the safely of the river bank. It wasn't long before the boy, now safely in the arms of Sir Bedwere, was back to a part of the bank where they could stand up and continue the remainder of the journey to dry land on foot. The boy's mother crying in relief ran into the river to take her son from the arms of the Knight.

A collective cheer rose from the crowd and the sense of relief was palpable. The immediate emergency over, Arthur turned his attention to the matter of Merlin's inability to use his magical powers to salvage the situation in the first place. "What do ye mean thine magic doth not work?" Merlin was exasperated; he simply did not know how to describe the situation in any other words. "Mine power to levitate, gone", he said simply. "Try something else then," interjected Arthur, still trying to grapple with the gravity of the situation. "Fire" he said pointing to a pile of nearby gathered twigs that must have been dropped by a villager in the confusion. Merlin turned his attention to the twigs that were tied neatly into a bundle. This ought to be simple enough. It was after all the very first feat of magic that Merlin had done as a boy. He motioned with his hand toward the combustible material. Nothing happened. The two men exchanged a look of worry. "Once more" commanded Arthur. Merlin furrowed his brow in concentration. Pointing at the twigs again he actually spoke the words of the fire spell aloud, something that Arthur had not heard before. Again nothing happened.

Maelgyn had become separated from them in the confusion and was calling for Arthur from somewhere in the now dissipating crowd. Before Arthur responded he had a thought that he shared with his sage. "Could thine powers be suppressed by all of these magical people?" Merlin considered the proposition for a moment and eventually shook his head. "I do not know Arthur. Such a thing is beyond mine abilities. I cannot stop Morgan from casting a spell. If these people were preventing me from using mine powers, I would feel it for sure." He then shook his head more fervently. "No Arthur, they are not stopping me from practicing magic. For some reason, it just will not work in this place." Merlin looked about him as if it would somehow help him understand the situation in which he found himself. Arthur wanted to pursue the point further, but was interrupted by Maelgyn. "King Arthur," he said. Merlin and Arthur turned to see Maelgyn approaching them. "Let us talk more, come to mine abode," he signalled a direction with his hand.

Arthur looked over and mistook the general directed indicated to mean the large turret and hall structure that dominated the township. "A fine building," he offered by way of compliment. Seeing the misunderstanding that he had caused Maelgyn corrected the King's understanding. "Our temple to the Father in heaven, Arthur. Mine house is behind it. I serve in the temple and administer to our Lord's flock here in Pen Rhionydd." This however caused another misunderstanding. Arthur enquired "Who is thine Lord whose sheep ye attends? What is his name?" Smiling benevolently, Maelgyn tried to explain in more direct terms. "I am a holy man that serves our Lord and Father in heaven. His flock are the people of Pen Rhionydd." Not having had any contact with this kind of ideology before Arthur could not help but look perplexed. Merlin offered his assessment of the explanation that Maelgyn had offered. "This is part of thine Christian belief?" He waited for confirmation of his account. "Aye" came the reply.

Further talk was indeed called for thought Arthur. It would not do to claim a new part of his Kingdom and have them follow some

Roman inspired religion. They would have to be made to adopt the old ways that he and Merlin were so eager to spread once more though the country. "Aye let us talk more Maelgyn" he managed a smile. The three walked toward the direction of Maelgyn's home.

Chapter 20: Sussex Coast - Dusk

Morgan had made good on her promise that the horses would be able to ride for much longer than normal. They had been hard at it now for the entire day, not stopping to drink, eat or relieve themselves in favour of carrying on as far as their endurance allowed. The pain of such and extended ride was showing upon all of their faces, but chewing on the willow bark had relieved it somewhat, although not completely. Legs and backs were the most affected by the continual motion of the horse. After a while it had become almost dreamlike, the rhythm of the ride and the inexorable motion forwards. The sensation of time passing seemed to melt away. The sun was disappearing slowly from the sky and soon they would be forced to make camp for the night, here in Aelle's territory. So far they had been lucky and not seen anyone of note; an occasional remote farmer from an even more remote village; nobody who looked like a Saxon.

"Wareham is ahead" shouted Galahallt to the others. "It marks the outermost border of Aelle's lands. Morgan took up the conversation "They were conquered by Aelle, there will yet be men and women that do not regard Aelle as their King." Morgan was referring to the natives that were basically occupied by Aelle's forces when he annexed his neighbour's lands. It was either Osulf or Byrhtwold, more unwelcome Saxons, Morgan couldn't remember which. The villagers would have scarcely showed any want or desire to have a Saxon rule them. Nevertheless, they would have accepted it rather than face persecution from their new overlords. "We must find a boatman that will take us to Insula Vectis" called out Gwenhwyvar. "One that has no love of Saxons."

It was a task that was more easily spoken than it would be done. Questions raced through all of their minds. How would they be able to find somebody to shelter their horses, and offer them safe passage to the island? How would they be able to identify a villager that was loyal to the old ways, and hopefully to the idea that Arthur was the rightful ruler of the entire land? Morgan and Gwenhwyvar tried to not let a frown of worry show on their faces. It would not do to look uncertain at this stage of their mission. The three Knights were still uncomfortable about taking the women on this perilous journey. What was needed now was a firm hand of decision and action.

"We should not race into the village" cautioned Guaen. "There should be no sense of urgency to our ride, 'twill attract too much attention." It was good advice. One that Gwenhwyvar was quick to praise. "Aye Sir Guaen, before we reach the village we shall dismount and walk in with our horses." With a definite plan of action more or less decided upon the party in unison slowed the pace of the horse's strides. The Knights had wisely left their chainmail behind at Cellewig so they did not appear to be warriors. The traveling tunics were bland and featureless, not showing their family crest. Hopefully with their swords adequately hidden beneath their flowing robes, they would be taken for simple travellers and nothing more. Their assumptions would all very soon be put to the test.

In the distance, on the road that they were now travelling they could make out a figure walking what looked to be a small horse. With a signal from Gwenhwyvar, they slowed to a stop and all dismounted. The horses still looked as if they could continue on with their frenetic pace, but it would be unwise to look as though they were in a hurry; giving rise to suspicion that they were running from something. The time dragged by with the distance between them not appearing to close as quickly as it should. It was perhaps the impatience of the group to see exactly who it was they were dealing with. Eventually they could make out that it was an old man leading a horse laden with goods no doubt purchased at the village that lay ahead of them, still out of view.

The old man was as curious about the travellers as they were of him. They could see him straining his aged eyes to get a better look at the men and women approaching him on the road. He was an unkempt old man, with dirty and almost tattered robes, the garments of a working man. When they were close enough to each other to hear without shouting, Gwenhwyvar spoke to him "Greetings old man." He immediately widened his eyes. "You come from the north." He stated with certainty in his voice. Gwenhwyvar and the others tried their hardest to not wince. Their accents would give them away for sure. Quick thinking from the Queen almost salvaged the situation of their being so readily identified. "Travelling to see relatives in Wareham; is it much further?" she skilfully tried to change the subject. He was having none of it though. "Where abouts are ye from?" he inquired. Morgan interjected "Deorham" It was a village within the borders of the Mercian holdings of the south Angles, yet it should almost account for their northern accents. Northern compared to his at least. He was clearly sceptical of the answer. "Ahhhh" he said, showing no sign that he believed Morgan's explanation at all. The three knights tensed. It would be a pity to dispatch this old man, but if he showed any sign of raising the alarm with his Saxon overlords, they may have no other choice. A knowing look passed between them.

"I know just about everybody in Wareham. Lived here mine whole life. Who is it that you seek. I can better direct ye." There was a definite edge to the man's voice. It was almost a challenge. Caught in her abject lie Gwenhwyvar was temporarily at a loss. What should she say in reply? Perhaps a randomly chosen name that was common to these parts? It was worthy of an attempt at least. Before she had settled upon a name to use he took a step much closer to her. He looked the Queen up and down and then over to the three men, lastly he looked at Morgan. His hand came up to his mouth in an absent minded gesture of concentration. He was thinking about something. Then in an instant his face lit up with realisation. "I know ye" he said. Gwenhwyvar could feel her head skip a beat. She was hoping with all of her might that the old man was senile enough to mistake her for somebody that he had met during his lifetime. "Oh?" she replied nonchalantly.

"Queen Gwenhwyvar Pendragon." Her identity laid bare the Queen could not help but look shocked. The knights as one reached beneath their tunics and grasped the handles of their swords. Tension constricted their pupils in the failing light, they readied themselves for the kill. Turning to Morgan he similarly clearly and perfectly identified the woman, "Morgan Le Fay sister to King Arthur." Morgan's mind was racing, what exact spell she could enable upon this seemingly harmless old man that would get them out of this situation. He continued on with his trail of thought. "Ye are spoken of in these parts, but only when those evil Saxon overlords are nowhere near." He actually seemed pleased to see them. "Mine dear ladies, what brings ye to these parts. Surely ye knows of the danger to such royal visitors?"

Looks as it turned out could be very deceptive. This was no simple farmer; he was clearly educated and knowledgeable of Arthur and his kingdom. For a brief second of time Gwenhwyvar though that it may be best to deny the insinuation and laugh it off somehow. But the old man looked so genuinely disturbed at the warning that he offered that she dismissed the idea. "Ye art loyal to Arthur, mine husband" she asked, confirming his summation. "Aye mine Queen." They all breathed a sigh of relief. Of all the people that they could have run into in these parts, a Briton that clearly had no love for the Saxon conquerors and is fearful of their safety; this was an amazing piece of fortune. Looking at her travelling companions she decided to offer the old man enough information to be able to help them, but no so much as to put them in peril. "We have need of a boat, and a place to stable our horses"

The old man was positively gleeful. "Certainly mine Queen. I hath a boat and stables. Mine hut is close to the shore. I bring in fish to sell at the markets in Wareham, and I train horses when needed by other villagers or farmers." He then looked somewhat ashamed "And for those Saxon dogs" Gwenhwyvar reached out and took the old man's hand in a gesture of forgiveness. Clearly he was only doing what had to be done in order to not have the Saxons metre out punishment for any disobedience. "Ye live beneath a cruel master and so what ye must." The kindly tone in Gwenhwyvar's voice gave the man a warm feeling. He looked furtively behind him "We should go before anyone else comes this way", he wisely advised; now protective of his royal companions.

"This way mine Queen" he gestured and led them back the way they had come. "There is a path further up the road that leads down to mine hut." As one they turned their horses and followed the lead of the old man. "What is thine name?" asked Morgan. "Cawshall" he responded. "Ye hath our gratitude Cawshall" she offered. "Yet I am still puzzled" began Gwenhwyvar. "How did ye know the identities of Morgan and me?" Cawshall's eyes lit up as he answered. "We have a scroll that came from Caerleon village. It shows Arthur and ye mine Queen, and Morgan; beautiful representations from a gifted scribe that has sadly passed over to the otherworld now. He lived for a year or so in Caerleon village before coming back to his birthplace, Wereham" he indicated behind them to the general direction of the village. "Great stories he told us of Merlin and Arthur, the knights and their battles" It was all becoming clear to them now. A former resident of the village must have been somewhat of an artist and storyteller. People like this were responsible for spreading the legend of Arthur far and wide across the land.

They continued to talk of the village of Wareham and how the Saxons ruled it with fear and intimidation. Nevertheless, it seemed that the villagers had managed to get on with their lives despising the overlords but building a thriving functioning community. Eventually they turned off the road down the path that Cawshall had described. It was a good thing that they had the old man leading them because they would not have found it on their own. The daylight was almost gone now and their eyes were becoming accustomed to the dark. Thankfully Gaelach was shining down tonight offering them some respite from travelling in complete darkness.

It was a further half hour or so before they came to the bottom of the gentle slope that led to Cawshall's hut. There was a straw roofed stable off to the side of his modest abode. "It is empty at the moment; the horses should all fit in there nicely" he said. The lapping of the ocean against the land could be clearly heard. "The path leads all the way down to the shore. There you'll find mine boat. But come inside, ye cannot travel across the water at night." Galahallt was the first to take up the kindly offer. "Wise words; we should leave at first light for Insula Vectis." Cawshall nodded, he had assumed that the island was their destination when Gwenhwyvar told him of their need for a boat. It was agreed between them all. They would rest here the night and set out at first light.

Guaen set about tending to the horses whilst, Garethe started a fire in the stone fireplace that was the main feature of the hut. The night was closing in all around them yet there was a feeling of homeliness that was offered by the kindliness of Cawshall, a roaring fire and shelter from the cold night air.

When they had settled in and eaten a meal together Cawshall couldn't help but be more curious about their arrival in the land of Sussex. "What could bring thee here? There is nothing on the island of value surely." Gwenhwyvar was reluctant to tell the kindly man too much but also did not want to brush off his understandable curiosity. "We seek to reclaim something that hath made its way to the island." It was as full an explanation that she was willing to give. He seemed satisfied that whatever it was, it was important to the Queen, therefore it was important to him. Eventually they retired to get some sleep, upon hastily made beds of straw on the floor of the hut. As they were falling to sleep rain began to pelt against the outside of the hut.

***

It was still dark when Galahallt shook Gwenhwyvar awake. She realised that she had fallen asleep and not moved once during the night, a sure sign that she was in a heavy sleep. "The weather?" she began to ask. "The rain hath passed by, t'will be a clear day" he comforted her. Excellent, she thought. Their journey to the island would not be impeded by inclement weather. Cawshall was not in his bed. Before the Queen had a chance to enquire as to his whereabouts, the door swung open. He entered carrying a bucket of water, no doubt drawn from a nearby well or brook. He was full of energy and set about stoking the fire once more and mixing up something in the iron pot that hung to the side of the fireplace. The entire party had awoken by now he looked across at them yawning and stretching. "I am making a broth for ye to fortify thee for thine travels."

There seemed to be no end to the generosity of the man. With some assistance from Morgan the broth was prepared and dished out in simple wooden bowls. It seemed to have a mixture of oats, and fruit cooked into it, almost in a stew like consistency. It was sweet from the apples that made up a large portion of it and very satisfying. "How long before ye return to collect thine horses?" he asked. The three knights all looked at Gwenhwyvar for guidance. "It may be some time Cawshall" she advised. "However long mine Queen, I will be happy to shelter thine horses. Should any of the villagers notice, t'will not seem out-of-place for me to have more horses to train."

"Sunrise is imminent." It was Garethe, he was looking through a crack in the shutter of the only window. "We should go now."

"How long will it take us to row to the island?" asked Morgan, "Hath ye been to Vectis?" Cawshall replied, "Aye, 'twill take the morning to row from here; ye should arrive around noon." They were a little crestfallen. If they could only ride further into Sussex and depart form a point that was much closer to the island it would not be so much of an effort. But the risk of discovery from Aelle's men was too great. There was little chance of coming across a Saxon travelling by water. They were not known to be fishermen. They hurried through the remainder of their morning stew and prepared themselves to leave. Gwenhwyvar was the first to thank Cawshall for his assistance. "We owe ye a debt Cawshall" she said. He shook the gratitude aside. "Tis mine duty to the rightful King of Briton and the Queen that rules at his side." She could see that he was absolutely sincere. The small party bade their benefactor goodbye and with Galahallt in the lead, moved single file from his hut down the well-worn pathway through the shrubs and to the stony beach below. There they found the boat just as was described by its owner.

The two women waited for the men to launch it before boarding the small vessel and settling themselves into the bow of the hull. Gareth and Guaen took up the oar positions in the centre and Galahallt the position of rudder controller. The sun was just peeping over the east of the horizon. The sky was clear and most of the stars had disappeared by now, except for the morning star. Their course would be easy enough to navigate. Follow the coastline eastwards until they rounded the point where Wareham was built and onwards to Insula Vectis. Soon the rhythmic slap of the oars pushing the water and the squawking of the sea gulls was mixed with the splash of water against the boat as they inexorably made their way toward their destination. Much like their previous day's journey on horseback, it became hard to tell how much time had passed. Were it not for the ever-present sun by which to judge the passage of time, it would have been hour merging into hour with little realization of how many had passed.

Curiously, almost the entire journey to the island was made in silence. Occasional exchanges were limited to a call to rotate the men between steering the propelling the boat onwards. Each took turn at the easier task of keeping them on-course, whilst the other two heaved and stretched their arms legs and backs to push the boat through the relatively calm water. They could not have hoped for a more fortunate turn of events that found them in this position. The weather could have been bad, creating a journey to the island which would have been not only more difficult, but quite frightening as well. For certain, the ancient gods were watching over them and ensuring that they succeeded in their mission. Excalibur must be recovered and returned to its rightful King.

Chapter 21: Pen Rhionydd, Maelgyn's House - Mid Morning

Arthur was exhausted. He and Merlin had engaged Maelgyn at length in the virtues of abandoning the Roman ways of life and once more embracing the old ways that their ancestors lived by before the Romans annexed Briton as their eastern most territory of the empire. That of course would include this bizarre Christian religion that was now spreading out from the Romans and into all of the parts of its land holdings. But Maelgyn would hear none of it. He was a forward looking man that held true to his religious beliefs and insisted that this religion was the one that the entire land should be adopting. "It does not matter that ye hath found the truth of God in heaven or not. We are willing to recognise ye as King of Pen Rhionydd." It was a welcome offer, but tinged with a caveat. "Providing ye allows us to worship our Lord without prejudice." Maelgyn stated his position as eloquently this time as he had the previous thirty or so.

Arthur took up the same argument that they had been having all night. "Ye wish to be part of mine kingdom, yet ye do not want to honour the gods that our forefathers worshipped?" He was flummoxed. "How can ye accept me as thine King without accepting all of mine rulings." Maelgyn raised a finger to pointing to the low-beamed ceiling of his hut. "A wise king recognises that his people hath hearts and minds of thine own. 'Tis the common law that the King upholds, not the beliefs of every man in the field." It was a typically clever retort to Arthur's assertion. Arthur took a breath and tried to defend his stance, "Mine Knights cannot be asked to hold up laws that do not come from the King surely." Too late Arthur realised that he was once more on the defensive instead of the charge forward. He groaned internally, how does Maelgyn keep twisting his arguments around so that it feels as if he is in the wrong somehow. He waited for the verbal parry that would push him into an untenable position. "Only a fearful King supresses that which he does not understand or that which he does not proclaim." It felt like a small dagger in his heart. Maelgyn had effectively put Arthur into the role of the former Roman rulers; absolutists that dictated language, religion and economy to the Britons. Basically, a list of everything that he had just argued throughout the night that he did not wish to be as a ruler. "The King need not fear transgression in common law from the people of Pen Rhionydd. There is no crime here. No theft, no revolution against a tyrannical rule."

Arthur looked over to Merlin for help wondering why he had been so silent thus far. Merlin lay slumped against a wall, still seated on a stool, fast asleep. It was then that Arthur realised that there was light streaming through the cracks of the window shutters above Merlin's head. Outside could be heard the daily life of another day in the township well underway. Arthur reflected briefly upon everything that had transpired overnight during the marathon conversation between them. He had learned about the founding of the township. Merlin had learned that the stones taken from Vallum Hadriani were carried by horse and cart to the village and used in the various buildings around. There appeared to be absolutely no magical ability in these people at all. Merlin had made it the centre of every question to Maelgyn, at least whilst he was awake and still asking questions. Arthur then briefly wondered exactly when the old man had succumbed to his tiredness..

"Come King Arthur. Let us eat a hearty meal to begin the day." It was a welcome invitation from his host. Arthur realised at that moment that he was hungry, thirsty and tired. He smiled his gratitude, "Mine thanks Maelgyn that would be very welcome indeed." Whilst Maelgyn set about making them a morning meal, Arthur stood up and stretched and yawned trying to overcome the tiredness that was beginning to overcome him. He stumbled a little at first but then made his way over to where Merlin was sleeping. "Merlin," he said gently. The old man's released a small snort and jerked awake. "Aye Arthur, what is it?" he queried in a feeble voice. "Tis morning," Arthur replied. For his part, Merlin gave Arthur a perplexed look and then looked over toward the door to Maelgyn's house. Light could be seen coming in from the beneath the door and at various points around the door itself where it did not join up with the door jamb correctly. Surprised that the morning had come around so quickly he made to get up as though he had somewhere to go.

Arthur put his hand on Merlins shoulder. "Stay seated old friend. Maelgyn is preparing some food." Merlin's face lit up. "Oh Good" he said with a boyish gleam in his eye. "What did I miss?" he enquired of the King. Arthur shrugged in acceptance of his defeat at the words of the masterful debater. "Maelgyn hath proven himself to be a wise and determined leader of his…" he hesitated for a moment, "flock," he concluded, using Maelgyn's own words to describe the townsfolk. "t'would seem mine kingdom will now stretch as far north as Pen Rhionydd, to encompass these Christian people." This was not entirely an unexpected result from Merlin's point of view. Having established that these people did not know the first thing about the magical arts, he then listened for hours as Maelgyn skilfully argued the point to retain their beliefs and yet install Arthur as their recognised king. He was unsure of exactly when he realised that Arthur was not going to win the verbal duel, and allowed sleep to overtake him.

"I see," he said giving Arthur a look of sardonic acceptance of the way that things had turned out. "A joyous day; thine kingdom is now enriched with more Britons." Merlin's tone was less than convincing that he was overjoyed. Arthur was unsure exactly how to react to his mentor's mordant acceptance of the situation. He altered the subject to avoid any further discussion upon the issue until they were able to speak in private. "What of thine feelings that these people are magical?" This was a subject to which Merlin was far more enthusiastic. He sat upright and took a moment to gather his thoughts. "Mine feelings could not be so wrong; yet here they are, a township of people that feel magical and yet do not know of, or are able to practice feats of magic; 'tis a quandary. I keep wondering; would I find the same thing with other settlements that practice this odd Roman religion?" He looked up at Arthur as though he was expecting an answer. Taken aback, Arthur shook his head and grasped for an answer to the question. "Perhaps if thee travelled to Magna Frisia and found a similar township?" he offered.

Merlin however had a different solution. "Closer than that Arthur", he said somewhat mysteriously. What was that supposed to mean thought Arthur. The King gave his mentor a look of impatient exhaustion hoping that it would be enough to elicit further information from the old man. He was correct, Merlin leant forward. "Did ye not hear? During the night one of the references Maelgyn made to a similar Christian village, lies across the water at Maan" Arthur tried to recall exactly when the mention was made, but was unable to recollect this piece of information. "Art thou sure?" he queried. "Aye Arthur. Maelgyn made a reference to the other Christian settlement across the water at the Island of Maan. I heard it clearly. A monastery, he called it. Ye do not remember?" Arthur did not. He had been so preoccupied with trying to win the argument for following the ancestral ways that he must have missed the reference to which Merlin was referring. He shook his head. "It does not matter. When we return to North Rheged, King Rhydderch can ferry us across to the island to see for ourselves."

The thought of undertaking a sea voyage was a little more than Arthur could think about in his present physical and mental state. "Surely we hath more pressing matters to attend to" he softly rebuked the old man. Merlin gave Arthur a quizzical look. Arthur motioned to the forgery of Excalibur that was placed against the entry door to Maelgyn's house. With that, Merlin seemed to snap back to the present from his musings about the Christian religion and its divorced state from magical prowess. "Hath Morgan appeared in thine dreams?" Arthur asked in the hope that his ethereal sister had somehow tracked down the sword and communicated its whereabouts to Merlin.

Merlin shook his head. "I hath heard nothing from Morgan. That too could be an ability that does not work whilst I am here in Pen

Rhionydd, much like mine powers to levitate or start a fire; or perform any magical act. That is even more reason to test mine theory that this Christian religion somehow inhibits mine powers. We should travel to Maan." Arthur was about to admonish the very thought when Maelgyn summoned them to the fireplace at the far end of his home. It seemed that the meal was now ready. Pushing aside his immediate reaction Arthur thought that a more level headed decision about their next steps would be made after they had eaten something. He and Merlin walked over to the fireplace. Maelgyn then offered a prayer of thanks to his Christian God before he motioned for them to sit with him. It wasn't entirely an unusual situation for Arthur. He likened it to the pre-meal thanksgivings that he himself would say. Somehow, it felt familiar enough to be comforting. At that moment Arthur entertained the thought that perhaps it would be workable, to welcome this township with its strange religion into his kingdom.

Chapter 22: Insula Vectis, Noon

The small boat was pushed ashore by Guaen and Galahallt whilst at the same time being pulled ashore by Garethe. The sun was directly above them. It lit the serene beauty of the island. The scraping of the hull against the small stone pebbles that made up the beach where they landed broke the idyllic scene that greeted them. The island was beautiful, even from this cove; they could all tell that it was a sight to behold. Birds could be heard filling the air with their song. Majestic white clouds in perfect blue sky added to the effect that the place that they had come to was in some way at the other side of the world, yet it was only a short distance from the mainland of Briton itself.

"What now; shall we search the island for Garlon?" the question was posed by Galahallt. It was an innocent enough question, but it seemed to put Queen Gwenhwyvar ill at ease. She looked over to Morgan as though seeking guidance. In turn Morgan gave a response that the knights could not fathom. "Find us a place to camp for the night." The three brothers were flummoxed. It was only noon. Gareth gave voice to their collective concern at such an undertaking. "Mine Lady. There are many hours yet of daylight. Surely we can search for the remainder of the day and set up camp should we be unsuccessful."

Gwenhwyvar supported Morgan's assertion. "Please Sir Knight's, there is another.....enchanted being that we must consult with before we can intercept Garlon. Do as Morgan says." That appeared to be an end to any further discussion. Nodding in baffled resignation the men divided up the tasks of finding a suitable location in which to set up camp for the night and guarding the women.

The rest of the day passed without incident. A suitable camp site was found and made ready for the evening, which was still a few hours away. With nothing further to do and no orders to scour the island for either Garlon or this other magical being that the Queen had earlier referred to, the Knights became restless. Gwenhwyvar and Morgan had been whispering together for some time when they noticed how uneasy the men had become. With a few more quickly exchanged words in hushed tones the two women turned to face the three brothers and together walked toward them. "Sir Knights, please capture some morsel of food and prepare it for the evening meal. There will be another dining with us if all goes well." Gwenhwyvar's proclamation was exactly the cure needed for the agitated men. They quickly divided up the task of hunting and guarding the women. It was decided that Guaen would remain whilst Garethe and Galahallt would hunt down a wild boar or other such creature.

The two brothers left to see what they could do about fulfilling the Queen's requirements. With them out of the way for the present, Morgan could commence trying to contact Alus. It had been agreed between Gwenhwyvar and her that they should be as discrete about this as they could manage under the circumstances. Morgan signalled to the Queen that she was ready to depart the camp. Gwenhwyvar accordingly approached Guaen to engage him in conversation so as to allow Morgan the opportunity to surreptitiously leave. After ensuring that Guaen's attention was entirely focussed upon the Queen, Morgan silently exited the clearing.

Morgan could imagine Guaen's alarm when he would eventually realise that she was absent, but it did not matter. The primary goal at this point was to secure the services of Alus so that they may continue their pursuit of Garlon. She moved quietly through the shrubs and into a wooded area. She could think of no other way to summon this mysterious creature other than making her way to the water and calling for him. Eventually the trees gave way to the shoreline of the island. This was a point further around the island from where they had landed in their boat. It faced out to the open sea rather than the strait of water between the mainland and the island. Morgan looked across the great body of water. It was a magnificent shade of blue and green mixed together. The sun in the west was low in the sky which was devoid of clouds.

Standing a short distance from the water Morgan called, in a voice neither raised nor hushed, "Alus, hear mine call. I am Morgan from Caerleon, sister to King Arthur. Please join us for an evening meal. There is a deal that we must strike. Queen Gwenhwyvar and I need thine services to carry us forth across the water to Gaul." Pausing for a moment, Morgan wondered whether or not she should mention the Knights as well. Best to be completely forthcoming she decided. "Fear not the Knights that guard our person, they are kindly brothers that will do ye no harm."

That was all that needed to be said she thought. Now if only she could be sure that he had heard the message. Morgan went on to repeat the message over and over again, pausing for a few minutes between each delivery. She was not sure if there would be a response other than this mysterious water-horse making his presence known to her. Nevertheless any effort to obtain his services would be worthwhile. After just over two hours of stating her plea, Morgan decided to return to the campsite. She was feeling a little defeated as her ambition and expectation was to have Alus accompany her. There was no other precedent for summoning a magical being that she knew of. Queen Gwenhwyvar had simply called for the Lady of the Lake and she appeared. Merlin had shouted for Nimue, albeit in a voice that only animals could perceive. There were no spells that Morgan had uncovered in Merlin's voluminous library that were specifically aimed at summoning other-worldly creatures.

With a last look at the setting sun, Morgan turned back inland and began her journey to the camp. She calculated that it would still be light enough for the return trip to find her way with ease, but she would have to hurry. Moving with purpose she retraced her steps. It was at the half-way point that she heard the loud snap of a branch from behind her, as though it had been trodden upon with some force. She spun around to see what had caused the noise. There was no one in sight. The trees that surrounded her were too thin of girth to hide anyone of substance. "Alus?" Morgan called in the hope that it was the creature that she was seeking; nothing.

Somewhat frustrated, she hastened her way back to the others. Morgan could see the light of the campfire that must have been lit in her absence. It was a beacon in the fading light, guiding her directly back to her destination. When she eventually broke through the tree line and into the campsite she was greeted with a heartfelt cry of relief from the party. "Mine Lady" erupted Galahallt, the alleviation of worry in his tone was palpable. "Safely returned, thank the gods" added Guaen. He had been feeling a little more than responsible for Morgan's disappearance as he was on guard duty when it happened.

The smell of a roasting pig filled the area. It was hung over the fire with a make-shift spit. Morgan could tell that it was ready to be eaten from the colour of the flesh. "Thank ye for such a warm welcome Sir Knights." She smiled letting them all know that she was indeed well. "Were ye successful in summoning Alus?" enquired Gwenhwyvar. Morgan stopped dead in her tracks. "Apparently so," she answered, looking past the group to the far side of the clearing. As one they turned to see where she was looking. Standing at the direct opposite side of the campsite to Morgan was a young man. He had shoulder-length hair, dark and tangled, like Arthur's. Even in the dim light brilliant green eyes could be seen almost glowing with unearthly light in their deep sockets. His jawline was strong, cleanly shaven. His physique resembled the Roman and Greek statues of Apollo.

His clothing was strange. Not faerie silk, Morgan and Gwenhwyvar could see that even from this distance. He was covered in some type of animal hide that seemed to be stitched in such a way as to form around his very pleasing figure. It showed up every muscle in his body. Nobody moved. Gwenhwyvar had prepared the knights for the appearance of Alus and had instructed them to not make any threatening or sudden moves. Morgan was the first to speak. "Alus?" she needed to confirm that this was indeed the being that they had sought.

"I am Alus, brother to Usla." This was exactly the confirmation that they were seeking. The reference to Usla validation that they had indeed managed to find the one that they had sought. Gwenhwyvar motioned for him to join them. "Please share in our evening meal, ye are most welcome here." With all eyes upon him, the handsome young man gracefully moved to sit upon a log that had been positioned near the fire. Gwenhwyvar sat to the right of Alus and Morgan to his left. Gwenhwyvar spoke, "Guaen, please serve the meal." Whilst the three brothers scurried to perform the service, the Queen and Sorceress were free to gently question Alus. "Hearty food to revitalise the body at the end of a busy day." The Queen's open-ended statement was delivered with an inflection at the end in order to prompt a response from the man. He smiled and nodded, but remained otherwise silent.

With a look from Gwenhwyvar, Morgan knew that she was to take up the challenge of finding out more about their guest. "Mine thanks to ye for heading mine call. I hope that we are not keeping ye from any other pressing matters?" Once more he responded with a smile, this time he shook his head. Morgan handed the next move back to Gwenhwyvar. The Queen thought for a brief moment and then gently proclaimed, "Let us eat now and we shall talk of our reasons for seeking ye afterwards." By this time Guaen had sliced off a succulent leg from the roasted pig and was offering it to Gwenhwyvar on a small metal plate that had been brought from Caerleon as part of their travelling supplies. In a move of clever statesmanship she accepted the food from the Knight and then offered it immediately to Alus. He did not hesitate; taking the plate from her he positioned it in his lap and lifted the leg to his face breathing in the aroma of the perfectly cooked meat. He let out an audible sigh of satisfaction before sinking his brilliantly white teeth into the tender flesh and tearing off a sizeable chunk to consume. Gwenhwyvar and Morgan were served by Guaen, they waited until the Knights had in turn availed themselves of the meal before beginning to eat.

The time passed slowly and in complete silence. The Knights were vigilant of the strange man, but he made no sudden moves, seemingly content to eat the food that was offered to him and drink the wine that they had brought with them on their journey. When at last the meal was completed, Gwenhwyvar made once again to engage the magical being in conversation. "We hath sought thee with purpose Alus…" she began. Alus interrupted, holding her gaze with his amazingly green eyes. "Sleep first; we shall talk later." He spoke the words then moved off a little way to lie down upon the ground, he curled-up almost like a cat and shut his eyes. With a deep breath he relaxed his body and gave the appearance of being completely and instantly asleep. An air of absolute serenity surrounded him.

Gwenhwyvar was a little flummoxed, but tried to not show it. With a gesture of surrender she bade the others to follow suit. It was strange, but Morgan felt a wave of immense tiredness come over her at that very moment. Perhaps it was all of the travel that they had done. With a small amount of resignation she wrapped herself in a blanket and settled down a little closer to the fire than Alus, but still a careful enough distance from him for the sake of her own serenity. Gwenhwyvar did the same. There was a hushed exchange from the brothers as the duty of watchman was meted out. Gwenhwyvar did not notice which one had taken on the responsibility of the first watch as she had suddenly felt very weary. Mimicking Morgan's actions, the Queen wrapped herself up and settled down close to the fire. Just as she was finding a comfortable position, she could perceive one of the knights stoking the fire and adding more fuel to it. Then she succumbed to the gentle arms of sleep.

Chapter 23: Insula Vectis Campsite, Midnight

Morgan awoke from what felt like an eternity of sleep. She stretched and looked up at the stars overhead. The night sky was filled with an uncountable number of glimmering specks. At that moment, there was the brief streak across the sky from a falling star. An omen, thought Morgan, of magical deeds being performed. She turned her head. The fire had become a pile of embers that was glowing but no longer alight. She felt good, alert. Raising herself up Morgan surveyed the campsite. Unbelievably all three of the Knights were sound asleep. Their heavy breathing could be heard in the still night. She was about to call to one of the sleeping knights when she heard the interrupted breathing of Gwenhwyvar awaking beside her.

Gwenhwyvar's eyes opened and she too stretched and surveyed the scene around her. Seeing that Morgan was awake she was about to speak but first looked over to where Alus should have been lying. He was not there. Alarmed she sat up and looked about. Alus was standing at the far side of the clearing looking back at the two women. Without words or even gestures they both knew that he wanted them to follow him. Morgan and Gwenhwyvar stood up without making a sound. With a reassuring look passing between them, they made to follow Alus from the campsite.

He moved lithely, almost seductively through the trees. There was hardly any light shining from Gaelach but it was just enough to see the way ahead. There was a smaller clearing a short walk from the one they had set up camp within. It was here that Alus stopped and turned to wait for Gwenhwyvar and Morgan to join him. They approached him together and stood a cautious distance from him. "Queen Gwenhwyvar, wife to Arthur. Hath ye provided thine husband with an heir?" It was not a question that either of them had expected. "Aye," responded Gwenhwyvar simply. Alus seemed to lose all interest in the Queen at that moment, a fact that was noticed by both of the women. He turned his attention to Morgan. "And ye mine Lady; a husband at Arthur's court?" Morgan shook her head, "No husband." She replied. This clearly pleased Alus who moved closer to Morgan. He continued with his questioning. "A maid in the service of the Queen?."

Alus's intentions were immediately clear to both Gwenhwyvar and Morgan. He was seeking a virgin, to satisfy his desires no-doubt. A knowing look passed between the two women unnoticed by Alus. "Aye" Morgan lied. "A maid-in-waiting in the Queen's court." Her instincts told her to give Alus exactly what he wanted in order to use his services to track-down and carry them to his twin Sister, and therefore to Garlon and Excalibur. The lie would have to serve as a means to an end. Alus was clearly pleased with Morgan's response. He closed the distance between them and reached out with one hand to gently stroke Morgan's cheek. Morgan appropriately turned away to give the impression of being shy. The ruse worked, it emboldened Alus. He held Morgan by her shoulders and pulled her toward him.

"What exactly do ye require pretty maiden." His voice was forceful. Morgan thought it best to continue her act of being shy in the presence of such a virile man. She looked over to Gwenhwyvar for assistance. The Queen, canny to what Morgan was doing took over the negotiations. "Thine Sister, Usla hath taken a man by the name of Garlon across the sea to Gaul. We seek passage to wherever in Gaul we may find Garlon." If Alus had any sort of curiosity as to exactly why they were seeking Garlon, it did not show. Instead he went straight to the heart of the matter. "What would ye be prepared to pay for mine service." His tone and expression were unmistakable. He intended that Morgan's 'virtue' would the recompense for the provision of passage.

Gwenhwyvar continued with the masquerade and did her best to look desperate for the young man's help. "What is it that ye wants; gold?" she cleverly offered him what she hoped he would assume was her ultimate level of payment. He turned to face Gwenhwyvar without releasing his grip upon Morgan. "What would I do with thine gold, Queen Gwenhwyvar? No. I seek something that is worth more to me than the most precious of stones or metal." They both waited for him to state his position, already knowing what it would be. "I want the virginity of thine maiden!" His voice was laden with lust. Morgan tried her best to look shocked at such a demand. She pretended to be aghast at such a suggestion and at a loss for words. He pressed his demand, "That is all that ye can offer Majesty. There is nothing more that ye possess that I want." He was brazen. Gwenhwyvar gave the appearance of being backed into a corner; of being offered a price that she was not quite willing to pay. Sensing that he had the advantage Alus pressed his demand. "How great is thine need Majesty? Safe and quick passage across the sea and land of Gaul; I know exactly where mine sister is. The journey will take a matter of hours."

Hours thought Gwenhwyvar, how great were the abilities of this magical being? Such a journey by longboat and horse would take the better part of three days at full sail and gallop. Alus mistook Gwenhwyvar's expression for one of near resignation. "Speak now," he demanded, "I shall not wait much longer." Morgan for her part, was already scheming as to how to best communicate exactly what she had in mind to Gwenhwyvar without Alus over-hearing. He was a water-horse that had the form of a man. There was no way to know how acute his hearing was. She prepared her thoughts and began to compress them into a package that could be surreptitiously communicated to the Queen. She looked down to the ground giving the appearance of being overwhelmed at the thought of being given to Alus. Instead she was hard at work mending her hymen and tightening the muscles in her vagina. She had to be sure that Alus felt he was penetrating a virgin.

It was a risk performing the magical art of healing in the presence of Alus, what if he was to detect her sorceress abilities. She made a quick decision to display her powers in some small way so as to cover up any such contingency. Gwenhwyvar had waited an appropriate amount of time. "Allow me to speak with mine maiden" she requested. Alus sensed that he had won his prize and assumed that the Queen was going to order Morgan to give herself to him. "Of course Queen Gwenhwyvar," he responded releasing his grip upon Morgan and backing off one step.

Morgan hurried over to the Queen and reached out with both hands. Gwenhwyvar appropriately took hold of them. In an instant she could hear Morgan's words in her head. "I shall mend mine body to allow Alus to have his prize. The advantage of such quick transportation to Gaul is worth having this man fulfil his lustful desires with mine body. And he is very pleasing to the eye. Had he been a Saxon or otherwise I would have cast a spell to beguile him into believing that he had conquered mine virginity. But I do not know the bounds of his magical prowess. We had best do as he says and be on our guard to ensure that he delivers his side of the bargain."

Gwenhwyvar gave Morgan's hands a squeeze to let her know that her message had been received. So that Alus had some verbal conversation to overhear Gwenhwyvar spoke aloud, "Morgan, our need to intercept Garlon is great. Will thee give thine self to this man so that we may achieve our goal." There was what both women hoped was a fitting pause of angst before Morgan replied, "Aye mine Queen, let it be done." They both looked over to Alus with resignation written all over their faces. They needed him to feel that they were paying the ultimate price for his services. He had won his prize.

Alus was completely fooled by the charade. His expression was one of victory. There was no time like the present for him to claim his prize. He strode up to Morgan, but she held up her hand for him to halt his advance. "Please Alus, give me time to prepare," she said. At first Alus was a little annoyed and it showed. Morgan hastily gathered some dry twigs together to form the beginnings of a fire. She assembled the branches carefully observed by the impatient Alus. When she was done, she stood back from it and cast the spell for fire. The branched ignited into a crackling blaze that lit the small clearing in which they were all standing. Gwenhwyvar made a strategic withdrawal from the immediate area, but did not return to the campsite. She wished to stay within shouting distance from Morgan just in case this mutually convenient unison went awry.

Alus was impressed at the showing of magical prowess by Morgan. "A Sorceress? Thought that there was a magical presence about thee.” He stated. Circling her like a predator circles its prey; he regarded Morgan with his lustful eyes. She did her best to look apprehensive about what was to come. In the mean-time she had completed all of her healing. She had successfully repaired and tightened everything in her vagina in preparation for receiving Alus. This masquerade would be somewhat difficult as she could not help but feel some desire for the handsome young man. Perhaps that would work to her advantage. Feign hesitation at first and then give herself over to his advances as though he had truly conquered her. Yes, that was it. That would complete the illusion for him. Morgan drew her arms up to cover her ample breasts that Alus was admiring through her travelling garments. She looked at the ground.

He reached out and gently pushed her arms to her side so that he could see her buxom chest. With one hand he lifted her chin so that she would look upon him. Her eyes were filled with uncertainty. It acted as an aphrodisiac for Alus. He could feel the desire for her well up within him. "Have no fear Morgan for I shall be gentle,” he offered the reassurance to Morgan. Morgan realised that she was now completely naked. There was no sense of her clothes being removed, no sense of any lost time. This must be a power of his she thought. She instinctively looked around her for her missing garments. She could see them strewn about her feet. She looked back to Alus with wonderment. He smiled at the reaction. No screaming, no disbelief at what had just occurred. He was very pleased with her demeanour. In the blinking of an eye, Alus too was now naked. Without realising it Morgan looked down at his growing penis. She unintentionally drew in her breath. He was large, much larger than Merlin. He laughed, whilst enveloping her with his muscular arms.

She could feel every muscle in his torso, waist and legs press against her body. Aroused, her nipples became erect and sensitive. The combination of her breathing and his generated a tingling sensation that spread from her breasts throughout her entire body. Her breaths became shorter and more hurried. He ran his hands up and down the length of her spine, ending by gently stroking her buttocks. This produced an entirely new sensation that threatened to overwhelm her. The combination of the two sensory inputs was enough to trigger lubrication of her reproductive area. It almost hurt, the force at which her virginal fluids began to excrete. But that too added to the overall effect of arousing Morgan to a height that she had previously never attained.

He swept her off her feet and lowered her gently to the ground, laying her upon their magically discarded clothes. With an arm around the back of her neck he began to kiss her lips, briefly at first and then with greater length, more deeply. She could hear herself moan with pleasure. Now she was not acting, it came from deep within her very being. She felt herself let go of any trepidation. These were not the actions of a man only concerned with his own satisfaction. He wanted to give Morgan as much pleasure as he received. She knew that now. She could sense it through the fabric of his perfect skin.

Her hands came up to clasp the back of his head and keep him in the perfect embrace that they shared. She felt the silky softness of his hair. Moving her hands she traced the back of his neck, his skin was smooth. The kiss was lasting an eternity and Morgan was completely lost to its power over her. The world about her began to spin just at the moment when Alus wrenched his mouth from suckling hers. Everything vanished from Morgan's view, there were no trees, fire, sky, there was only Alus, and her entire attention was focussed upon him. His emerald green eyes looked into hers in a way that nobody's had before. It felt as though he knew her more completely and intimately than anyone else during her entire lifetime.

The tangled mess of his hair had fallen forward and he bent down to run the tips of his hair over her face, then down her neck and to her bosom. She closed her eyes and allowed herself to become enraptured in the moment. He traced her lips with one finger. Then beginning with her neck ran his fingertips down between her breasts and over her stomach stopping at her pubic hairline. There was a pause, just long enough for Morgan to open her eyes, and then he entered her with one of his fingers. She let out a loud moan of pleasure. He felt inside of her Vagina, there it was, the assurance that Morgan was indeed a virgin.

Alus was now fully aroused, but he wanted to take his time with this rare prize. He ran the tip of his tongue down Morgan's stomach and over the external surface of her vagina. Morgan let out a combination of a sigh and a guttural animalistic growl. He placed the palms of both of his hands on her thighs and with a light pressure moved them upwards over her waist and stomach finishing by gently massaging her breasts. The sensations that he was evoking within Morgan both energised and made her weak, simultaneously. Morgan wanted the absolute pleasure that Alus was bestowing upon her to go on unabated. There followed what seemed like an eternity of similar foreplay. Both of them completely lost track of time. Only Gwenhwyvar, listening with some curiosity to the carnal sounds emanating from the clearing had any sense of the lengthiness of the love-making.

There came a point when both Alus and Morgan knew it was the time to end the overture to penetration. It was an unspoken moment that was communicated with absolute clarity between their gazes. The expectation from both of them was as tangible as the environment around them. Alus moved himself to the position of dominance above Morgan. His hard penis was now at the point of entry, through which he would feel the quivering anticipation of Morgan's erect clitoris. Inexorably he pushed himself slowly, deeply into Morgan's body. She felt her labia get stretched open, her hymen tear through. The pleasure that she felt was so intense that it was agonising. He drew back and thrust himself again deep into her. It was unbelievable, but it felt even better the second time. And so it went on, each penetration becoming incrementally more pleasurable than the last. Morgan could not have dreamt of such perfect intercourse. The crescendo of sensuality rising relentlessly to a level previously unattained and then greatly surpassed. Bit by bit Morgan and Alus were pushed into a point of absolute singularity.

Chapter 24: Insula Vectis, First Light of Morning

"Morgan?" It was a distant voice that was calling her name. There was a blissful moment of silence where she forgot that she had been summoned. Then it came again, more urgently this time, "Morgan!" She recognised the voice, it was familiar yet the knowledge of who to associate it with was lost upon her. Gradually, her eyes opened. It was light; the brightness of the world broke into her consciousness. Morgan's mind began to perceive what she was seeing. The top of the trees touched the early morning sky above. A beautiful woman's face was staring down at her, with a look of concern painted firmly upon her features. Morgan recognised her, but couldn't quite remember her name or how exactly she knew the woman.

"Morgan please, wake up!" once more, a now almost frantic plea from the woman. Something happened. In an instant Morgan remembered what had occurred prior to this moment. Alus had made love to her in a way that she had previously been incapable to imagine or perceive. She was in a clearing with Gwenhwyvar looking at her with a great deal of anxiety written on her face. She was covered with her former discarded garments. Clutching her gown to her breasts she sat up and looked about her. There was a further moment of orientation. The afterglow of the perfect intertwinement with Alus still present, Morgan took a breath and tried to overcome the feeling of utter contentment. There was work to be done, she knew that. "How do ye feel?" enquired Gwenhwyvar. Morgan's glow of contentment was evident, yet it still seemed the correct thing to ask. Morgan's voice was filled with the serenity of complete gratification. "Beautiful" was the single word of reply.

There was no need to elaborate upon the situation, both women knew that. Gwenhwyvar's expression altered from concern to one that could almost be described as envious. But she was too demure to either admit it or allow it to show on purpose. "Alus is at the campsite. We should go" Gwenhwyvar pragmatically stated the current situation. Morgan stood up and clothed herself. When she had tidied her appearance up to the point of hopefully not arousing suspicion from the Knights, she gave a single nod of readiness to the Queen. They departed the small clearing, Morgan looking back at the point where Alus had made love to her with a wry smile.

The journey back to the campsite was taken up with scheming as to how to break the news to the brothers that they were to be left behind on Insula Vectis. Both of them knew that the Knights would be horrified at the very thought of allowing them to depart the island riding a magical beast. Nevertheless, it had to be done if they were to have any hope of intercepting Garlon. Eventually it was decided to attempt reason with their guardians first, and if the situation became intractable, a royal command would have to ensue.

When they arrived at the campsite, the three brothers were regarding their morning meal guest with a good deal of suspicion. There was more than enough meat left-over from the previous night. It was once more undergoing further roasting above a neatly prepared fire. Alus had not waited for the meat to be further cooked. He had taken a considerable chunk and was eating contentedly. The knights looked up with relief at seeing the women return safely to the campsite.

In answer to the unasked question, Gwenhwyvar assured the men that they were unharmed. She further instructed that they should eat a morning meal before any further discussion as to what was planned for the day ahead. Galahallt set about carving up the remains of the pig and distributing it amongst the party. In what was a re-enactment of the previous night's repast, it was eaten in a somewhat awkward silence. At the conclusion the three knights looked to Gwenhwyvar for further information as to what would come next. Disguising the nervousness in her voice, the Queen began her summary of the plan of action. "The next stage of our journey will take us to Gaul." With this the three knights leapt to their feet in astonishment. A chorus of "What"? and "Gaul"? erupted from the men. Holding up both her hands in a gesture to calm the situation, Gwenhwyvar continued. "We intend to ride with Alus across the water to Gaul. Speed is of the essence if we are to catch-up with Garlon."

Garethe was the first to seize upon the relevance of the information that had just been presented. "Mine Queen, ye know for certain that Garlon is now in Gaul?" For her response Gwenhwyvar elaborated upon the information that she was privy to. "Garlon is an insidious fiend. He seeks to secure the object that we seek behind the magical powers of a faerie. He does not know that we are in pursuit. Nor does he understand that Morgan is more than a match against the meagre powers of any faerie." She embellished her statement with a motion toward Morgan, who emphasised the point by agreeing with the Queen's summation of her abilities. Secretly though, Morgan had grave concerns that she would be any match for a faerie of such great age. Just like Matrona, he will have amassed a vastness of power over the centuries that he had lived through. But the Knights did not need to know any of this information just yet.

"We shall encounter Roman soldiers in Gaul for sure mine Queen," Guaen stated his greatest concern at such an undertaking. This point was taken up by Galahallt "The five of us will attract unwanted attention. And we do not speak the language." Garethe followed his brother's statement concluding the knight's overall fears as to the proposed journey, "The journey will take days. And how shall we ride with Alus without our horses?"

Gwenhwyvar addressed the concerns. "Morgan and I speak Gaulish. We shall not ride with Alus to Gaul, we shall ride Alus across the water to Gaul. And we shall ride alone. Two women travelling together will attract less attention than our party of five." The Knights simply could not believe what they were hearing. It was hard enough coming to terms with what the Queen was relaying to them, much less the full meaning of how such a journey would be accomplished. As if adding an afterthought or perhaps to pre-empt any question regarding the involvement of Alus Morgan interjected, "A bargain hath been struck with Alus for passage across the water and land, and payment made."

This only served to raise a whole new set of questions in the minds of the brothers. The Knights were drawing breath, ready to let loose a tirade of new concerns and clarifications when Alus transformed into a horse. It was as quick as it was dramatic. He visibly blurred and reformed into the animal. There was no sound, no glimmering light as there would have been if he was a faerie, nothing but the sudden metamorphosis. He was no ordinary horse, either. Alus was big; larger than a Clydesdale. His streamline body towered above them. Alus in this form was at twenty-five per cent larger than the greatest horse in the Caerleon stables. He had a magnificent white mane that ran the entire length from his head over his back and merged into his tail. The off-white fur shimmered in the morning light in a way that none of them had seen before.

Completely taken by surprise the group instinctively backed away. Even Morgan, more accustomed to witnessing such feats of magic was intimidated by the show of power. Alus shook his head and let out a loud 'neigh' followed by a huff through his sizeable nostrils. He seemed to be indicating that he was impatient to begin their journey. All of the misgivings and queries that the Knights had on their minds were temporarily blotted-out by the occurrence. Morgan indicated to Gwenhwyvar that they should take advantage of the situation and make a hasty departure.

With all of the authority that she could muster Gwenhwyvar instructed the knight standing nearest to her, "Sir Galahallt; assist me onto the horse." Still Galahallt hesitated, even though he initially made to move to fulfil the command. There was one last ploy that Gwenhwyvar played at that moment in order to tip the situation to her favour. "And give me thine dagger so that I may adequately defend mine person should the need arise." Accordingly she held out her hand to the bewildered knight. He instinctively reached into his outer tunic and untied the sheathed dagger. Bundling it up the Knight obediently handed it over to the Queen. "Now, help me up" she reiterated. The mechanics of exactly how to do this now dawned upon the hapless fellow. He looked up at the distance that he would need to boost the Queen in order for her to have any hope of taking the mount. And she would be riding bareback, holding on only to the mane in order to stay on the beast.

Fumbling with various solutions to the problem that came and went in a flash, he settled upon falling to one knee as closely to the horse's torso as he could. "Step upon mine knee then shoulder and grab the mane Queen Gwenhwyvar." He instructed. In effect the knight was using himself as a human step ladder. Not wanting to show any hesitation Gwenhwyvar did exactly that. Galahallt easily took the weight of Gwenhwyvar on his knee, and then he steadied himself as best he could before she set foot upon his shoulder. Grabbing Alus's mane she hauled herself into a mounted position. "Now Morgan" she commanded from on high.

Morgan followed the manoeuvre and soon joined the Queen upon the magical beast. It was obvious in spite of his size, that there would be no further room for any of the burley knights to join them upon the mount. "Return to Wareham and stay with Cawshall; wait for one full week before making thine way back to Caerleon." The Queens instructions were delivered in somewhat of a hurry as Alus had begun to turn toward the direction that he was clearly intent upon taking. Without any hope of arguing the point the three Knights watched dumbfounded as Alus leapt into motion. Morgan holding onto Gwenhwyvar for dear life and in turn Gwenhwyvar clasping the voluminous mane with all of the strength that she could muster. In a few steps Alus had departed the clearing and they were racing at an unbelievable speed through the woods that separated them from the nearby shoreline.

The ride was much smoother than either of them had expected. Alus's powerful legs took bounding strides each time, soon the water was in sight. There was no time for Morgan and Gwenhwyvar to exchange suppositions as to how Alus was going to navigate the water. Would he swim as a normal horse? What exactly was a water horse? Merlin's scrolls made only a small mention of the beast. Whatever was to come it was upon them in an instant of time. Alus reached the shoreline and jumped into the water with a huge splash. Gwenhwyvar and Morgan were pushed forward with the sudden loss of momentum. Both women could see through the clear water to the horse's limbs below. They were transforming in the same blur of motion that Alus had used to take on his horse body. The legs were replaced with what could only be described as lengthy flat diamond shaped fish-fins.

With incredible force they were leaping to the surface of the water as surely as a boat's oars would have done, reaching out as far ahead as they could, and diving into the water to drive them forward. Once more the women were shocked at the speed at which Alus could travel. With each passing arc of both front and rear leg 'oars' they accelerated faster than a long-boat under full sail in a storm. The water splashed onto the legs of the women. It was cold, but Alus's body was warm. It was much warmer than that of a normal horse. In fact now that it had come to their attention, they could feel his body temperature enveloping the both of them. It acted as a shield of warmth against the coldness of the water and the speed of the wind. They were safely encapsulated in an invisible cloud of comforting heat. It did not matter that their legs were now saturated. Also, Alus's body floated much higher in the water than that of an ordinary horse. Most of his body was above the waterline. Therefore the water only reached up to the thighs of the women, so their waists and torso's remained dry.

Morgan managed to look behind them to the island that they had so rapidly departed. She could just make out the three knights standing upon the shore. They must have pursued them to ensure that all was well. She could only wonder what the Knights were thinking of the sight which beheld them.

It was exhilarating. Alus was able to build upon the already incredible speed at which they were travelling. Gwenhwyvar managed to turn and look at Morgan. They both had smiles affixed to their faces. It was terrifying but exciting at the same time. "At this pace I can now believe that the journey will take only hours and not days", observed Gwenhwyvar. Morgan responded, "I shall be able to update Merlin's library with first-hand experience of travelling by water horse." Gwenhwyvar was able to relax her grip a little. She now realised that much like travelling over land, Alus's movement through the water was uncannily smooth. Even Morgan had ceased to grab Gwenhwyvar's waist with fearful vigour. They were both relaxing and enjoying the experience. Perhaps that too was part of the magic that Alus was working. They did not know.

Their journey became a blur of water, speed, comforting warmth, blue sky and sunlight. Seagulls squawked in the air above them. Morgan had the presence of mind to keep a close eye on the position of the sun. It was the only way to ascertain how much time had passed. She needn't have bothered. Much sooner than either of them could have suspected, land was in sight. It was the coast of Gaul.

Chapter 25: Pen Rhionydd - Late morning of the same day

Arthur and Merlin were busy with final preparations before their departure from the newly, and peacefully acquired township of Pen Rhionydd and surrounding lands of Galloway. Arthur should have been ecstatic. He had added a new land to his Kingdom without the need to battle Saxons, Angles, Gaels or Scoti. In fact, it had been handed over to him through the course of simple conversation. But it was an odd situation that he had been somehow forced to accept; a Christian religion within his own borders. No matter how cleverly he had debated the situation with Maelgyn, he was not victorious. Christianity would remain here as the overriding religion.

His demeanour did not go unnoticed by Merlin. "Still brooding?" he queried, his tone more like a rebuff than a question. Arthur stopped tying the food that Maelgyn had supplied to his horse and turned to face the old man. "Why will they not embrace the old ways which served our ancestors well, long before the Roman's invaded? And now that we have the opportunity to go back to the lives that our forefathers lived, this village chooses not to. I simply do not understand why." Arthur completed his complaint gesturing with both hands in the air.

If Merlin had head a single word of Arthur's rhetoric it did not show. His reply did not intimate that he shared any of the King's concerns about the situation. "King Rhydderch keeps a longboat moored directly south of here on the coast of Galloway. It is attended to by a small band of his soldiers; Ganieda hath told me so." Merlin looked expectantly at Arthur for some kind of reaction. For his part,

Arthur returned the look with a somewhat annoyed expression. Brushing off the lacklustre non-verbal response Merlin continued more animated this time. "Do ye not see Arthur? I know that there is a small Christian monastery on the Island of Mann. If I can see that there too, mine powers do not work then I have proof that there is something about this religion that inhibits mine abilities. As it stands now, all I have is conjecture. I need to be able to repeat the occurrence, then I shall have proof that the two things are somehow connected."

Arthur found the rather large hole in Merlin's reasoning. "But ye shall still not know how thine magic is suppressed. The Christians seem to have no abilities themselves to do so; nor any inkling that they are having this effect upon ye." Arthur's summation of the obvious problem with Merlin's thinking was brushed aside with a wave of Merlin's hand. "First let the connection between Christianity and magical inhibition be proved; then the source of the matter can be explored." Merlin turned back to complete tying his horse reigns. Arthur almost continued to be critical of their present course of action, but stopped himself. He realised that he and his Kingdom relied upon Merlin and his abilities. In fact, the current situation of the missing Excalibur was sure to be solved only by magical prowess. Resigned to this sudden forthcoming journey across the sea to Mann, Arthur groaned beneath his breath and turned to complete his preparations.

When they had finished Arthur suggested that they locate Maelgyn to bid him farewell. Leaving the barn together, they came across Sir Alynore. "Sire" he said, relieved to have found the King.

"Maelgyn wishes to bid thee farewell. He is in the great hall." Arthur received the news gratefully and added to the knight "Sir Alynore, administer Pen Rhionydd in mine name but allow them to continue to practice their unusual religion" He was in fact re-stating the directions that he had already imparted to the Knight. But Sir Alynore, a little nervous at his first posting as the King's representative was grateful for the reiterated instructions. "Aye Sire" he said bowing his head slightly. Arthur added as a final statement "Should there be any sign of invasion by land or sea, deliver word to King Rhydderch who shall send help." Satisfied that Sir Alynore had headed his commands he slapped him heartily on the back. "Ye shall be a worthy Administrator Sir Alynore, of that I am certain."

The three of them walked side by side toward the main hall. They could see that a large crowd of the townspeople had gathered to see them off. The crowd was gathered around the open entrance to the hall. Passing through the sea of smiling faces and well-wishers, the three men entered the hall. Maelgyn and all of the men considered to be the elders of Pen Rhionydd were clustered together awaiting the presence of the King. As Arthur approached they spread themselves into a semi-circle around him. Arthur noted the configuration of the men as a reflection of the round table in Caerleon. He assumed that it was homage to the famous table from which he ruled his kingdom. It pleased him. As per usual, Maelgyn did all of the talking on behalf of the natives. "Hail to Arthur, King of Galloway", Maelgyn's voice echoing slightly in the large space. In response the entire assembly responded as one "Hail to Arthur." It was loud, taking Arthur aback a little. But it did lift his spirits. He responded not directly to Maelgyn but to all of them. "Send word throughout this land; Galloway shall be protected by mine rule. Sir Alynore shalll administer in mine absence, supported by a small band of soldiers. King Rhydderch of North Rheged stands by to assist should the need arise. I shall return within the year. Rest assured that ye lives will be better by inclusion into mine Kingdom. Ye will be able to practice ye Christian religion without fear of persecution. Farm ye lands without fear of paying tribute to Saxons or any other." Arthur's summation of the benefits of becoming part of his Kingdom brought a substantial cheer of joy from the crowd.

Even through the delivery of his brief speech Arthur was working on the logistics of his rule. The foot soldiers could be rotated within the year as well as Sir Alynor's role as administrator. In this way he would not earn the ire of the wives and mothers of the Caerleon villagers from which they came. Perhaps Sir Bors De Ganys would do well as the next representative in this far north land. In turn each of his Knights could spend a year here in Galloway. There was perhaps even the chance of recruiting some of the locals to enhance the soldier's numbers. That too would better cement the land and its people to Arthur's rule. He made a mental note to leave this further instruction to Sir Alynore. When the cheer had died down he addressed the semi-circle of townsfolk elders. "Farewell; until I return once more to this fair land." He raised his hand.

The elders, Maelgyn included all returned Arthur's gesture. Amongst the numerous bids of goodbye from the group, Maelgyn's voice could be heard above them. "Safe Journey King Arthur." There was much clasping of hands in physical bids of valediction. It took quite some time for Merlin and Arthur to make their way through the crowd and out of the hall into the afternoon sun. Arthur's Knights were waiting for him upon their horses. They had fetched Arthur's and Merlin's horse and were crowded together along with the now greatly diminished number of foot soldiers. Best that he let them all know his final instructions. "Sir Alynore" he said in a voice loud enough to be heard by all. "The soldiers and thine self will return to Caerleon before a year passes. I shall accompany the replacements in person." There was a grateful sigh and motion of understanding from the Knight.

With nothing further to be said, the King and Sorcerer took their mounts. Arthur took the lead and pointed his horse in the direction of south. The party departed followed by a throng of townspeople. They followed the band to the outskirts of Pen Rhionydd before falling away bit by bit. Arthur took the time to look over the township once more. He had not succeeded in stopping the townsfolk dismantling Vallum Hadriani and using the stone in further construction. He had not succeeded in converting the people back to the ways of their forefathers. But somehow he felt victorious. Galloway was a considerable prize.

"What shall I tell King Rhydderch of Vallum Hadriani?" enquired Arthur of Merlin. "Tell him that it is being put to better use," replied Merlin. For the first time Arthur actually felt that it was. The stones would contribute to building formidable structures here in Galloway. There seemed to be little use for it now as a barrier between two components of his expanded Kingdom. Hopefully King Rhydderch would see the sense in that. In fact, now that the wall was no longer needed, North Rheged could benefit from the ready-made supply of building materials that it offered. He pondered that thought for a moment. Surely Rhydderch would like to avail himself of that opportunity. Anyhow, further conjecture on this thinking would have to wait until they returned from the Island of Mann. There was a new directive that must be explored; the regional loss of Merlin's magical powers.

As if reading his thoughts, Merlin spoke, "If we push the men and horses hard enough, we should reach the coast by nightfall. We can rest for the night before setting sail for Mann tomorrow morning."

"Aye Merlin," Arthur confirmed his approval of the plan of action clear from his face.

Chapter 26: Gaul - One hour past noon

Alus had transformed his oar-like legs back into those of a horse when they were close to the shore. He had leapt onto the dry land and without stopping for breath and began a spritely gallop across the sand and onto the firm grassy land beyond. The rolling fields flew past with unbelievable speed. Alus was able to move faster on land than in the water. Gaul was a beautiful place; it evoked memories of her upbringing by her grandparents within Morgan. They had not seen anybody during the entire journey across water, and now across land. This thought must have occurred to the women simultaneously because Gwenhwyvar turned to Morgan to comment upon it. "Do ye think is coincidence that we have not come across any people thus far?" Morgan indicated that she agreed and offered a potential explanation. "Alus must be able to sense people so that he may avoid them. After all, how many folk hath seen a water horse?" Convinced by this argument Gwenhwyvar indicated that she agreed with Morgan's assessment of the situation.

It was another two hours at least before Alus began to slow his pace to a trot. They had entered a slightly wooded area and there seemed to be what looked like a road just ahead. Gwenhwyvar estimated that they had penetrated the inland of Gaul many hundreds of milles. Alus appeared to be sniffing at the air as he approached the road. Satisfied that they were alone he stopped just short of the well-worn track. He turned his head and gave the women a snort which they took as an instruction to dismount. They did so. In an instant Alus transmuted back into his human form; miraculously he was once more clothed in his form-fitting attire. Morgan dismissed the event in her mind as inconsequential. His clothing must be like faerie silk and could appear and disappear at the will of the magician using it. Gwenhwyvar was more disappointed in the fact that Alus was not completely naked. She had just assumed that he would be. And her curiosity was piqued after firstly hearing the rapturous love-making that Morgan and he had performed the previous night; and secondly finding Morgan the following morning in a state of absolute contended bliss.

Refocussing her mind on the task at hand, Gwenhwyvar asked Alus, "Where to from here?" He was forthcoming with a complete explanation. "This is as far as Usla carried Garlon. There is a village further down this road. Our agreement is at an end." Without allowing the women time to respond Alus transformed back into the form of a horse. Gwenhwyvar and Morgan instinctively moved back as he turned around and galloped back in the direction they had come. "Wait!" Morgan managed a feeble cry as he sped away from them. "It appears that from here we find our own way" she concluded, watching him disappear from sight. Gwenhwyvar was already analysing the situation. "Garlon would have come here with purpose. The villagers most likely know the location of the Minotaur. Much like the villagers in Caerleon know about the faerie forest through hear-say and rumour. Although they may not know the exact form of the beast, just that it is there; we must be careful in finding out anything that they do know. We are outsiders, and will not earn their trust easily."

Morgan considered the Queen's words and followed in the same train of thought. "Perhaps we can offer something to give them comfort." Her suggestion intrigued Gwenhwyvar. "Such as…?" she asked. Morgan seemed to ponder some more upon her thought. "Villagers everywhere are the same; superstitious and fearful of magical beings. We shall offer the following explanation of ourselves. A healer and her apprentice travelling the land, mending the sick and ridding villages of magical beings in return for lodging and food." Morgan outlined her plan with a flourish of her hand and a satisfied smile. Gwenhwyvar was impressed. "Morgan, that is a brilliant strategy! It is not so far from the truth either. By offering such assistance to the villagers we shall gain immediate acceptance for sure; as well as finding out what they know of the being that Garlon has made his alliance with." Emboldened by the tactic that they would soon implement, the two women walked side-by-side down the road and toward the village that Alus had indicated was there.

They had not gone very far when Morgan noticed that there was a rhythmic noise emanating from somewhere far off behind them. There was something familiar about it. She turned around to see where it was coming from. Off in the distance there was a cluster of men, they were marching in formation and the gold and red of their clothing could be made out even at this distance. Alerted by Morgan, Gwenhwyvar too turned to see what the Sorceress was looking at. "Roman soldiers," Morgan identified what they were both seeing. They must have been marching at a fairly rapid pace. The distance between the women and the advancing battalion began to close with unnerving rapidity. Quickening their pace, Morgan and Gwenhwyvar were keen to avoid the swathe of Roman foot soldiers whilst they were alone on the road. There was comparative safety in the village if they could just reach it and win over the villagers with their story before the Romans caught up with them. The woodlands either side of the road offered insufficient places in which to hide and allow the soldiers to pass. And by now, the women would have been spied by the soldiers for sure.

The women came over the top of a hill and saw the village below them. On the outskirts of the cluster of huts and other buildings was a structure that would most surely be a tavern. "Do ye think that would be a tavern?" queried Gwenhwyvar. "Aye" responded Morgan; she was calling upon her local knowledge at this point. It had the same look as most of the taverns that she and her grandparents visited whilst she lived here. "From this point on we should only speak Gaulish," warned Morgan. The Queen nodded and they hurried onwards to their immediate destination. "Let us not mention the forthcoming Roman soldiers until we hath won-over the inhabitants with our story," said Gwenhwyvar. Morgan was a little perplexed at this stratagem. She objected "Surely we can aide our cause by offering advanced warning of the Romans?" she was beginning to pant at the frenetic pace that they had taken. They were now safely over the rise of the hill and on the downward slope to the tavern, and therefore out of sight of the Roman battalion. It was safe now to quicken their pace all the more, at least that way it would not look to the Roman's that they were trying to avoid them.

"What of the villagers, surely they will see our hurried entrance." Morgan saw the gaping hole in the Queen's idea. Gwenhwyvar mentally kicked herself for such an obvious mistake. "Of course Morgan, ye are correct; best then to admit that we intend to avoid the Roman's, two unaccompanied women, fearful of our virtue." Gwenhwyvar hurried out her recourse between now laboured breaths. She thought to herself that hopefully this would help to portray them as helpless women who were in need of sanctuary. This could work to their advantage after all. They would know soon enough. The tavern was in sight. And they had indeed been sighted by an individual, maybe the inn-keeper, who upon their approach entered the building.

When they had hurried up to the door and opened it, the villagers inside all stopped talking and turned to face the newcomers. It was a typical Gaulish tavern; low ceilings of seasoned timber, roughly rendered straw walls and a thatched roof above. A large stone fireplace took pride of place at one end of the long narrow structure. It was not lit, the weather was warm enough to be comfortable without it. The silence seemed to last a little too long. Morgan looked to Gwenhwyvar for guidance; would they just blurt out their story and hope for immediate acceptance? What looked to be the inn-keeper was busy lighting a pipe from what looked like bruyere wood. A freak accident gave Morgan her chance to establish their credentials. Perhaps over packed, or with the wrong mixture in it, the pipe fizzled and hissed loudly; a large flame spat out and burnt the nose of the man.

He screamed in pain. Everyone forgot the two women momentarily and turned to see what had happened. The man had thrown the pipe down and was clutching his nose in agony, the smell of burnt flesh now apparent in the room. Morgan shouted at her loudest in her best Gaulish. "Stop, do not move, I can help ye!" She rushed forward and wrenched the man's hand away from nursing his wound. He was about to object and instinctively pull away from Morgan but something made him hesitate. Morgan concentrated as hard as she could and spread the palm of her hand over the man's injury. It stopped hurting as much. He became aware that she was uttering words in some language that he did not understand.

The pain receded even more. He shook his head in amazement. With a few more utterances, the pain had disappeared completely. He could not believe his fortune. It took a moment for him to compose himself. Morgan removed her hand from the man's nose. It was uninjured. A collective gasp of "Ooohh" arose from the onlookers. There began hushed whispering between people unable to believe what they had just witnessed. "Mine nose, it is no longer sore?" said the man. He looked at Morgan with astonishment. She allowed the situation to sink-in to the crowd before speaking once more in fluent Gaulish. "I am a healer. Mine apprentice and I travel the land curing the sick and ridding the land of mischievous faeries and other magical beings. All that we seek is safe lodging and food in return." There was an approving "Ahhh" from the villagers. They had just witnessed for themselves the truth of this strangers claim. Morgan continued turning to face the majority of the room. "Yet we are two women alone and cannot fend-off a Roman battalion. They are approaching even now." Her expression was needy. "Please find it in thine hearts to offer us sanctuary in ye village." Morgan offered her empty hands in a gesture of help.

The ploy worked. The miraculously cured inn keeper was the first to side with the women. "That is the second time mine pipe hath done that this month. It must be the mixture that I am using. Thanks to ye, I am cured of an injury that would have taken months to heal." He turned to face his customers. "I believe that this woman is a healer and needs our help." There was another approving "Hmm" from the group and much nodding of heads. "Ye are very pretty mine ladies and we hide our maidens from the Roman's whenever they pass through. I say that we hide these women with our own." That was clearly all of the encouragement that the villagers needed. There was a resounding "Aye" from many of them. It was only then that Morgan and Gwenhwyvar realised that the tavern was full of old men and old women, there was not a youngster to be seen anywhere. It was very odd.

The news about the approaching Roman soldiers sent a flurry of activity through the tavern. Some of the villagers left immediately, maybe going to secure their homes or warn the rest of the local population. Roman soldiers would be common enough in these parts but there would still be a great deal of apprehension about their presence. Morgan remembered being hidden by her grandparents after she was old enough to look comely to the men. Fear of her virtue being taken by the overlords was an ever-present danger. This was clearly the case here too. The inn-keeper strode up to one of the nearby men. "Take them to hide with the rest of our maidens." There was no argument, clearly the decision had been made that Morgan and Gwenhwyvar would be offered what protection the locals could provide. He motioned to the women to follow him from the tavern. They did so, looking up the hill as they exited. The advancing soldiers could be seen beginning to appear, heads, shoulders and torsos rising into view.

They followed their guide behind the tavern and down the road to the village itself. The pathway that they were taking put the tavern between them and the soldiers, blocking them from view. They moved quickly past chickens and pigs, goats, sheep and cows all coexisting happily in the space between the tavern and the main part of the village. Soon enough they had entered the main cluster of huts that made up the centre of the community. Other young girls and boys were being herded by the older folk. Morgan and Gwenhwyvar joined the throng surging forward. Morgan looked over her shoulder to see if the Romans could be seen from this point. Now it was the cluster of huts that stood between them and the hillside view that the soldiers would have. Morgan wondered if the buildings had been constructed in their places for this very purpose.

There would be time enough for conjecture when they were safely secreted away. The small group made towards a large structure, raised from the ground. Morgan recognised it as a grain storage building. The entrance to it was on the far side, further concealing from view what was happening. They followed their guide around to the far side entrance and he stopped short, pointing the way up the stairs, "That way quickly!" he ordered. The women moved as fast as they could up the stairs, followed by the last stragglers of the contingent that they were part of. When inside, they could see that it was a very large structure holding large sacks of grain on a wooden floor covered in straw. At one side there was an internal structure build to hold further sacks of grain in a mezzanine-style arrangement. There was a ladder leading up to the landing above.

The youngsters however were not hiding up in the loft as Gwenhwyvar would have thought; instead they were making their way through an opening in the piles of grain-filled sacks to a secret room at the centre of the largest pile. It had cleverly been structured with wood but clad in the sacks. There were what appeared to be the tops of bulbous sacks full of grain over the top of the room, giving it the appearance of a dense cluster of the storage bags. If the bag that concealed the entrance had been in place the women would have not suspected that there was a secret room encased in the bags. A man was motioning for them to go inside. "Quickly now!" he said, annoyed at their slowness. Morgan and Gwenhwyvar obeyed. They had to duck down low in order to get through the entrance. Inside were the village's young, boys almost old enough to be conscripted into the Roman army, and girls coming of age and a temptation that may prove too great for the Roman soldiers to resist.

There was a solitary candle in the centre of the gathering. It had been lit by one of the boys. Once inside and settled, the door which had opened inwards was closed. It too contained a sack of grain secured to the outside; it was a perfect disguise. They could hear a large sack being dragged into place covering the secret door, and straw being shuffled around to disguise the foot traffic that had just gone through the barn. The villagers were clearly adept at protecting their most vulnerable members.

Nobody spoke; all eyes were upon Morgan and Gwenhwyvar. "We hath come to help; but we too need protection from the Romans," Gwenhwyvar offered a simple one line summation of their situation. The shared experience of needing protection from the soldiers gave the two women acceptable credentials with the youngsters. One of the young girls, perhaps fifteen years of age reached out and gave Morgan's elbow a reassuring squeeze. Now all they had to do was wait until the Romans left the township. Morgan wondered how long that might be.

Gwenhwyvar was calculating in her head the last point where she saw the Roman soldiers, and estimated that it would be some minutes yet before they reached the heart of the village. She chanced to speak to some of the youth nearest to her in a hushed tone. "How often do the Roman's come to thine village?" One of the boys answered her, "Once, sometimes twice a season. Come to collect the taxes for the Emperor Flavius Anastasius. Our elders pay what we are able. We feed them and they leave soon enough." He did not seem too concerned with the situation. She enticed further information from the young man. "Ye hide for fear of conscription?"

He indicated that she was correct. "It is enough that they take our money, food and wine. They should not feel free to help themselves to our people as well. None of us want to serve in the Roman army, nor do our women wish to become the wives of Roman soldiers. They have yet to uncover our hiding place." He offered the women reassurance that they were indeed safe.

Gwenhwyvar and Morgan had come across a village full of very clever people indeed. The two women felt secure huddled together with these people. There were crude mattresses here and there. They had settled upon one. At least waiting out the current situation would not be without some comforts.

Chapter 27: The Galloway Coast - Sunset

Arthur's contingent had made excellent time through the land of Galloway and to the coast. Guided with unerring accuracy by Merlin, they had reached the secured long boat that King Rhydderch kept at this location. The soldiers from North Rheged that had been posted to maintain the boat were surprised to see the young King. But he was easily recognised by both his standard flying high above, held by one of the Knights and the fact that Arthur was no stranger to the court of King Rhydderch. Most of the eight men on duty recognised Arthur from his many visitations to the castle. It was the one that must have been in charge that was running forward to greet the King.

"King Arthur; this is a surprise. We were not expecting ye," he managed to say before coming to a halt in front of Arthur's horse. Arthur duly brought his mare to a stop and signalled that the troop should do the same. He dismounted. "I hath need to borrow King Rhydderch Hael's long boat for a mission to the Island of Mann." There was no question from the soldier. After all King Rhydderch was sworn to recognise King Arthur has the true ruler of all of Briton, which included North Rheged. "Aye Sire," he bowed in obedience. King Arthur continued, "We shall rest here for the night and make sail at first light." Once more the soldier bowed in acknowledgement and compliance. "Prepare some extra campfires for my knights and foot soldiers" the King further stipulated. "Aye sire; we have plenty of dried wood. Please accept the comfort of the guards hut for your royal slumber this night." The offer from the soldier was welcome. Arthur would have normally eschewed such comforts, not wanting to either take the use of the hut from the entrenched soldiers, or sleep apart from his Knights and men. But he was weary and the thought of sleeping in the comparative shelter of the soldier's hut was appealing enough for him to graciously accept the offer. The soldier, whose name Arthur still did not know, hurried away to see to his newfound chores.

Merlin and Arthur's knights had by this time dismounted and joined their King for a further briefing on their actions for the morrow. The light was soft; the sun had now set in the west. A cool wind had whipped up from the sea. The red clouds were a harbinger of a fine day tomorrow. "'Twill be a good day for sailing. With favourable winds we can make landfall on Mann well before noon. Where on the island is the monastery that we seek Merlin?" Merlin gave them all some welcome news. "According to the elders in Pen Rhionydd it is on the close side of the island, barely an hour's walk from the coast." He delivered the titbit of information with his usual hand waving and gleeful smile flourishing the information. The King gave a visible sigh of relief. "That is excellent news Merlin. Knights prepare the camp and the evening meal; we have an early start tomorrow." Arthur gave his instructions and the Knights obeyed without hesitation.

When they were out of hearing range Merlin let loose with an update to his magical state that took Arthur completely by surprise. "Mine powers hath returned," he announced. "What?" replied the startled King. "When?"

"As soon as there were no more townsfolk near to me", he replied. Arthur was miffed that the old man had not told him this minor revelation as soon as it had happened. "So then it is the presence of the people of Galloway that somehow inhibits thine magic; not the land itself" observed the keen-minded ruler. "Aye. But the visit to the monastery will be the true test. They too are worshipers of the Christian religion that springs from Antioch. Should my powers fail in their presence too then the hypothesis is proven. Christians unknowingly, as far as I can tell, prevent me from practicing the mystical arts." Arthur was trying to think forward to all of the ramifications of this if it was proved to be true. He began to pace up and down in front of Merlin. "Surely then, we should do our best to limit the spread of their religion, so as to assure your continuance as mine Sorcerer."

He expected Merlin to be completely in favour of this plan of action; however Merlin was thinking more broadly that that. "Consider this Arthur. The religion can only spread so fast. And from what I could gather from the people of Pen Rhionydd, they hath never seen a faerie, nor any other type of ethereal being." He finished off the sentence almost trailing off in sheer wonder of the implied consequences. Arthur however did not see the obvious connection. "So?" he said. Merlin admonished the young King. "Do ye not see Arthur? 'Tis not just mine magic that does not work on or near the people of Galloway, it is *all* magic. That is what I seek to prove by this trip to Mann."

Arthur was now beginning to see the advantage of such a useful tool. "Where ever there are Christians, there are no faeries?" he pondered the corollaries. "Exactly" smiled Merlin. "So ye thinks that we can deploy these Christians to rid our borders from the faerie pestilence?" Arthur looked to his sage for confirmation that this was indeed his thinking. Merlin gave Arthur the satisfied look of a master that had successfully taught a complex problem to a student. "Aye Arthur. We shall finally possess a weapon that can be deployed against the faeries in response to them aiding King Aelle in the battle for Anderidae."

This was very welcome news. Arthur's mind was already racing forward with thoughts of wresting Anderidae away from Aelle. But guessing his thoughts Merlin interrupted him. "If this correlation turns out to be true, then we can invite some of the Christian's living in Galloway to set up a village in the faerie forest to the north of Caerleon castle. They will be far enough away from me to not inhibit mine powers, but the forest will be cleared of the wretched things once and for all." Merlin finished and outlined his immediate goal should his hypothesis prove correct. Arthur could see that Merlin wanted to proceed cautiously with this newfound strategy. He appropriately adjusted his thinking. "Aye Merlin; a good plan," he praised the old man's tactical thinking. He tried to reach the logical conclusion that Merlin was aiming for. "Then any thoughts of faerie allegiances with Saxons, Angles or Jutes can be effectively thwarted. All that we need do is introduce Christian observers to our battles. Thine magic will be ineffective, but so will that of any faeries present." He looked to Merlin for confirmation that he had indeed reached the outcome that the Sorcerer was hoping for. "Exactly" replied the wily sage. This introduced an entirely new way for Arthur to consider battles with the invaders. He would have to rely upon skill and military prowess alone. There would be no ethereal intervention from Merlin in such battles.

The obvious question then sprang to Arthur's mind. "Excalibur; will it still be able to slice through chainmail with Christians present?" the very question then reinvoked the deficit that he felt without it at his side. Merlin looked furtively about them to ensure that nobody was within hearing range. "When," he said with conviction, "we recover Excalibur, that question can be answered. It may be that Excalibur is somehow immune to this influence. After all, it comes from the most mysterious of magical beings. Perhaps the Lady of the Lake's sword will be unaffected by the suppression that this religion emanates. Arthur I just do not know. First let us complete my experiment, recover the sword, then we can think of the best way to use our new-found weapon." They were wise words. It would not help matters to rush ahead and make definite plans at this stage. Arthur allowed himself to relax a bit and tried to let go of the anticipation that he had built up inside him during the course of this exchange.

Arthur decided that it would be best to distract himself from these thoughts. He altered the subject of conversation completely. "Let us help set up the camp for the night," he said. Merlin indicated that that would be a good idea and they set about doing just that.

Chapter 28: A Market Town South of the Chalk Caves in Gaul - Night

Garlon looked up at the sky. Gaelach was hanging in the darkness; her face a crescent. He did not expect it to look any different, but it was difficult to not look. The signal that he had pre-arranged with the beast was that the orb would look blood-red after Merlin arrived at the creature's lair and had been dealt with. All that he had to do was to wait until the signal was given. Merlin would be dead, and he could recover Excalibur from the beast's caves and take it back to Briton. He imagined himself brandishing it about before a meeting of the Saxon warlords. Arthur's magical sword stolen; Arthur's Sorcerer dead. He would be proclaimed a hero amongst his people. The scheming that he had begun in this very town only two short years ago was coming to fruition. From this point his victory was only a matter of time.

Chapter 29: The Village to the West of the Chalk Caves in Gaul - Night

Far away from Garlon, in the small village in which Gwenhwyvar and Morgan had taken refuge, the Roman soldiers had exacted their taxes. The Roman commander had ordered that his men stay for the night and set out to the next morning to continue their tour of duty. This fact had been guessed by the refugees taking sanctuary in the hidden room in the grain-store. They had begun to settle down to sleep for the night. A few of the more mature youths had worked out a roster to keep watch over the sleepers. Any unnecessary noise or snoring would be quashed for fear of giving away their hiding place. Morgan surmised that this was a situation that they had faced before. She was impressed at the forethought that had gone into managing the situation.

Morgan was settling down on one of the mattresses. Queen Gwenhwyvar had insisted upon taking the first 'watch' along with a couple of others in the group. It was a wonderfully comforting feeling being in the situation that they found themselves in. Although discovery by the Romans would be catastrophic, it was clear that the villagers were well practiced at hiding successfully from them. Secure in this snug hiding place, Morgan found the onset of sleep with abundant ease. She drifted into a deep sleep. It felt like she was floating above the floor. The sound of water lapping against the wooden hull of a boat seemed distant, but somehow disturbing. Gradually Morgan became aware of the smell of the sea. Gulls squawked overhead. She opened her eyes. She was standing in a long boat that was out at sea. There were oarsmen that bore the crest of King Rhydderch Hael of North Rheged. Morgan was disorientated. Somebody was shouting about something.

It took a moment for Morgan to realise what the words meant "Gael raiders!" came the scream of warning. Morgan looked to where the noise was coming from. It was the one of Arthur's Knights, Sir Dagonet. He was shouting a warning about the raiders called the Gael that came from across the sea to wreak havoc, usually in the communities of the Picts at the northern most part of the land. Is this where she was right now? Morgan couldn't tell, there was nothing but water all around. She concentrated upon Sir Dagonet. He was pointing off to the larboard. She followed the direction of his finger. There in the distance was another long boat. It was coming towards them.

Morgan groaned almost imperceptibly in her sleep. Gwenhwyvar looked over to her and guessed that she must be dreaming. Maybe she was witnessing a vision? The Queen thought for a moment about waking her, even though it was barely any time at all since she had fallen to sleep. Morgan rolled over onto her side. There was silence. Gwenhwyvar decided to not disturb the sorceress in case she was having a vision of Excalibur or something else that may help them in their quest.

It was almost like a fog had rolled in over the boat. There seemed to be a cloud preventing Morgan from seeing what was happening. She was aware of voices, rising tensions. Then it all became crystal clear once more. There was no fog; in fact it was a brilliantly clear day. The long boat of Gaels that was the cause for so much concern was almost upon them. Morgan had a sense of having lost a great deal of time. It simply was not possible for the boat that she saw earlier to have travelled so far so fast. What did matter was that the crew of the boat were making to board their long boat. Then she saw them; Arthur and Merlin. How was it possible that she had not seen them before on this small vessel? Nevertheless, there they were alongside Sir Dagonet, preparing themselves for battle with swords drawn, even Merlin!

Morgan could scarcely believe her eyes, Merlin with a sword in his hand? Her instincts were to call out and plead for an explanation. But her throat was numb. No sound emanated from her mouth. The Gael boat had begun to swing around to make it parallel to theirs. There was much shouting from both sides, angry cries of war. A few more moments was all that it would take for the Gael boat to get close enough for the raiders to jump across to their long boat. King Rhydderch's oarsmen were using their oars as weapons. They had lifted them out from the water and were trying to push the Gael boat away to no effect.

"This is it," Morgan heard King Arthur shout; "we fight!" his voice clear over the growing melee. Morgan rapidly assessed the situation. Both long boats were similarly sized, but the Gael boat was laden with raiders; bloodthirsty men armed and ready for battle. Arthur's boat had only the six oarsmen that appeared to carry no swords with them, Merlin, Sir Dagonet and the King. They were hopelessly outnumbered. Morgan looked with absolute horror as Arthur raised his sword to begin battle with the first of the Gael that had hurled himself across the narrow stretch of water between them and onto Arthur's boat. He fought with the experience of a seasoned warrior. But his sword-play was more cumbersome than usual. The mock version of Excalibur that he brandished was much heavier than the actual magical sword. If he had been holding Excalibur he would have easily sliced through the Gael's sword, leather armour and even his torso with one mighty swoop.

Instead there was the sound of metal upon metal clanking once, twice, again and again. The angle that the first Gael had come onto to the boat almost excluded Merlin being able to use his sword. Arthur was between him and the aggressor. Sir Dagonet was busy running the length of the boat to the stern where another raider had made the leap across to the boat. They too engaged in heated battle. The oars men were grouping together to try and fend off any more raiders coming on board. They were successful in thwarting the attempt of one of the Gael's who was knocked off balance mid-flight and pushed down into the water by a combination of the oarsmen. They then began to beat the head of the man with the blades of their oars; there was blood in the water, on the oars, and a dying scream of a man being killed.

Arthur had in the meantime outmanoeuvred the Gael that he had engaged in battle. The raider, clearly less of an accomplished swordsman, had made a desperate bid to overthrow his opponent with a parry and a thrust, countered by Arthur. The Gael attempted to use his entire weight to push Arthur back. Arthur dropped to one knee causing the Gael to become unbalanced; it was the precious second that the raider took to try and regain his composure was his undoing. Sliding his sword back just enough to reposition it against the riders throat, he thrust it into the man who gargled a bloody scream and Arthur pushed him off the boat and into the water.

Two down, and what looked like twelve or fifteen more to Morgan. Sir Dagonet was now fighting two Gaels, whilst some nearby oars men did their best to render assistance with their oars. Another raider jumped onto the stern of the boat, and another. Swords drawn they focussed their attack upon the nearest oarsmen who was quickly and mercilessly dispatched by the both of them. Another raider joined his friends on Arthur's boat. Morgan looked back to Merlin and Arthur. Each man was engaged in battle with a raider. It was hopeless, there were too many of them, Arthur and his men didn't stand a chance.

A feeling of mounting dread filled Morgan. She was powerless to help, her limbs seem to not work, arms at her side. It was that moment that seemed to slow and hang in time. Merlin was engaged with the Gael that he had been fighting. Morgan was transfixed with this vision. He fended off blow after blow from the much younger and more aggressive fighter. The Gael raised his sword for yet another pounding cut of his sword. Merlin took the opportunity to levitate the sword up and out of his opponent's hand. Surprised and dumbfounded, he stupidly looked up to where his sword should have been. Merlin took only a second to swing his sword from left to right and cut the man's arm deeply at the outer area of his bicep. The Gale screamed in agony. Merlin lifted his foot and used his weight to push the injured opponent off the edge of the boat.

Merlin turned to see how Arthur was faring with his latest battle. It was at that moment his eyes met Morgan's anguished stare.

There was a flash of acknowledgement from him, shock at seeing her on the boat. He was completely distracted by the presence of Morgan at the stern of their long boat. And that was all that it took. With Arthur otherwise occupied, another Gael had made the leap onto their boat to replace the one so cunningly dispatched by the old Sorcerer. Merlin became acutely aware of the movement in his peripheral vision; but by the time he had turned to face his new enemy it was too late. The Gael plunged his sword deep into the chest of the old man.

Withdrawing the bloodied sword resulted in a spurt of red life-force from Merlin. He became limp. There was no sound, no scream. He collapsed to the deck of the long boat, his head making a sickening thump audible to Morgan above the noise of battle.

Drawing in her breath, Morgan sat upright from her sleeping position and screamed at the top of her lungs. "MERLIN!"

***

There was a mild state of pandemonium in the hidden room in the grain storage building. The young men and women, boys and girls that had been sleeping were shocked awake by the cry. The few watchers that had stayed awake to keep guard were all leaping forward to cover the mouths of those that had been stirred by the shout. Gwenhwyvar had done her best to travel the small amount of distance between them when she saw Morgan sit upright. But she had been too late. The exclamation had escaped from Morgan before the Queen had a chance to muffle it with her hand.

Realising that she was still in the hiding place Morgan did her best to compose herself. She clasped at Gwenhwyvar's hand wrapping her mouth. There passed a look between them; one of assurance from Morgan that she had indeed regained her equanimity; and one from Gwenhwyvar pleading for an explanation, when it could be done safely. The other inhabitants of the secret room were shocked at Morgan's outburst. She looked around to give them assurance that she was once again in control of her poise. There came an agonising time of complete stillness whilst they waited to see if their hiding position had been betrayed by the shriek. And just as they had begun to dare think that Morgan's call had not attracted any unwelcome investigation they heard a dreaded sound of footsteps in the grain building. Someone had entered through the door. There were footsteps up and down the length of the room. At one point they came to the area where the concealed door was. The tension in the room escalated. One of the smaller children whimpered what could have been the beginning of tears of fear.

One of the elder girls gently clasped the little girl's mouth and pulled her in closer to offer more comfort. The footsteps moved away from the doorway and then circled around the room to the other side. A voice cut through the darkness. "I heard ye in here mine pretty. Come out lest I summon the remainder of the garrison to help me find thee." The words were spoken in Latin. Morgan and the Queen were able to understand as they were both versed in the language. They were unsure of how many of the youngsters in the room had understood the words. However, hearing the Latin words left all of them in no doubt that a Roman soldier had entered their sanctuary. Something had to be done to remedy the situation. Gwenhwyvar moved to the concealed door, she knew exactly what had to be done. All eyes were upon her; she turned to face all of them and motioned with her finger over her lips for them to remain completely silent. Noiselessly, she unlatched the door and opened it. Looks of horror ensued from everyone inside the room, including Morgan. What was the Queen doing? Gwenhwyvar signalled to Morgan to come and shut the door behind her after she had exited. Moving as quietly as she could, Morgan made to comply. Gwenhwyvar in the meantime had crawled into the space between the top of the sacks and the roof of the mezzanine level. There was just enough room for her to squeeze her lithe body over the sacks and through to the other side.

The Roman soldier was still on the other side of the conglomeration of sacks, still unaware that it hid a secret chamber. However he did hear the sound of two feet landing upon the wooden floorboards around the other side to his present position. He ran around to see who was there. He was holding a small oil lamp lighting his way. Just as he suspected, there was a woman here. She must have been the one that he heard cry out. He held the lamp up to her face. She was beautiful. He thanked the gods for his fortune. This prize must have secreted herself in this grain store to avoid any unwelcome advances from his compatriots. He spoke perfect Latin to Gwenhwyvar; she translated it in her head. "What a beautiful woman. Why hide in here mine pretty, when ye could enjoy comfort in the arms of a soldier?" He was half expecting a fearful reply but instead she smiled at him. Encouraged by her response he moved closer. “You are a pretty morsel,” he continued, then hesitated for a moment as a thought occurred to him. “Do you understand my words?” he asked, and was delighted when she signalled that she did.

Looking around him he motioned for his prize to do the same. “We are alone,” he began as he used his free hand to stroke Gwenhwyvar’s hair. “What is thine name” To his amazement his soon-to-be conquest was distracted. She seemed to be assuring herself that he was indeed alone. She spoke perfect Latin to him. “Are you sure that you were the only one to hear my cry?” Her voice was just as beautiful as she was. Her accent was strange. Not as he would have expected of a Gaulish woman. But he was too overcome with desire to give it much thought. Eager to assure her he offered this summation. “I was walking back from the tavern alone and towards the hall where we are sleeping. There was no one else behind or ahead of me. I saw no sign that anybody else heard your call.” This was all that Gwenhwyvar needed to know. “Excellent!” she said with a broad smile. He was not only encouraged by this response, but he could feel his loins moving with a surge of blood. “Put down the lamp,” she instructed. He hurried to comply and looked around for a place to rest the flickering light. He settled upon a thick beam that was just about at the height of his head.

He was eager to begin ravaging his newly discovered prize. A stray thought entered his head as he deposited the lamp securely on the beam. Why had they never found any beauties like this in the village before? It was the last thought that he ever had. Gwenhwyvar had used the fleeting second to reach into her robes and draw out her dagger. She put her left hand on the soldier's shoulder and just as he turned his head downwards to once more look upon her, she stepped forward at the same time as she pulled him toward her, thrusting her dagger deep into his throat. There was no cry of alarm, just a muffled gurgle of blood that oozed from his mouth. Thinking quickly, Gwenhwyvar used the man's robe to staunch the flow of blood. She did not want any to fall upon the floor as evidence of the quiet murder.

The soldier buckled and fell at Gwenhwyvar's feet. Wiping her blade upon his robes, she re-sheathed her weapon. She moved quickly to the concealed door. "Morgan come out and assist me with the body." Then walking back to ensure that the man was not depositing copious amounts of blood over the floor, the Queen barely noticed as the sacks behind her moved out of the way with otherworldly power. Morgan appeared from the secret doorway and came up to Gwenhwyvar and whispered, "He is dead?" The Queen indicated that he was. Before Gwenhwyvar had a chance to move into position to help Morgan lift the body, the sorceress had already begun to levitate him. Just a tiny amount from the floor, but he glided silently across the thick floorboards and into the hiding place. She could both hear muffled gasps of shock at the appearance of the floating corpse, followed closely by Morgan.

Gwenhwyvar took the lamp and was using it to check for blood. There was some where the man had fallen. She looked about her for something to help dry it up. Thankfully the very place in which they were hiding afforded her the perfect solution. Reaching into a nearby sack of grain that had not been properly sewn up she took a hand full of the contents and spread it over the blood. That would dry up the tell-tale sign. Then gathering up some straw that covered the floorboards she positioned it over the grain. Checking her handiwork and satisfied that it would be undetectable, she made her way back to the refuge. When inside she bid for Morgan's attention, "Put back the sacks of grain in place", she instructed. Morgan dutifully levitated the sacks back into place. Contented that everything looked as it did before, she shut and latched the door. Addressing the wide-eyed youths she offered comfort; "This hiding place is still safe and unknown by the Romans. When, in the morning, they realise that he is missing I suspect that their leader will believe that he has run off. It happens, even in the paid ranks of the Roman army. We may have to remain hidden for longer than ye are accustomed; but they will eventually go on their way." This was welcome news and was received with obedient and relieved nods.

Turning her attention to Morgan she was now able to address the reason that they were in such a precarious situation. "What made ye scream out so loudly?" Gwenhwyvar could see that her words had reinvoked whatever nightmare the sorceress had prior to waking so abruptly. The look of horror on her face told the Queen that it must have indeed been a terrifying dream. Composing herself as best as she could, Morgan tried to keep her voice low. "I saw Merlin die at the hands of a Gael's sword," she said. Gwenhwyvar moved around the dead soldier that Morgan had deposited upon the floor and subsequently covered up with his own cloak. She knelt down in front of Morgan. "Tell me," she said.

Chapter 30: The Coast of Galloway - Night

Merlin awoke startled. He grasped at his chest where the Gael's sword had penetrated him. It took a few moments to realise where he was. It was still the dead of night. His heart was beating rapidly. He sat upright and looked about him. Gaelach was in crescent above him. She shone enough light for him to see Arthur sleeping at his side. They had been offered the soldiers hut in which to sleep. The window was open and through that the light of Gaelach was shining. The other knights were strewn about them also fast asleep. His sudden waking had not disturbed any of the others. Gently he shook Arthurs shoulder. Arthur awoke instantly, with a small jerk. He looked up at Merlin his eyes still heavy with sleep. "What is it?" he asked in a small voice.

"I hath had a vision of the morrows voyage" answered Merlin. The tone made Arthur sit up in anticipation. He had been privy to many of Merlin's visions over the years. They had proven themselves to be the source of much strategic foreknowledge. Arthur was eager to hear what the old Sorcerer had to say. "Tell me" he ordered. Merlin tried to moderate his tone, he was still a little shaken at seeing his own demise. "During our crossing to the Island of Mann we shall encounter the long boat of a Gael raiding force. In mine vision, we had not taken sufficient men and arms to defend ourselves from attack at sea. We were overthrown and I….." he paused recalling the moment; closed his eyes "I was killed in battle." Merlin let out a breath of angst. Arthur was horrified. "Killed, at the hands of a Gael?" he sought confirmation that he had indeed heard the terrible truth. Merlin nodded. "Then," said the king," we shall take our entire contingent with us, as many as the long boat can hold. And we will be prepared for battle." He was shocked and was saying the first thing that came into his mind in the hope that it would alter the outcome of the vision and comfort his old sage.

"Aye Arthur; a wise strategy, the Gaels will be easily overthrown by our Knights and soldiers. Remember though," he raised a cautionary finger and simply pointed to the replica of Excalibur that was beside the King. "Ye shall need to fight according to the current circumstances," his warning was in code, lest any of the Knights were not asleep and listening to their conversation. It would not do any good to alert them to the fact that Excalibur was missing. Giving Arthur the warning provoked a distant memory about the vision that he had just witnessed. "Wait!" he said, "there is more." The old man struggled to recall exactly what it was that was irking him. "What is it Merlin? What more?" pleaded Arthur. Merlin tried his hardest to concentrate. He recalled the Gael boarding the long boat, and the battle. He had levitated the sword from a Gael's hand and dispatched him with ease, but then he had seen something; something that had distracted him.

Like a flash of lightening in a storm it seared through his brain and pushed the vision to the forefront of his mind. "Morgan!" he said a little too loudly. They both looked around them to ensure that the cry and not disturbed any of the sleeping knights. Their heavy breathing could be heard in the absolute silence that followed. Then after a moment, assured that no one had stirred, Merlin turned back to Arthur and leant-in closely to him. "I saw Morgan in mine vision.

She was on the long boat; she looked into mine eyes before I was slain." Arthur grappled with the potential meaning of this turn of events. "What do ye think it means?" he queried. "Is it not obvious," he said his tone equally impatient and joyous. Arthur indicated that whatever it was that had occurred to his magical advisor was not indeed obvious to him at all. "Morgan must hath word of the other matter that we seek to resolve," he said with some amount of glee. Nodding toward the fake Excalibur "Why else would she attempt to contact me in a vision?" Arthur could feel the hope in him rise. If only he could ascertain the veracity of Merlin's supposition. Had his sister managed to find Garlon and recover Excalibur? What a wonderful outcome if it were true. He could return to Caerleon and once again hold the very symbol of his Kingship.

"Is there any way to ensure that this is so?" said Arthur, his voice filled with anxiety. "Be calm Arthur, Morgan would not contact me otherwise." Merlin was clearly very sure of the conclusion that he had reached. The sorcerer was obviously overjoyed. Once more his former pupil had surpassed his expectations. Matters were now better. "We shall sail to Mann tomorrow, battle the Gaels and be victorious. And when in due course we return to Caerleon, all will be back in place as it should be." Merlin's eyes were gleaming in the light of Gaelach with such certainty of how things would unfold; that it was impossible not to get caught up in the moment. "Aye Merlin," affirmed the King. "That is the way that it shall be." They were both energised by the conversation and scheming. It would be difficult to sleep now, and yet there seemed to be some time yet before the morning would come. Sensing the king's thoughts, Merlin once more offered a ready-made solution. "A simple calming spell Arthur, as I used on ye when ye were just an infant. A good night's sleep in preparation for tomorrow's victory."

Arthur smiled and dutifully placed his head upon the folded blanked he was using as a pillow. He heard the first few words of the calming spell but then nothing. He was fast asleep.

Chapter 31: Gaulish Village - Morning

Aurelius Bato Reburrus was both furious and astounded at the same time. Could it be that he had a deserter from his ranks? "Search the village again!" he barked at his second-in-command "Find Vedius Casca!." Although the Roman leader and his next highest ranking soldier had become good friends, he was still taking out his frustration upon the man. Not wanting to add to the Centurion's dark mood, the soldier managed a typical Roman salute, turned and hurried away. The Roman centurion was once more left alone whilst his troops were scurrying throughout the village trying to locate their missing compatriot. Reburrus looked up at the building nearest to him. It was the store-house for all of the grain harvested from the fields surrounding the village. He knew that it had only just been searched, but nevertheless he entered and looked around in the hope of spotting some clue as to why Vedius Casca had suddenly disappeared without a trace.

It was dusty in here. He could see it hanging thickly in the air through rays of sunlight coming through cracks in the walls. He walked around the base of the mezzanine level and studied the bags upon bags of grain that were stacked here. He leant in to see how far they went back, but his view was blocked by even more sacks of grain. There was no way a man could secret himself in there. The bags were packed together too tightly. Vainly he looked up at the mezzanine level. There was a ladder at one side that he could use to climb up. He moved almost without thinking toward the ladder and began to climb. He was a tall man and had to stoop so as to avoid hitting his head on the thick beams and the masterfully thatched roof. His sandals of hard leather made a combined shuffling and thumping sound on the rough floor boards.

Inside the secret room below him, all eyes were staring at the roof of the sanctuary. People were barely breathing in the hope that their absolute silence would somehow protect them. And it would. Reburrus was tired. There was nothing here but grain. He and his men had appropriated enough of it, along with a fair sum of currency as taxation that would be paid to Rome and its presiding Emperor. He had never failed to gather the amount that was due to Rome. In all of his years as a Centurion he had never before had to suffer the humiliation of admitting to having a deserter from his men. He shook his head for what felt like the hundredth time. Why now? Why desert at all? Was there some Gaulish wench nearby that had taken Vedius Casca's attention? Had he gone to seek refuge with her somewhere nearby? The questions were never ending causing a cacophony inside of his head. Unable to reach any conclusions, he descended the ladder. The morning light streamed through the open doorway hitting the floor. If only Aurelius Bato Reburrus had not been so preoccupied with his musings, he may have noticed the darkened patch of straw, just at the edge of the framed sunlight on the floor.

Still with questions going around and around in his head he walked to the entrance. His sandal scraped away a small patch of straw on the floor as he moved. He did not see that he had partially uncovered a smear of dried blood that was upon the floor. He stood in the doorway for a long time. Occasionally some of his men would pass by and acknowledge him. He could hear them nearby and in the distance calling the name of Vedius Casca. The Centurion had no idea how long he stood in that doorway pondering his situation and how he would report it to his superiors. But the longer that he stood there, the higher the sun moved into the sky. The light that was being cast upon the straw covered wooden floor was moving accordingly. More importantly, the tell-tale sign of human blood was moving into the shade. And with the Centurion standing in the doorway, none of the soldiers bothered searching the grain store again. Unwittingly the Centurion was helping to conceal the one clue that there was to see as to the fate that had befallen the missing soldier.

Eventually though he had to give up the search. It was hopeless, the missing soldier could simply not be found. It was nearly noon when he called his men together and ordered that they leave the village and continue on to their next destination. With a heavy heart, and still with no answers Aurelius Bato Reburrus and his men left the village.

***

It was the innkeeper and a number of the villagers that came to let the hiders out of their self-imposed captivity. When the door was finally opened there was a great sense of relief. Mothers and fathers were reunited with their children once more. There was a great outpouring of emotion and quickly whispered stories about the goings on. The innkeeper was trying to make sense of it all. "Calm down" he called. "What happened?" he demanded to know. It was Gwenhwyvar that answered. "A Roman soldier almost found the hiding place, but he was soon dispatched." Gwenhwyvar motioned to the inside of the darkened secret room. There followed a complete amazed silence from the crowd. Taking charge once more the innkeeper marched inside to inspect the scene. He bent down and flung off the cloak covering the dead man that lay upon the floor.

When he remerged from the room his orders were simple. "Burn the body and bury the remains. But wait until dark; we do not want the Romans to see the smoke." He turned to face Morgan and Gwenhwyvar. "Ye did this to protect our secret?" They indicated that they did. "Then," he said, "Ye hath our thanks mine ladies." He stood regarding them for a moment. People looked at one another unsure what to do next. After a while the innkeeper turned to Morgan. "Ye said that the sick in our village……" he was cut-off by Morgan who took the initiative. "Bring me thine sick and I shall heal them." It was more important now than ever that the two women proved themselves to be as good as their word. The villagers had exposed their secret to them and now it felt as though Gwenhwyvar and Morgan owed them something in return for the sanctuary they had been granted. Besides, they needed to know more about the surroundings, and the potential final destination of Garlon when he passed through here. The women needed to win more trust from the locals if they were to continue their quest for Excalibur.

Chapter 32: The Sea between Galloway and the Island of Mann - Noon

"Soon," Merlin replied to Arthur. The King had become impatient to engage the Gaels. They had travelled across the sea for half the day so far and seen no other boats at all, much less a Gael raider. The wind was against them, so the sail was not raised. No oarsmen were aboard the boat. It was packed with Arthur's knights and soldiers. None of them were exhausting themselves rowing though. Merlin insisted on moving the boat inexorably forwards against the prevailing wind using his otherworldly powers. He was showing signs of becoming weary. It was then that Arthur had asked the old Sorcerer when they would encounter the Gaels that he had prophesised. Almost as if in response to Arthur's exasperation there was a shout from one of the Knights. "Sail!" he shouted. Everybody on board looked to see where the Knight was pointing. It was Sir Ectorde Maris. Sure enough, now visible was the unmistakable sail of a longboat. It would have benefited from sailing with the favourable winds, and was making its way toward them.

A sense of anticipation filled the boat. Reinvigorated by the sighting, Merlin concentrated and pushed their long boat onwards. There was no doubt in his mind that this meeting with the Gaels would happen. He had absolute faith in his abilities to see possible futures. However, unlike his vision, this battle would be won by Arthur.

It soon became apparent that the Gael boat was just as keen to engage with the stranger that they had encountered in the middle of the sea. It wasn't long before shouts from the oncoming boat could be heard. Perhaps taunts or orders being barked to prepare for battle. Whichever it was, the tone was aggressive. The preparations on-board Arthur's boat were more measured and orderly. They would be fighting at close-quarters, on board a boat rocking up and down on the waves. This would be no ordinary battle. No commander shouting orders from atop his horse whilst surveying the oncoming force. No way to retreat, not that retreating had been a part of any of Arthur's battles, except for his encounter with Aelle. But this also meant that there was no way to surround the Gaels and prevent them from retreating. The tension on-board was palpable. This was not the kind of fighting that any of the knights or soldiers had done before.

The moments marched by slowly, but the Gael boat made quick headway through the water. Eventually the individual people could be seen more clearly on the Gael boat. They looked a fearsome lot; long flowing hair and beards. They were actually growling and barking across the water, in their own language. It sounded angry and guttural. They brandished their swords and before too long they were within a distance that could have been crossed by skipping a rock across the surface of the choppy water; if that were possible given the rough conditions. Merlin left his place at the front of the boat and picked his way through the now mostly standing Knights and soldiers toward the rear of the boat. Clearly he was going to supervise the imminent fracas from the position of rudder controller. There was no need for further words from Merlin to Arthur. They had had sufficient time during the morning and the ensuing voyage to fine tune their battle strategy.

And then like a hunter leaping upon his prey, the trap was sprung. The four knights aboard produced their shields from what seemed to be out of nowhere. They had been resting against the inside curve of the hull. Each took up a position on the wooden slat benches that the oarsmen would have normally occupied. Taking deft steps backwards and holding their shields out in front of them, they each ran the short length of the bench and jumped across the almost impossible distance between the two boats. With screams of primeval attack now filling the air, the knights landed on-board the Gael boat taking the raiders completely by surprise.

Arthur may not have needed any last minute reminders of the battle strategy but that did not stop Merlin shouting above the clang of metal on shield, "Remember to leave a few of them alive!" It was an order that was lost on most of those aboard both vessels. At the same time he was steering the bow of the boat directly toward the Gaels. The knights would not last long without re-enforcements and Merlin was going to deliver them as soon as possible. Sirs Ectorde Maris and Bors De Ganys along with Lyonell and Bedwere were a joy to watch. Each had managed to land with shield forward knocking off balance the Gales that they hit with the flat metal protective armour. Swords in their other hands had simultaneously lashed out in a clean swipe across their other side from their shields. The effect was that all of the Gaels on the close side of the boat had been knocked off their feet. Raiders tripped backwards and further knocked off-balance those that had taken up positions behind them. This had given the four knights the valuable seconds that they needed to group up in the centre of the boat.

The knights effectively annexed this section of the Gael long boat and with their backs to the water began the fight in earnest. Sword clashed with sword in excellent and well-practiced form against hurried and brutish blows from their combatants. It was then that the King's voice shouted above the melee the warning that the knights had been expecting. "Knights down!" Two simple words delivered to forewarn the knights that phase two of the battle strategy was about to begin. As one, the four knights dropped to their haunches and steadied themselves against the hull of the Gael long boat. All aboard Arthur's boat did the same. At that very moment Arthur's boat collided with the Gaels. The raiders who had all been standing were hurled once more off their feet. The sound of wood splintering and cracking ripped through the air, masking the sound of iron upon iron. Once more the knights on board had the advantage. They leapt to their feet and each of them chose a flailing Gael and ran him through. Blood stained swords were pulled from the sinew and muscle of the hapless victims. Screams of anguish and death could be heard all around.

The foot soldiers began their invasion of the wounded Gael boat via the point at which the two vessels had become joined. Swords drawn and shouting "Attack" they could cross over into the intruders craft two abreast. The Gael raiders did not stand a chance against the superior numbers and skill of the Knights and soldiers combined. Arthur had by this time managed to leap across the short divide from where he was positioned and onto the Gael boat. It could be felt sinking low into the water beneath the combined weight of Arthur's invasion force. Arthur's knights instinctively parted to allow their king to engage one of the Gaels. They now formed a semi-circle of five aggressive swordsmen and the foot soldiers were pushing the remaining Gaels toward them. It must have become apparent to one of the raiders that they were hopelessly outnumbered and out manoeuvred. The rudder controller on the Gael boat dropped his sword and leapt into the water to avoid the oncoming onslaught.

His panicked cry and actions were mimicked by another of the raiders who, seeing the futility of the battle turned from the fight and jumped into the water as well. Two of Arthur's soldiers had ganged up on one of the Gaels and unable to fight on two fronts was run through, blood pouring from his mouth. No cry of defeat in his death, the soldier that speared him had done so in the front of his throat. Similar scenes were enacted in rapid succession. The soldiers had been paired up beforehand by Arthur and instructed to fight in this manner. One by one the Gaels were slain.

The Knights and King were soon left with only the one-to-one fights that they were currently engaged in. The clashing of metal swords on swords seemed to be feeble even though there were now five simultaneous fights occurring. Merlin could be heard shouting orders at the foot soldiers "Leave them to the Knights." This was more than an act of fair-play or chivalry. It was clear to everybody that the Gaels were outmatched by their opposing adversary. The knights and King were almost playing with their rivals. It was Sir Bors De Ganys that slew his enemy first. The death of his compatriot distracted the raider that was doing battle with Sir Lyonell; it was enough of an opportunity for the knight to slice the raider's leather armour with his iron sword. The Gael cried out in pain. He was soon quietened permanently by the Knight with one final thrust through the convenient opening in the man's leather armour that the knight's sword had just made. The Gael slid backwards off Sir Lyonell's sword and fell to the deck of the boat, blood pouring from the fatal wound.

"Enough!" called Arthur. The two raiders that remained alive on-board and engaged with the King and Sir Ectorde Maris froze. The King had shouted the word in the native Gael language. They were breathing hard, shaking. The look on their faces told of their absolute defeat at the hands of those that they had sought to slay. Arthur pointed at the raider opposite him and continued in perfect Gaelish "Go back to where ye came from, and know this, King Arthur rules this land and these waters. Any Gael who trespasses here will die by mine sword." The two men looked like trapped wild animals. Arthur shouted further orders at them. "Throw thine swords overboard." There was a moment of hesitation from the men. But the king was in no mood for procrastination. "Now!" he bellowed. The looked at each other as if for confirmation as to what the other was planning to do. A moment of tension filled the air. Would they rather die in battle than admit defeat? Nobody knew. One of the men seemed to break the deadlock, he slumped his head. He could not bring himself to face his fellow Gael when he flung his sword backwards. It made a small splash in the water. The remaining man looked horrified at what his friend had done. He surveyed the scene. Surrounded, all of his fellow raiders aboard were dead. There was no hope. He too must have reached a pit of depression and the darkness that came over him could be seen clearly in his face. He turned and hurled his sword off the far side of the long boat as far as his muscles were capable of throwing it.

"Turn thine boat around and return to thine land, and pick up ye two cowardly friends that even now lay thrashing about in the water." One of the men made his way toward the rear of the boat to obediently take up position as the rudder controller. The other looked around him not sure of what to do. The sail was down; it had been dropped about the same time that the Knights from Arthur's boat jumped aboard. The oars were stored, and he was just one man. How could he row the longboat by himself? The magnitude of the journey before him began to dawn upon the hapless man. He decided to pick up an oar and attempt to rescue his two drowning ship mates. With three of them on the oars, they had a chance of putting some small distance between themselves and the King's boat. Arthur meantime had departed the Gael boat and was ordering those closest to him to help push the invaders stricken vessel away from theirs.

It took a concerted effort of nearly one third of the crew to push down the Gael boat in the water at the same time as pulling their boat upwards and then kicking off so that the two would separate. It happened with excruciating slowness. Eventually the long boats were separated and began to drift away from each other. "The oars" shouted Arthur. His soldiers scurried to take up their positions and ready themselves to row. The extent of the damage to the Gael craft could now be seen in its entirety. Although a huge gash cut through the near-side of its hull, it did not continue downward to the waterline. At least the boat would stay afloat to carry the men with their warning message back to their homeland; contingent upon them not encountering stormy seas along the way. There would be no guarantees in that situation. Arthur further barked an order to his men and they dutifully began to row in absolute unison.

The king kept his eyes on the beaten enemy. The two Gaels that had been in the water were in the process of being hauled aboard one at a time. There was a verbal fracas when both of the deserters were safely aboard. Arthur could make out the scalding of the two for being so cowardly. Inexorably Arthur's boat powered through the sea and the Gael boat was left behind. There was talking aboard here and there, recounting the battle just fought. Arthur heard his knights discussing the finer points of each kill. It wasn't boasting or gloating, but scrutinising the swordplay and the overall battle strategy. Exploring and evaluating it piece by piece. Arthur encouraged this type of examination. He would eventually participate, but for now he wanted assurance that all was well. He made his way to the back of the vessel. Merlin was steering the long boat onwards to its destination.

"Do ye think the Gaels will have second thoughts before sending more raiders?" he queried of his sage. Merlin shook his head, "Aye; for a short time at least. If we ever need to bargain with the Picts to join forces with us, that battle can be given as an example of thine ferocity" he said with a mischievous glean in his eye. To Arthur though, the thought of striking up an alliance with the Picts at this stage was too distant to factor into his planning. "What of thine vision?" Arthur asked. Merlin responded "We hath transformed defeat into resounding victory mine King." It was exactly what Arthur had been seeking. "And now....?" Enquired Arthur. Merlin looked steadily at Arthur and said "Onwards to Mann. I grow impatient to meet the Christian monks."

Chapter 33: Gaulish Village - Sunset

Morgan was exhausted. She had spent the entire afternoon drawing upon her powers to heal the sick and injured in the village. Farmers and ironmongers, bakers and the like. There was no end to the amount of bones that had been broken and set incorrectly. Unusual rashes when certain foods were consumed. Failing eyesight and hearing; mostly due to the onset of old age. Morgan had much to do. But eventually the flood of people that had come to the inn to take up her offer of healing dwindled to a trickle and finally there were no more villagers to avail themselves of her abilities. Throughout the entire session, Gwenhwyvar had adopted her assumed role of apprentice to the Sorceress. She worked out who had the greatest need and dutifully brought them forward to be consulted with by Morgan and then healed.

There were often words of caution following each ethereal consultation. "Do not drink red wine, it is the cause of the pain in thine head, drink ale instead;" "If ye should break thine fingers again they must be strapped against a straight plank of wood until the bone knits together properly;" Do not eat any foods that use the eggs of chickens, that is what causes thine swelling and rash around ye mouth;" Gwenhwyvar would be careful to repeat the instructions to the magically cured individual whilst escorting them away from Morgan, and before fetching the next.

Now it seemed that there was an entire village that was grateful for the intervention of the good Sorceress. The mood in the tavern was jubilant. A good deal of food was prepared for the two women by way of appreciation for their service. There was talking and even singing over near the main fireplace. It was a very festive scene. Morgan, although drained of her energy, was beginning to feel a little reinvigorated at the goings-on around her. Gwenhwyvar meanwhile was ensuring that Morgan ate, hoping that it would bolster her strength. The innkeeper, who they had since found out was named Garrone, was in attendance, warranting that his prized guests were left wanting for nothing. "Thine powers are truly incredible mine lady Morganna." Morgan had thought it wise to adopt the more Gaulish version of her name. In doing so she had begun to attribute the name Gwen to Gwenhwyvar. The legend of Arthur and his Queen may have spread to this land; best to be cautious about using her full name. It would have at the very least, sounded foreign to the Gauls. The small deception would effectively cover-over any use of the Queen's full name that had already slipped out whilst hiding in the grain storage building. "It would appear that our work here is done," smiled Morgan. Garrone was however in no hurry to see the newfound village magicians finish up so soon. "Can we convince thee to stay with us here in Avyze? Ye would be most welcome," he offered, the hope apparent in his tone. Gwenhwyvar and Morgan had the same thought simultaneously without knowing it. Avyze must be the name of the village; strange that they had not thought to ask anyone. Rather than refuse Garrone's generous offer outright, Morgan used the situation to try and gather more information about the whereabouts of Garlon. "We were hoping to come across a friend of ours that would have travelled through Avyze. Garlon, hath ye heard of him?" Garrone stroked his chin and furrowed his brow in concentration. "The name is not familiar," he answered staring off into the distance. "What business would he have had?" he further enquired. Morgan phrased her answer carefully. "He would have sought knowledge of other worldly things."

Both Gwenhwyvar and Morgan caught a look of apprehension upon Garlon's face. His eyes darted to the far side of the tavern wall, the direction leading to the east. Both women turned to look at each other and confirm that the other had noticed the unguarded moment. Morgan pushed the point with him further. "Garlon sought to find magic wherever it may be found." Garrone was pensive. He looked about him and realised that there were others within earshot that were now silent and taking a close interest in the conversation. The two women also looked about them to the faces that were now covered with concern. Garrone eventually interjected. "I am sorry Morganna and Gwen; I have no knowledge of thine friend." It felt like an incomplete answer even though it stated an absolute. Gwenhwyvar pushed for further detail. "But there is something….?" She held Garrone's gaze steadily. The revelry in the tavern was becoming quieter with each passing moment. Morgan and Gwenhwyvar could see people whispering to each other. It spread throughout the tavern like a cloud covering the land on a sunny day. Soon all of the talking in the tavern had ceased altogether. The villagers present were looking from the women to Garrone.

Morgan stood up and addressed them all. "Please dear villagers of Avyze. If ye hath knowledge of magic that is nearby then take Gwen and I into thine trust. We may be of further assistance." There passed a moment of collective contemplation. Then one of the old village women that Morgan had cured of her aching joints stood up from where she was sitting and spoke to them. "The old Roman chalk caves to the west of our village are haunted with a foul beast." The reaction from all of the people present was intense. Some who clearly did not want this to be spoken of brought their hands up to their ears. Some others chastised the old woman to "be silent" and "do not talk of it." She almost hissed at her detractors, "Morganna is a sorceress. Who better to protect us from the creature?" Another moment of contemplation filled the inn. Villagers looked to each other for guidance. Garrone took up the point. He could see and feel that there was a need to confide in the friendly Sorceress. "Perhaps 'protection' is not the correct word." He said.

"Tell me," pleaded Morgan quietly. Garrone sighed and began, "The chalk caves to the east have long since been abandoned by the Romans. They have found richer deposits and moved on leaving behind them a labyrinth of caves. It is good farming land and grows the richest crop of grapes to be had in all the land. But around twenty years ago a creature took up residence in the caves. A beastly thing that few have seen and lived to tell of" He looked for affirmation once more from those present that he was allowed to continue the story. Finding absolution in the eyes and faces of his fellow villagers he continued. "We dare not farm the land in that area for fear of the creature. It devours people that stray into the caves. We hath found the remains of some of its victims through the years. Never more than one for each year that it hath lived here, but even that is too many. Although it never seems to venture from its home, we live in fear that it may someday do just that. If ye friend, Garlon, hath sought-out the creature he may have fallen victim to it." He finished his summation of the situation with a regretful shake of his head.

Morgan seized the opportunity before them. "I can defeat this creature for ye and return the land that ye now fear to farm, to any who would do so." The tone of confidence was so prevalent in her statement that it was difficult to not get caught up in the potential outcome. The very thought of being rid of the ever-present danger that they had lived with all these years was tantalising. Gwenhwyvar though, was puzzled. "Hath ye not sought deliverance from the Romans. Surely they could send in the garrison that was just here to help ye." Garrone indicated that they had tried this very approach many times. "They hath no bravery amongst them to face such a beast. They see no downturn in the taxes they exact for the Emperor, so it does not matter to them. Why would they risk a single Roman soldier's life to ease our burden?"

She persisted with her line of questioning. "Surely the combined force of men in the village would be enough to overcome this beast?" She had unknowingly hit a nerve. There was an uncomfortable silence. Men and women all looked at each other. There was shame written on their faces. Even Garrone seemed hesitant to provide a suitable explanation to their lack of action. The old woman who had started the village confession must have felt obliged to offer their paltry excuse. "One death a year, Morganna. Sometimes a villager, sometimes a traveller. It seems an easier burden to carry than to face a creature with powers beyond our understanding. We are too afraid." There followed another stretch of silence as yet another secret that the village kept was laid before the two newcomers.

Gwenhwyvar contemplated the people around her. There was real angst in their expressions. There was a want to do something about their situation; but too much fear to overcome in order to act. She felt compassion. These were after all simple farmers, and trades people without the benefit of a posse of knights to protect them. They knew nothing of fighting. "With Morganna and I leading ye; the beast will not have a chance." It was a bold claim from Gwen. It felt like absolution from their shameful secret.

Garrone turned his attentions once more to Morgan, "Morganna, if thine magic is truly powerful enough to battle this creature, then we will find the courage to stand with ye." He was sincere, the women could tell. There was an echo of agreement from the villagers. This was perfect, thought Morgan; all the villagers needed was a magical leader to rally behind. Now she and Gwenhwyvar had a ready-made supporting attack force to aide them in their quest. It would be mutually beneficial. Excalibur would be recovered and the village would be rid of the malevolent force that had pervaded them for so long.

"Then let us waste no time Garrone. Spread the word throughout the village. We wage war on the beast tomorrow morning." Her words produced an immediate response from the now shocked looking villagers. Some not wanting to argue the point left the tavern immediately, no doubt to spread the word as instructed. Others shocked that their salvation could come so quickly were so taken aback that they wanted to delay the proceedings. Those entered into immediate simultaneous debate with Morganna and Gwen about planning the undertaking more carefully and perhaps making a future date for the attack to happen. But Morgan and Gwenhwyvar were having none of it. They realised that time was not on their side. Morgan motioned with her hands for the voices talking over one another to be calm. "The only plan we need is that ye bring anything that can be used as a weapon, and stay behind me as I face the creature. I shall use mine powers to the best of mine abilities to ensure our victory." This had the effect that she wanted. Argument was silenced and opposition was turned to support.

Further people left the tavern to help garner the other villagers to the new-found cause. Garrone still looked stunned at the sudden onset of the initiative. He made to say something and then cut himself off. Then as though he had once more gathered his thoughts said, "Very good Morganna. We shall follow thee to the lair of the beast and be rid of this blight once and for all." It seemed now all that was required was for the night to pass by and then the mission could begin.

Chapter 34: Insula Mann - Sunset

Arthur's boat had taken a further two hours after the battle to reach the shore of their destination. That was mid-afternoon; now the boat lay on shore with most of the knights and soldiers wondering around it. Some were still swapping battle stories from the successful skirmish earlier in the day. The tide was going out so the boat was in no danger of floating away if not watched each moment. The sun was setting and the men were beginning to wonder if they would see King Arthur and Merlin again. The king and his sorcerer had set out to find the monastery immediately upon landing upon the island. Surely they must have happened upon it by now. With any luck, they would be well on their way back to the boat. It was sir Dagonet that took charge of the situation.

"Should the King and Merlin return we shall not be able to set sail for Galloway until morning; gather some wood and make camp fires. We shall stay here tonight." Now that the soldiers and knights had a purpose, they set about to do what Sir Dagonet had ordered. It was not as if anybody had left him in charge in the King's absence. But the very sense of his instruction was too rational to ignore. Until the tide came back in, there would be little hope of re-floating the long boat anyway. Sir Dagonet watched the men organise themselves according to his instruction. He looked at the setting sun. It was beautiful; painting the sky a myriad of warm colours. Then he looked inland in the direction that Arthur and Merlin had disappeared and wondered what the two of them had found.

***

Merlin and Arthur were studying the monastery. It was further inland than either had anticipated. Merlin however, was able to home-in on the same feeling of magical prowess that identified the Christians of Pen Rhionydd; so they knew that they were heading in the right direction. The monastery was a stone building with a thatched roof. It was low and long and hung on to the side of a steep hill. The wind must beat upon it constantly. There were some goats on a small plateau at the rear of the building. Also a chicken coop made of low thatched twigs was at the rear of the building. It all looked quite normal except for its exposed location and lack of neighbours. "How does this bring them closer to their God?" asked Arthur. Merlin had no answer to provide. Arthur asked a different question. "How will ye test thine theory that Christians somehow block magical powers?"

Merlin was one step ahead of Arthur. He was already well into his experimentation. He was holding out his hand and had a look of concentration on his face. "What are….." Arthur began yet another question just as Merlin, excited with the lack of a result, shouted out half a curse. "By the eyes of mine father!." He was clearly very surprised at something. "What is it?" Arthur enquired cautiously. "The spell to create fire; nothing!" answered the old man. The King surmised that his friend had been trying to start fire on a nearby fallen tree, now old and desiccated by the constant wind. It should have erupted into flame beneath the Sorcerer's spell. But nothing eventuated. Arthur was a little sanguine.

"So thine theory is proven?" he asked rhetorically. Merlin continued the thought. "These Christians need only be nearby to dampen mine abilities. They do not need to be witness to mine conjuring. This is exactly the result that I had hoped for. Now I need to know if it is just mine own powers or those of all magical beings that are affected?" He paused and stroked his beard for a moment. "We need to find a faerie or other magical being and expose them to the presence of Christians. If they suffer the same effect, then I will be certain that Christians can be used as protection from interfering faeries and any others that would use magic to foil us." Merlin was very clear about what he wanted to do next. He was not so clear on how that would be achieved. This prompted the response from Arthur. "Do ye intend to invite Christians into Caerleon Village?" The ramifications for his sage, Sorcerer and military adviser were obvious: his powers would abandon him. Arthur was concerned. Merlin could see that the King was taking the wrong direction with the planned outcome of his scheming.

"We set up a new village at the border of the faerie forest populated with Christians and drive the scourge of the faeries from our land." Merlin's plan seemed quite simple. "Of course we forbid Christianity in Caerleon village lest it inhibit mine and Morgan's powers." He hastily added a caveat to his proposal. Arthur pondered the idea for only a moment before nodding in agreement. "Aye Merlin, a good strategy," he affirmed. "For now though, let us seek refuge for the night with the Monks. It is too late to make our way back to the boat and I do not wish to travel the sea navigating only by the stars." Arthur had never been fond of sea faring by night, Merlin and indeed all of the knights knew that fact. Merlin looked once more at the steepness of the hill that now faced them. All of a sudden the trip overland back to the boat didn't seem too onerous by comparison. He hoped that there would be a warm bed and a cooked meal as compensation for the long climb. They moved forward bracing themselves for some hearty exercise.

Chapter 35: Avyze Village - Sunrise

Everyone in the village had risen long before the sun was up. The excitement, anticipation, and terror of what the day held for them made it difficult for most to sleep. The grain store was set as the meeting point for every man that was willing and able to accompany Morganna and Gwen to the chalk caves. Women and children accompanied their loved ones to the site to wish them well in the endeavour that was to come. The place was as busy as a bee hive in the middle of spring. Garrone was doing his best to muster together the volunteers, but the goodbye wishes from their various loved ones were interfering with his attempts to corral the men.

Gwenhwyvar pulled Morgan aside for another strategy meeting. They had barely slept trying to figure out how they would battle a faerie that was almost as old as Matrona, and surely very powerful. By the time both of them had managed to fall asleep, shortly before first light, they had not come up with a definitive plan. The flight from Caerleon to Llyn Callyfyrth, subsequent consultation with Matrona, then the frantic ride to Wareham, boat ride to Insula Vectis and water horse transportation to Gaul now seemed as though it were an ill-conceived folly. Gwenhwyvar once more put the situation into the simplest possible terms so as to make it somehow seem more solvable.

"The beast is expecting Merlin; it must therefore be more than a match for his powers," Morgan completed Gwenhwyvar's summation. "And I am not as powerful as he. I know this Gwenhwyvar. But we hath the strength of numbers. I can do mine best to keep the Minotaur busy with a battle of magic whilst the men attack the creature with all that they can. I agree that it is not the most assured battle plan, but we hath not been able to devise a better one." Morgan let a little of her frustration come through in her tone. Gwenhwyvar was not annoyed to hear it though. She understood the situation that they had both put themselves in. However, neither knew when they first began their pursuit of Garlon that it would result in a battle with an ancient and evil creature. They now had to face the consequences of their actions if they hoped to succeed in recovering Excalibur for Arthur. This was the best that they could do with the resources available to them.

Garrone had managed to separate the well-wishers from their loved ones and was looking to Morgana and Gwen with expectation in his eyes. Morgan saw the plea and dutifully responded. "Citizens of Avyze!" she shouted. The throng of talking subsided as a sea of faces turned to look at her. Morgan climbed the first two stairs that lead up to the grain barn. Everyone assembled could see her clearly now. "With brave hearts we march to rid this beautiful village of the pestilence that hath plagued it for these many years." There was a cheer from the crowd. Morgana was telling them exactly their desire was. "With mine magic to protect thee, and the strength of this courageous company, success will surely be ours." This elicited a rapturous applause of praise and approval from everyone gathered. Morgan thought that she had best lead by example and finished with a simple but effective call to arms. "Follow me, all who want to be free of this evil!" Another raucous collective cry of support and approbation gushed forth from the men, women and children present.

Morgan couldn't help smiling; the feeling emanating from the villagers was palpable. She could sense the good will surrounding her and enveloping them all. Striding down from the steps the crowd parted to allow her and Gwenhwyvar through so that they could take the lead. Further hearty confirmations and valedictions merged and helped lift the general mood even higher. The band moved with purpose behind Morgana and Gwen, arms raised in hope and defiance. Soon the group had separated from those that were to stay behind and wait for them. Women and children waved at their fathers, husbands, brothers and sons as they slowly left the relatively safe confines of Avyze village.

***

It took an hour to reach the area in which the chalk caves were carved. The caves where now just ahead, hewn by Roman miners exploiting the chalk on behalf of the empire. The sun in the sky disappeared behind billowing white clouds every now and again, only to re-emerge and smile upon them and their quest once more. For the entire journey both Gwen and Morgana had faced what seemed like a never ending retinue of men who had come up to them seeking further assurance on an individual basis; that collectively they would be more than a match for the fearsome beast. Morgan and Gwen did not let the constant need for comfort and encouragements dissuade them. Instead they offered support to each one that sought some kind of guarantee that all would indeed be well. It was very different to marching with Arthur's knights and foot soldiers. Neither Gwenhwyvar nor Morgan had done that very often over the years; however there were some few occasions when it had been necessary.

The comparison between marching with seasoned trained fighters and farmers and artisans was quite dramatic. In their current situation, the two Caerleon women did all that they could to be inspirational to the men.

Now the moment of truth was almost upon them. Garrone had made his way toward the front so he could walk with Morgana and Gwen. "There used to be many more entrances to the caves," Garrone pointed out, "but most of them seem to have collapsed. There is only the main entrance now; the one that the Romans dug first when they found the deposits of chalk beneath our farming land. We are fortunate; it is the largest and easiest to traverse. The slope leading into the earth is gentle and wide." Morgan's suspicions were raised. How convenient that all of the other entrances had collapsed. There certainly was no reason for them all to have done so. She suspected magical intervention but thought it better to not voice her concerns. Garrone added as an afterthought, "We hath brought torches to light so that we may see our way in the darkness." This was something that Morgan did feel the need to talk about.

"I shall use magic to light our way Garrone. The thought of facing a mystical beast by the flickering light of a flaming torch could cause undue fear in the men. Light them by all means, they can be used to hurl at the beast should it become necessary." Morgan gave him a reassuring smile. Garrone was impressed as always with the resolve shown by the Sorceress. "The entrance is just ahead,' he said. Morgan and Gwenhwyvar would have missed it had it now been pointed out to them. There must have been a field of wheat abandoned, because the fronds now grew so high that it obscured the entrance to all but the most discerning eye. Morgan felt a tingle; something that she had felt before, the same feeling that she had looking over Llyn Callyfyrth. She could feel the presence of a magical being; a powerful one at that. This was not the pleasant but eerily awesome feeling that Matrona had invoked within her. The feeling was different, it made her feel uneasy. There was something dark and foreboding ahead of them. She wondered if the beast could detect her as she could it.

Garrone was busy giving orders for the way to be cleared and the torches lit. People did their best with pieces of flint, but Morgana felt it was time for a demonstration of her power, to offer communal comfort to her followers. She stopped and turned to face the crowd. They all looked expectantly at her. "Hold up the torches" she commanded. The men did so. They could be seen rising up above the heads of the throng. Morgan raised her hands and mumbled something beneath her breath. Simultaneously all of the torches blazed into life. There was a collective sound of awe from the mob. This was the kind of encouragement that the men needed at this particular moment. They were surely following a powerful Sorceress that would defeat the creature in the cave. Some men that were not holding torches moved forward and used their farming and other instruments to clear the wheat away from the entrance to the cave. In complete contrast to the brilliant light bearing down upon them, the cave looked dark and foreboding. Anxious to capitalise on the feeling of awe she had just created within the group, Morgan strode forward and instinctively ducked her head, even though she did not need to, and entered the cave. Gwen followed closely behind.

Chapter 36: The Creature's Lair

Morgan's followers filed into the cave two abreast; the cave was wide enough for that, but no more. There were still white deposits of chalk to be seen streaking through the clay and soil. There were no braces, just a cleverly formed archway of a tunnel that lead downwards; the typical Roman simplicity of the design giving the cave its structural integrity. Everyone paused after entering the cave at first, to allow their eyes time to adjust to the gloom. Morgana and Gwen were the furthest down the opening. They proceeded cautiously. Then at a point that seemed no more remarkable than any other, Morgan stopped and once more turned to address the village 'soldiers.' The flames of the torches were doing exactly what Morgan had predicted. They cast moving images into the walls. There was a moment of expectation. Was Morgan about to reveal how she would magically light their way?

"I promised thee light" she announced in her typically authoritative tone. With one hand pressed to the nearest wall she said something in a language that none but Gwenhwyvar had heard before. It was a slow process but the chalk components in the walls began to glow with a soft white light. It was even toned and spread itself forward and backwards from them lighting the way ahead and the path to the exit. There was a loud murmur of astonishment from the men. Garrone voiced clearly what so many were mumbling beneath their breath. "Amazing Morgana, amazing!" The cave did not seem so frightening now. It could be seen approximately fifty or more paces ahead of them. But no further. Morgan moved forward and correspondingly the light ahead of her moved forward too. "I shall keep the walls aglow for at least this amount of distance ahead of us. Forward men; with me!" the last part of her sentence almost shouted in defiance. Fears were allayed yet again thanks to Morgan's show of magical ability and confidence. Her band of supporters either purposely or unconsciously bunched up toward her. Together they moved brazenly deeper into the caves.

***

Somewhere deep in the labyrinth that it called home, the Minotaur stood at what may have been a shrine or altar. It was hewn from a single piece of white marble. The large slab was carved with precision that was unknown to the best marble artists of the world. It was smooth, so smooth that it reflected the room in which it took centre placement. Glow worms covered what seemed like every measure of the vaulted ceiling of the cave. Their combined light amplified by a spell that the Minotaur had cast many years ago. In the exact centre of the altar lay Excalibur. The beast reached out with its hefty arm. Its muscles rippled as its thick fingers grasped the handle. Raising it up from its resting place he brandished it briefly in the air before adjusting his grip. Now the sword was bearing downwards towards his huge chest. He brought the magic sword down and it made to pierce the beast's chest. Hitting the hide of the creature it made no mark and deflected away instead of striking the ancient faerie down.

The Minotaur laughed a loud and boisterous, but evil laugh; almost maniacal. No weapon could pierce its hide. Centuries of casting spells of protection and strength and draining the life-force from many humans had seen to that. This toy of Matrona's was no different to any other that he had faced. Assured that he had nothing to fear from this over-crafted piece of metal, he threw it once more onto its resting place. The weighty sword clanged against the hard surface of the marble. He turned his attentions to the presence that he could feel in his abode. There were many humans, he could feel them, and one magical being, he could feel that too. This must surely be Merlin, the very reason he had not immediately taken the life of Garlon when he first arrived in the beast's home. Just as the perfidious human had promised, he would soon be in the presence of the world's greatest magician. It was time to make good on the arrangement that he had made with Garlon. There was a tripod of iron poles from which an iron pot hung toward the right of the marble slab. Beneath it some dried twigs lay. With barely the flick of one large finger the twigs burst into flame. His black eyes reflected the dancing fire. His huge feet thudded against the compacted ground as he stomped over to where he kept some dried herbs, flowers and other sundry ingredients. They were in small alcoves carved into the chalk walls of the cave. Choosing some with great care he carried them over to the pot and threw them in.

He chanted something with his slobbering animal mouth and a red smoke began to rise from the pot. It streamed in a perfect column upwards. Reaching the top of the cavernous space it began to absorb into the ceiling. He was satisfied that his spell was a success; all that he needed now was for the moon to rise tonight. It would turn blood red as was the prearranged signal with Garlon. The treacherous human would see the sign and know that he could return to collect the sword. By then Merlin would have already met his fate and been absorbed into the fabric of the faerie Minotaur. Perhaps he would renege on his deal with Garlon and absorb him as well. There would be time to consider his position after he had stolen everything that Merlin was.

***

There were many twists and turns to the chalk caves. It was exactly as was told in the Greek legends that both Gwenhwyvar and Morgan had studied as girls; a Minotaur living in the centre of a labyrinth. Was this one, even though they knew it was a faerie, just as certain to devour them? It was an uncomforting thought that neither knew the other was sharing at that moment. Morgan stopped her party. "We should mark the walls to ensure that we can find our way out again." Her suggestion held all of the weight of a royal command. One of the men drew out an iron-mongers instrument of some sort. It looked like something used to do finer work, but was nevertheless sturdy enough to carve a sign in the soft chalk walls. He hurriedly drew an arrow that faced backwards the way that they had come. When done almost collectively everyone looked to Morgan for approval. She nodded and smiled; her face even more beautiful in the eerie light that she was causing to emanate from the walls. She moved forward once more bringing along her troop of loyal followers.

This way and that they turned and turned and turned again. Without the regular markings being scratched into the walls, there would have been no way any of them could have remembered the path back to the surface. Time and again they came to intersections in the caves and had to choose between them. Morgana always made the decision. Eventually all nervous but softly spoken talk in the group gave way to an ominous silence. They had been walking for the better part of one quarter of an hour before one of the men spoke up. "Morgana, surely the beast is not here or we would have found it by now." Morgan couldn't see which of the men had spoken. She addressed them all. "Our numbers and ferocity have it scared. It is hiding from us!" There was a murmur of satisfaction with her answer. It suited all of them to think of themselves as more frightening to the beast that it was to them. "Come, see, the cave widens ahead, more of us can walk side-by-side," she assured them.

The cave had indeed widened somewhat and was becoming much more roomy. The glow that Morgan was making come from the walls cast even more light because of the increased surface area. The ceiling of the cave was lifting. Ahead they could now see what looked to be the entrance to something. A flicker of a fire could just be seen in the distance. More of the men, emboldened by the earlier summation of their situation offered by Morgan, joined her in the lead of the band. This section of the cave seemed to come to an end, except for a carved archway. It was from there that the fire light could be seen. Pulses quickened. Was this it, a campfire lit by the beast? Weapons were raised in expectation. The archway was not wide enough for more than two of them at a time. They closed the distance and were at it soon enough. As one they all stopped. It was Morgan and Gwenhwyvar that broke ranks and stepped through the archway into the room beyond. It was cavernous. Glow worms covered every conceivable part of the ceiling. There was no need for

Morgan's otherworldly light in this room. There was a fire heating a pot over to one side of a large stone block. Two by two the men filed into the room. Each amazed at the sight of such beauty above them; then cautiously looking at the fire and stone altar. It took a few moments for Gwenhwyvar to realise that lying on the huge slab was Excalibur! She grabbed Morgan's arm and indicated with her eyes. Morgan saw the object of their quest. It appeared to be lying on the dais abandoned, unguarded and just waiting for them to retrieve it.

But caution prevented either of them from simply walking over to it. They felt a dread that was dripping from the very air that they breathed. Garlon broke the uneasy silence. "The beasts altar?" It was a question, not a statement. Morgan looked at him and responded. "Perhaps it gives worship to something. But I see no carved figure of a deity." One of the men who was closer to the platform than the others pointed. "There is a sword. Perhaps it worships that." He was a young man. Boldly, before Morgana or Gwen could stop him, he took the remaining steps toward the stand and reached out for the sword. "No! Stop!' they exclaimed. He had just managed to touch the handle of the sword when the beast jumped up from crouching behind the slab. With a chilling bellow of a kind that none of them had heard before it slammed its hand down clasping the boy's arm with a grip so tight it felt to the boy that his forearm would surely be crushed as a result. He screamed with terror, barely a second before the Minotaur's other huge hand clasped itself over his face.

People screamed and jumped with fright. Something that seemed like the lightening in a fierce storm shot through the body of the terrified boy. It could be seen lighting up the body of the youngster as brightly as the noon-day sun. The light was drawn into the hands of the hideous creature, in waves it left the boy and entered the Minotaur through his contact points with the villager. Although his face was covered by the beast the cry of absolute agony could be heard coming from him. It seemed like forever but in reality was over in less than one long moment. At least half of the contingent that had followed Morgana and Gwen into the caves turned and fled in a screaming mass. The others perhaps frozen with pure fear or maybe braver than the others watched as the boy's body melted out of the grasp of the beast. The stink of rotten flesh filled the room. As one, the congealed heap of what was left of the hapless villager slopped to the cave floor.

Gwen screamed at the limit of her ability "Attack!" She pointed dramatically at the object of her loathing. Her war cry galvanised the remaining force into action. Pitchforks, make-shift spears, arrows and other assorted weaponry were readied in an instant. Morgan saw the opportunity to assist. She would capture the weapons in mid-flight and greatly increase their speed and accuracy ensuring that each of them found its target. The creature could surely not withstand the brutal onslaught of so many weapons hurled with deadly accuracy and speed.

"Now!" came Gwen's follow-up command. Spears and arrows and blades of all sorts were hurled in the general direction of the demon. Morgan's reactions were sharper than the keenest of them all. She stretched out both hands to feel the motion of the barrage in flight. Done, she could perceive the shape and construction of each of them. Turning her head she set her now glowing blue eyes on the living target. Then with a sweep from left to right of her arms she hurled the phalanx at the creature at a speed that could not be achieved by any man or woman. Some found their target in the beast's torso, others its head, but uniformly they all bounced off the incredibly tough hide of the Minotaur. It bellowed a blood-chilling howl of what could have been either anger or disdain. The would-be instruments of death thudded on to the compacted chalk and dirt floor of the cave.

That was all that the remaining villagers could take. Just as before, they screamed in abject terror and ran; the faster villagers pushing the slower ones out of the way as they exited. At least one or two of them fell in the melee that ensued. However the sheer terror of being left in the presence of a thing that could not be killed ensured that they managed to recover themselves from the floor and limped hastily after their compatriots. Gwen looked to Morgan for guidance. The two of them were the furthest from the entrance to this underground miniature cavern. Morgan's eye's said everything that Gwenhwyvar needed to know. They were in deep trouble. Without a word they agreed to run as fast as they could. The Minotaur however had other plans for this magical woman. The entrance to the cavern closed. It was as though the solid walls had become malleable like a tapestry. The exit, their only means of escape closed before their terrified eyes. Gwenhwyvar and Morgana huddled together facing their captor. Morgana forced herself to concentrate on the spell of fire. She willed it into existence before the two of them. A white hot ball of flame as large as a man's head appeared from nowhere. With a flick of her fingers she directed the flame at the Minotaur. It flew at him. He disdainfully swept it aside with a mighty blow from the back of his hand. It was knocked into a wall causing it to glow with the dissipated heat. There was a moment of stillness. Then the rasping growling voice of the Minotaur cut through the air. "Is that all ye hath mine pretty? No more?"

Morgana and Gwenhwyvar's terror gave way to shock. As the beast had the torso of a bull they had unconsciously assumed that it would not be able to speak. Faeries cannot speak when they are in their animal forms. There was no reason to think that this one could. It was a surprise to them both. It took a few moments for Morgana to recover her composure enough to formulate an answer to the question. "Tell me then beast. What magical feat must I conjure to defeat thee and reclaim Arthur's sword?" In response the Minotaur almost purred like a cat, but a much more fearsome sound, more guttural. "Why try to defeat me Sorceress? I hath lived for over one thousand years. What hope for ye is there?" He continued in his gargling deep voice. "Instead, why not try to amuse me? I hath fed on a healthy young human. I shall not need another for at least a year." Gwenhwyvar and Morgana listened intently to the creature. Was it offering them a way out? This must be why more of the villagers hadn't mysteriously disappeared over the decades. It only feeds once a year.

Grasping the seeming opportunity that was presented to them Gwenhwyvar took the initiative, "What then would amuse ye? How can we offer ye a distraction?" The beast looked like it was moving toward them but then turned and raised a hybrid human/bull hand to its mouth, giving the impression that it was contemplating the

Queens question. It slowly turned to them once more and spoke. "Tell me something that never was and never will be?" The words echoed slightly in the small cavern.

It was a riddle. Think of something that has never existed and never will. Surely it was puzzle without an answer, thought Morgana. But Gwenhwyvar 's mind was working at a frantic pace. She blurted out her solution to the quandary. "A mouse nesting in a sleeping cat's ear." This answer pleased the Minotaur. He laughed loud and long. It was almost ear-shattering. When in time the noise had subsided he directed his question to Morgana. "Now Sorceress, what say ye?" Morgana was quick with her reply "A chicken coop guarded by a fox." This too amused the hideous beast. Once more he erupted in a laughter that sent shivers down the spines of the two women. Morgan noticed something about their captor. He had developed a silver shadow along one side of his head. It traced the muscular form of his bull head and neck down to the half bull and half human chest; sitting just proud of the beast's left side. She wondered for a moment what it could be.

Morgana's musings were cut short by the ancient faerie. "Excellent!" he verbalised his approval of their answers to his riddle. "Thou are clever. But ye will need to prove thine intelligence more if ye are to win thine freedom from mine labyrinth. Answer me this then. There are two sisters: one gives birth to the other and she, in turn, gives birth to the first. Who are the two sisters?"

Gwenhwyvar's memory called out to her. She had heard this conundrum before; but where? Similarly Morgana thought that it sounded just a little too familiar. It was too much to contemplate at the moment however. Something that the Minotaur had said; 'win thine freedom'? Could it be possible that they could bargain their way out of their current predicament? The Queen spoke first, her tone not giving away exactly how fearful she actually was. "If we answer correctly will that be enough to win our freedom?" She regarded the beast carefully. He snorted indignantly. "No!" he said, dashing their hopes. "Answer mine riddle and then we shall bargain for thine freedom." His terms sounded absolute and not open to negotiation. Gwenhwyvar took a second to puzzle why this faerie from the old Grecian civilization would be so amused by riddles. And then the thought struck her. It had something to do with the old Greek teachings that formed part of her formal education as a young girl. More specifically it was the studying of Greek mythology that entered her mind.

This faerie was after all the living embodiment of a Greek myth. Or perhaps he was the cause of this particular myth; a Minotaur living at the centre of an impossible labyrinth that trapped those who entered so that he may feed. The words that he had spoken, Gwenhwyvar had read as a girl. Her mind raced, she knew the answer. It was one of the oldest of the Greek myths. Boldly she spoke to the creature. "The sisters are day and night" she responded. Morgan snapped back into the present from her frantic thinking. Gwenhwyvar had cracked this code. The Minotaur was citing ancient Grecian riddles. She too had studied them, more recently than Gwenhwyvar, whilst studying beneath Merlin. Morgan could have kicked herself for not realising it sooner. If all it took was to correctly solve mythological puzzles, then they would succeed in giving the beast what he wanted. Morgan sought to trick the creature into giving them similar problems to work upon. "Minotaur, we are more intelligent than the villagers that ye use for nourishment. There is no riddle that ye can pose that we cannot solve with ease." It was an arrogant boast from Morgana.

Gwenhwyvar heard Morgan's words with mild shock, what was Morgan trying to do, anger the beast? It once more moved toward them. And again the silver shadow on the bulls head raised itself. Morgan hadn't noticed, but whilst they had been contemplating the shadow had receded into the form of the Minotaur, and was showing again. What could it possibly be?

Gwenhwyvar and Morgan instinctively took as many steps backwards away from the creature as it took toward them. He stopped moving but his gurgling breathing could still be heard plainly. It was full of mucus and saliva. Morgan feared that her ruse had not worked. But then in an irritated tone the Minotaur spoke. "Ye will need to correctly answer two riddles each. Then solve one puzzle each. Only then shall ye be granted thine freedom." It was dangled before them like a piece of jewellery just out of reach. There was a price to pay for their freedom. It was only then that Gwenhwyvar figured out what Morgan had been doing. She had ensured that the price to be exacted was something that was within their collective abilities to deliver.

"Very well then, a bargain hath been reached" declared Gwenhwyvar. "Two riddles each and one puzzle each for our freedom." There was a feeling of some relief for the Queen and Sorceress. It now seemed that they would not be the meal of this ancient faerie. If only their memories of the Greek myths proved to be good enough, then they may yet prevail. But what of Excalibur lying abandoned on the stone altar? Gwenhwyvar was already working on a plan to include that as part of their prize for overcoming the Minotaur's dilemmas.

He spoke once more turning his head and sharp protruding horns toward Gwenhwyvar. "A dreaded and a dangerous whirlpool am I; swallowing up ships as they pass by without favour or fear." This seemed the most obscure of anything that the creature had yet said. It did not seem like a question. Morgan however knew the answer she looked to the Queen in the hope that she also knew. Gwenhwyvar paused and frowned in concentration. There passed a few moments that seemed to be an age. Morgan began to worry, Gwenhwyvar must have studied the Greek myths as a girl, her memory would not be so clear as her own. Summoning her strength, Morgan closed her eyes and concentrated on Gwenhwyvar. 'Can thee hear mine words?' she said to the Queen without speaking. Gwenhwyvar looked directly at Morgan, then back at the Minotaur returning once more to the Sorceress. Morgan knew that Gwenhwyvar had heard her thoughts. 'The answer is Charybdis', she prompted.

Gwenhwyvar broke into a broad smile and looked directly into the Minotaur's eyes as she delivered the solution to the problem. "Charybdis" she stated with confident repose. This only had the effect of further irritating the hideous being. "Thou are astute for one so very young," he said in what sounded like a mocking tone. The beast turned the great bulk of his body and walked back toward the altar. Once more Morgan could see a silver shadow protrude from the bull's head and then recede once more. Reaching the stone structure he turned with greater poise than something with that mass should be capable of. "I am a sea-living female, with an ugly face, and barking dogs all around mine waist." The next of the riddles was posed for Gwenhwyvar to solve. She was concentrating on only her teachings of Greek mythology. Gwenhwyvar tried with all her might to recall anything and everything about them. This question seemed to be a little more familiar than the first. The Minotaur was clearly referring to a sea-dwelling being. There was only one that she could think of, it was the Hydra. But the reference to barking dogs at her waist level was a conundrum. Just as she was opening her mouth to utter the name, Morgan's voice filled her head and she cut herself off. 'The answer is Scylla,' hailed the secret prompt from the Sorceress.

Once more Gwenhwyvar smiled in victory and announced 'her' answer, "Scylla of course." The Minotaur was even more aggravated than before at the woman's cleverness. He snorted with frustration that both his riddles were so easily dispatched. Turning his attentions to Morgan he barked at her. "Are ye as gifted as thine companion?" Morgan was not sure if it was a rhetorical question so elected to give a vague reply. "Ask, and we shall see." She was feeling more confident now. Collectively they were one third of the way through their challenge, and so far it was looking good for the two women from Caerleon.

The Minotaur stamped one of his bulbous feet upon the ground, annoyed at Morgan's self-assuredness. He stretched his neck by circling his head this way and that, snorting as he did so. "I hath one hundred watchful eyes; 'twas to Hermes I owe mine demise." The roar of the beings voice filled the cavern. Morgan did not even take time to think about the answer, this riddle posed a question about one of her favourite stories in Greek mythology. "Argos" she said triumphantly. "Arrrrrrrrgggg!" cried out the beast in anger. He clenched his fists at having the answer to his clever enigma so quickly delivered. Turning he rammed his right fist upon the stone altar. Gwenhwyvar and Morgan gave each other a look of worry. Morgan thought that it would be a better strategic move to not answer so quickly the next time. They waited barely breathing for the beast to deliver the next brainteaser.

He turned back toward them "We nine cause storms and fog and mist, if killed by Odysseus we would never be missed." Morgan deliberately looked worried. She gave Gwenhwyvar a theatrical questioning look. Frowning in concentration she brought a hand up to her décolletage and covered it, giving the impression of someone who was struggling for an answer. This pleased the Minotaur and he could be heard grunting with pleasure. "Not so fast with thine answer this time Sorceress?" Another rhetorical question; this being was beginning to get on Morgan's nerves. The moments passed slowly. How long could she drag this out before she announced her answer? There had been no talk of a forfeit time limit to the riddles. Nevertheless, feeling that she had given the Minotaur enough of a show she proclaimed her answer, "Hydra." Success; they had answered all of the set riddles.

The beast screamed in frustration long and loudly. He shook his head from side to side; it was terrifying. "Thine skill with puzzles of words is one thing," he declared, "but how clever are thine hands mine ladies?" He stomped across the cavern to the far side. There for the first time the women noticed that there were carved niches containing various things. The light was perhaps just not quite bright enough to help distinguish them. The creature was looking for something amongst the small openings. Too soon he found the object of his search. Holding it up he turned to face them and display it. It was a length of rope. Not particularly long, but very thick. It gave the impression of belonging to a long-boat sail rather than any farming equipment or the like.

"I shall tie a knot into this length of rope. Untie it and ye will have fulfilled the first of thine puzzles." Up until this moment neither Gwenhwyvar nor Morgan had stopped to ponder exactly what form the two puzzles would take. This seemed innocuous enough. How good a knot could the beast tie that could not be undone from such a short length of rope? He began to loop the rope and pass ends through in what seemed to be a haphazard manner. In hardly any time the rope had become one complete knot. The ends could no longer be seen. They must have been tucked into one of the loops. It was the only explanation. He hurled the knotted rope toward Gwenhwyvar; she instinctively intercepted it before it impacted on her body. The force at which the rope was thrown ensured that her hands stung from catching it. Her hands throbbed with pain that she was determined to now show the Minotaur. Instead she casually held it up before her to inspect the work of the creature more closely. It was bizarre, there seemed to be no beginning and no end to the rope anymore. Gwenhwyvar was engrossed in the puzzle. She frowned with concentration and bewilderment. She had thought that the great strength of the beast may have to be overcome should the knot be tied so tightly that her abilities to undo it would be compromised. But the knot itself did not seem to be particularly tight, just well-formed and incomprehensibly without an obvious starting point to unravel it.

She was still pondering the dilemma when Morgan's voice once more filled her head. ‘It is a trick Gwenhwyvar. The beast hath used magic to tie a Gordian knot. Once tied it cannot be undone. There is no beginning and no end. This too heralds from his civilizations mythology.' Gwenhwyvar resisted the urge to look up with surprise at what Morgan had surreptitiously told her. Instead she gave Morgan an almost imperceptible nod to signal that her message had been heard. Matters were grim. The Minotaur was clearly trying to ensure that they failed their tests and were never granted their freedom. Perhaps that too was just wishful thinking in the first place. Better that their energies be directed toward looking for a weakness in the being, some way to overcome it's brutal power and bring this farce to an end.

Morgan interjected Gwenhwyvar's thoughts once more. 'Since the beast hath used magic to tie the knot, it is only fitting that magic be used to untie it. I shall sever the rope at one of the buried points. Ye shall know which when it happens. The Minotaur could be heard almost purring with pleasure at the wonderment that his conundrum had caused. Morgan in the meantime was concentrating with all of her might upon the rope. She pictured her fingernail growing to mimic an iron cast arrow head. Now she pictured it hewn with stone to the sharpest of edges. Lastly she imagined her nail penetrating the rope and finding a point to cut. There, she could feel it against her nail now. Bit by bit she pushed the miniature dagger into the same point on the rope. Gwenhwyvar became aware that there were fibres in one of the folds that were beginning to sever by themselves. She had no doubt that it was Morgan's doing. It was slow but steady work. Gwenhwyvar thought to buy some time by casting a look of bewilderment at the Minotaur.

The creature received her perplexed look with great and noisy satisfaction. That was all of the time that Morgan needed to complete her secretive magical task. The rope had been severed. Now all that Gwenhwyvar needed to do was untangle the mess that the Minotaur had tied. They were acutely aware that this was a task that they were meant to fail. How would the creature react when it realised that they had succeeded in achieving the impossible?

With no exit available to them, Gwenhwyvar decided to distract the beast for a short time. "Perhaps the sword could be of assistance in this matter?" she asked, sure that the creature would refuse such an obvious ploy. Her assumption was correct. "No!" he bellowed and turned to march over to the altar and recover the sword from its resting place. Gwenhwyvar used the time to hastily begin unbinding the rope. But she would need more time if she were to succeed before the Minotaur reached the altar, picked up the sword and turned to once more monitor Gwenhwyvar's 'progress.' Morgan acted instantly. "What is thine name Minotaur?" she asked and separated herself from Gwenhwyvar, walking away from her in the hope that the beast followed her with his eyes and not the Queen. The

Minotaur had by this time reached the stone block and with a swoop of his bulging muscular arm snatched the sword from the slab. Spinning around he faced Morgan. "Name?" he asked almost confused at the question.

"Surely ye had a name in the times gone by, when ye were a mischievous faerie?" prodded Morgan. This disturbed the beast. How could this human know that he was a faerie? He growled with displeasure. Morgan pushed her advantage. She walked closer to him, which the Minotaur did not expect. He was much more accustomed to people running in fear of his hideous form. "Were ye a handsome man when in thine human form?" She stopped her advance; keeping the creature at more than his arm's length. The Minotaur snorted loudly with contempt. "What does it matter what I looked like in centuries gone by Sorceress? Now solve the puzzle of the knot or face mine wrath!" he bellowed, impatient at the pointlessness of the inquiry.

"Solved!" Gwenhwyvar's voice echoed slightly in the surrounds she spoke so loudly. The Minotaur's eyes widened visibly. His gaping mouth dropped open like a surprised child's. "What trickery is this?" he screamed. Gwenhwyvar was proudly displaying the now completely unfurled rope. Lurching forward he made to cover the distance between them with as few steps as possible. Surprised and fearful of the consequences of angering the Minotaur Gwenhwyvar threw the solved puzzle at him. He instinctively raised his free arm to catch the rope. The Queen had in the meantime circled around the beast and joined Morgan close to the altar. The beast was staring at the unsolvable knot at first with wonderment then absolute fury. He spun around and pointed Excalibur at Morgan. "This is thine doing Sorceress. Magic hath been used to solve this puzzle." He stamped his foot with resentment.

Morgan took up the challenge. "Magic was used to tie the Gordian knot; it was only fair to use magic to solve the problem." There was no sense in pretending that she had no part to play in the outcome. The creature let out a scream of rage. He had been bested by a slip of a girl with some rudimentary powers. Morgan and Gwenhwyvar braced themselves for the worst. But the Minotaur's next move was completely unexpected.

With a wave of his huge hand the entrance to the cavern was reinstated. The sound of rock bending and reshaping itself filled the air. It was too good to be true. Was the fearsome creature allowing them to leave? The way-out lay tantalisingly close to the women. Between them and the exit, was the creature. It stood ominously, silently; the being's annoyance clear in its laboured breathing. The moments crept by with agonising slowness. In the flurry of happenings that had occurred since encountering the Minotaur neither Morgan nor Gwenhwyvar had noticed that the creature was completely naked. Only the torso was that of a huge bull with horns; the remainder of the massive body was that of a man; a man that was becoming slowly erect; his pendulous appendage thickening with the rush of blood. As the women watched in horror his penis began to drip with pre-seminal fluid. It was clear that his intention was to rape the women.

"The final challenge is simple mine ladies," he began. "Find the way safely out of mine labyrinth before I mate with thee and then consume thine shattered bodies!" It was the final insult to them both. They had played his game as best as they could up ‘till now, but the beast revealed his true intentions. They were to satisfy his lust and serve as additional fodder to the creature's most recent meal. Gwenhwyvar and Morgan's felt their hearts sink within them. What hope was there for them?

Mocking them in their despair, the Minotaur stood aside to allow the two women egress from the cavern. Seizing upon the opportunity the Caerleon women ran skirting around the beast as widely as they could without slowing their escape from the cavern. Morgan instinctively pushed the spell of luminosity through her hand that was closest to the wall. It lit up the cave in which they were running. Even in this desperate state of panic they had the presence of mind to look for the arrows that had been drawn onto the surface of the cave walls. They would surely find their way out of the caves and make good their escape. As one they formed a similar grain of hope that no others that had come before them had had the presence of mind to do something similar. Surely they would be the first to navigate the labyrinth and achieve their salvation.

Chapter 37: Between the Minotaur's Caves and the Village of Avyze

Morgan's followers were ashamed but grateful to still have their lives. They had abandoned their recently adopted Sorceress in the heat of battle. But they were telling themselves, it was with good reason. Garrone was in council with some of the elder villagers. One of them was speaking to the small group. "Nothing could survive the powers of that hideous thing," the old man lamented. "Morgana and Gwen are most surely dead by now." He hung his head with nothing further to say. "Weapons were useless Garrone," offered one of the men. "We had no choice but to flee and save ourselves lest we enrage the beast any more than we already had." All in the small band that were in earshot nodded and grumbled in agreement. They had hoped to rid themselves of the burden of fear that was always present in their community, but they had failed. Garrone wondered if there would be recourse from the beast that they would be forced to face for their aborted attack. He shuddered, pushing the thought from his mind. It was too much to face at the moment. "Onwards to our homes," he called out to the bedraggled party.

Chapter 38: The Coast of Galloway, Midday

Arthur and Merlin were debating the possibility of deploying Christians near the faerie forest. "Surely the risk to ye powers is not worth the reward of banishing the faeries from their abodes?" queried Arthur. Merlin was sanguine in his response, "There is much to consider. Now that we know there is a way to nullify the magic of faeries, indeed all magic, we hath an advantage over them previously unanticipated." It was a typically thoughtful but non-committal reply from the old man. They had spent a night with the Monks on the Island of Mann and then returned to Galloway the next day. Now they were busy readying themselves for the journey back to North Rheged, and then home to Caerleon. "We hath much time to discuss the usefulness of our latest discovery on our way to brief King Rhydderch about the goings-on in Pen Rhionydd," Merlin further offered. Arthur took the point and rather than continue the conversation busied himself with preparing his horse for the journey ahead.

Chapter 39: The Minotaur's Labyrinth - Evening

Morgan and Gwenhwyvar had followed the arrows marked in the walls to what should have been their original entry point to the caves. Instead of that there was nothing but more caves, however. "The walls move, I hath heard them whilst we have been running," surmised Morgan. There was a note of defeat in her voice that the Queen would not allow her to wallow in. She replied almost sternly, "If the beast is using magic to trick us out of finding the exit, then use magic to create an escape for us!" It seemed a simple enough solution. Morgan reached out and grabbed onto Gwenhwyvar's arm in a signal for her to stop. They had been running for what seemed like an eternity. There was no end in sight to the caves. Their 'clever' arrows were not intelligent enough to defeat a magical labyrinth that could change its shape whilst they ran through it.

Morgan and Gwenhwyvar were exhausted. They were breathing heavily. "I can try," offered Morgan. She thought about the scrolls and scrolls of spells that she had studied. Picking the most likely of spells she thought, perhaps this one; a variation of the spell that Morgan had used to secretly cut the rope allowing the Queen to untie the Gordian knot. She stood before a wall with both hands pressed together by the back of her hands. She pictured her hands as many times bigger than they actually were. Mumbling the spell of amplification she imagined her hands able to dig through the hardest surface as easily as sand. With elbows held high she reached the climax of the spell and thrust her hands forward. Immediately before her the walls gave way in an oversized impression of her hands penetrating them deeply and completely. Thrusting her hands apart, the chalk, soil and rock similarly parted with her command. Rock exploded outwards to the surface revealing the evening lit sky. A perfect tunnel was presented to them. Morgan was amazed at her success. It must have shown in her expression because Gwenhwyvar actually laughed. In spite of their desperate situation the look on the Sorceress's face was a sight to behold. Gwenhwyvar's hearty laugh was a mixture of amusement and relief that an escape route was now available to them.

Hope welled up within them, but it was to be short lived. From all around them the mocking voice of the Minotaur bellowed. "Do not leave mine home beautiful women; I hath yet to show you the full extent of mine hospitality." He finished the ominous sentence with a raucous laughter. As the women looked on in horror, the walls of Morgan's escape tunnel folded in on themselves, the tunnel was no more.

Morgan stated the very obvious. "The beast will not let us leave," her exhaustion apparent in the tone of her voice. As usual the Queen was not going to hear of defeat or surrender. "Then we must find an alternative," she stated firmly. It was clear that Gwenhwyvar was about to elaborate on her quixotic solution but she cut herself off. Jerking her head to the left she signalled Morgan to listen. There, she could hear the sound of feet stomping. The sound was coming closer. It must surely be the Minotaur seeking them out. With barely a nod, they fled in the opposite direction. They ran through twists and turns in the hope of putting as much distance between them and their captor as possible. The minutes seemed to stretch into hours. Again they had to stop from fatigue.

Morgan felt out manoeuvred, and overwhelmed with by the age and power of the faerie that terrified them. Surely there was nothing that she could do to overcome the beast? She voiced her fears to Gwenhwyvar. "This faerie hath been alive for longer than any other save Matrona. I fear that even Merlin may not be a match for its power. What hope is there?"

Gwenhwyvar was about to launch into a typical majestic speech about not giving up regardless of the odds, but thought the better of it. She could see in Morgan's face that defeat was at the forefront of the Sorceress's mind. Unless that self-defeating premise could be eradicated then they really would have no hope. She took Morgan's hands into her own and looked into her eyes. "Sometimes the cleverest people are fooled by the simplest of tricks." It was all that she could think of to say, and feared that it was just not enough to conjure hope in her sister-in-law. But she was wrong. Morgan tilted her head slightly as though the Queen's words had had a physical impact upon her. Morgan squeezed Gwenhwyvar's hands in thanks.

"Mine Queen," she said mysteriously, "tis time that we stopped running." Morgan was looking decidedly more of her usual confident self once more. Gwenhwyvar was happy that her anecdote had such a positive effect upon the woman. She was about to query the meaning of Morgan's instruction when once more the distant sound of approaching steps interrupted them. Morgan was staring intently at the opposite wall of the cave. "What.." began Gwenhwyvar in a hushed tone, but Morgan interrupted. "I am unsure if this will work, but we must try. Stand against the far side of the cave wall," she instructed. Gwenhwyvar looked backwards to the way that they had come. There were definitely the striding sounds of the approaching Minotaur emanating from that direction. How could he catch up with them so quickly?

Without another word she obediently followed Morgan's instruction. Morgan began to chant a spell in a whisper. It was that ancient language that she had heard before. Morgan was tracing the outline of Gwenhwyvar's form against the wall with her hands. Unseen by Gwenhwyvar, but visible to Morgan, an image of the wall appeared between them. "Press against the wall as close as ye can," instructed the Sorceress. Gwenhwyvar did so. She watched as Morgan walked toward her. She seemed to be pushing something that Gwenhwyvar could not see. From Morgan's point of view a perfect image of the opposing cave wall was floating between the two of them. Now she pressed in over Gwenhwyvar like a blanket. Perfect. Gwenhwyvar now could not be seen. Only the cave wall was there.

Morgan stood back to admire her handiwork and smiled. "Perfect" she said. The Queen was perplexed. She looked down at herself, she appeared no different. But to Morgan a part of the rock wall in the shape of Gwenhwyvar's head was moving and looking down at itself. "No! No!" she cautioned. "For the spell to work, ye must remain completely still"

"What spell Morgan, I can see nothing," replied Gwenhwyvar, perplexed at the goings on. "Allow me to show ye, what hath been done to ye," answered Morgan. With that, Morgan began the spell once more, but this time regarded the cave wall directly opposite Gwenhwyvar. The image of the cave wall appeared. This time Gwenhwyvar could see it and Morgan could not. The Sorceress pressed her body against the wall and with a stroking motion the image wrapped itself over her form. Morgan had effectively disappeared. Gwenhwyvar was astounded. "Ye hath become rock," whispered the Queen. Morgan responded by raising her finger to her lips and shushing the woman. Gwenhwyvar saw an outline of the arm raise to make the gesture. It was the strangest thing that she had ever seen. In an instant it became clear to Gwenhwyvar that she too must look like this to Morgan, as though she were the cave wall itself. Morgan's outlined arm returned to its place and the cave wall was still once more.

Footsteps closed in on them. Gwenhwyvar and Morgan could hear the breathing of the Minotaur as he approached. Neither of them dared to shut their eyes even though the feeling was almost overpowering. Bit by bit the beast drew nearer to them. Then he was in sight. Again both women had to resist shutting their eyes as hard as they could. He loped into the spot that was exactly between the two women and stopped. Ominously he looked up and down the cave. Raising his head he sniffed at the air. He grunted. It was difficult to tell as the bull face gave nothing away, but Morgan thought that he looked perplexed. Again he sniffed the air. He spoke making both the Sorceress and Queen shudder slightly. "I can smell ye," his voice boomed.

The women were perspiring with fear. Would the beast be able to see through a simple spell of beguilement? Time seemed to stand still. The Minotaur was confused. He could clearly identify the scent of his quarry, but they were nowhere to be seen. He became angry. He stamped his feet and swung Excalibur around in a frenzy nearly slicing through the disguise that both women were wearing. With a loud roar he bent over and twisted his head side to side. He was sure that they were here somewhere. It took every bit of strength they both had to not turn and run from the fearsome display. With a final drawn-out snort and roar of frustration he turned and strode back the way he had come. His footsteps were loud. He was stomping quickly away from them. Morgan waited until she could no longer hear the Minotaur's egress before she flicked her arms out and the image of the cave wall that so adeptly hid her frittered away into small parcels and disappeared.

She stepped forward and brushed the beguilement spell off of Gwenhwyvar, who looked both scared and puzzled. "Can ye see me?" she queried. Morgan almost laughed in response, "Aye Gwenhwyvar," she responded. The Queen posed a question, "What now?" Morgan sounded much more confident than she had before. "Sometimes the cleverest of people are fooled by the simplest of tricks," Morgan paraphrased Gwenhwyvar from only minutes before. For her part, Gwenhwyvar was grateful that she had been able to inspire the Sorceress. "The spell of beguilement," she began, "that Nimue used so effectively on Arthur and ye and me those short years ago." Morgan nodded. "Exactly," she said with pride. "But," continued Gwenhwyvar, "I thought that it was used to mimic people, not cave walls?" Morgan's answer surprised her. "So did I, but it was worth trying."

Gwenhwyvar's eyes widened as she realised exactly what Morgan had done. The Sorceress had taken a chance that the spell could be used to mimic something other than a person, and it had worked. Gwenhwyvar briefly thought about the consequences if the risk had not been justified. It did not bear thinking about. Instead she returned to her original question to Morgan. "What now?" she repeated. Again Morgan's answer caught the Queen off guard. "Now we take back Excalibur"

Gwenhwyvar could scarcely believe her ears. "Take Excalibur?" she exclaimed, "from the Minotaur?" she said her tone dripping with incredulity. "Aye," came Morgan's one word reply. This would have normally angered Gwenhwyvar had it not been for the dire circumstances in which they found themselves. Instead she opted for a more moderate criticism. "Morgan, I am sure that we will barely save ourselves from this situation. How do ye expect us to prevail with Excalibur as well?" It was a fair enough question.

"First let us find our way back to the cavern." It was another almost unbelievable statement from Morgan. Gwenhwyvar shook her head in disbelief. But now it was Morgan's turn to bolster the spirit of the Queen. "Quickly," she said. “I am anxious to spring mine trap for the beast." She gently grabbed Gwenhwyvar's forearm and pulled her in the direction that they were originally heading. "Wait!" objected Gwenhwyvar. "How do ye know that this is the way to the cavern?" Talking as they hurried through the passageways Morgan replied, "In the Greek myth, all of the passageways in the Minotaur's labyrinth led to its centre and the waiting beast." It was not the inspiring plan that the Queen had hoped her question would invoke.

Now becoming more worried and frustrated as well, she pushed her point. "What is ye plan Morgan?" For her reply the Sorceress only gave a cryptic answer and an instruction to continue with haste. "Always show respect to ye elders. Hurry!"

Morgan was moving faster than Gwenhwyvar. They scurried through the labyrinth of caves turning left and right with what seemed like wild abandon. Then without warning Morgan stopped and turned, signalling for the Queen to not utter a sound. She pointed ahead of them. This area looked familiar. Yes, they were both sure of it now. The archway ahead led to the Minotaur's cavern containing its altar and other sundry things that looked like they were for the casting of spells. Perhaps this was the beast's equivalent to Arthur's study or Merlin's tower room. Gingerly Morgan pressed her form against the wall and chanced a quick peek into the room. Sure that she had seen nothing, she again moved her head into the cavern and looked all about for any sign of the creature. Nothing. Excellent, it was empty. She signalled for Gwenhwyvar to join her.

Morgan pointed at the altar on the far side of the room. If the beast was hiding from them, then it would be there. They tip toed into the cavern. Morgan again silently signalled for Gwenhwyvar to walk around the far side of the altar to her. They would approach it from both sides. Walking in a circle they leant forward with trepidation, hoping that the beast was not lying in wait for them. They gingerly tread their separate paths. Morgan noticed that where the remains of the hapless boy from the village should have been there was now nothing. She briefly wondered what the beast could have done with such a disgusting mess. Better to never find out she thought. The back of the stone bench was coming into view with painful slowness. The more that was revealed the higher their spirits were. Then there came the point when they could see clearly. The Minotaur was not lying in wait for them.

"This is perfect," said Morgan. She looked Gwenhwyvar directly in the eyes. "Here is what I want ye to do…."

Chapter 40: The Minotaur's Labyrinth – Night

The Minotaur prowled his familiar cave pathways. He concentrated and used his powers to ensure that the entrance could not be found. He was frustrated. He knew that the women were here but he could not find them. The sport of hunting his victims had lost its shine. These two had evaded his capture far longer than any before them. Perhaps the infantile powers of the Sorceress were stronger than he had anticipated. Something cut into his trail of thought. 'Minotaur.' For a brief moment he wondered if he had imagined it, until it repeated; 'Minotaur.' It was a woman's voice calling for him. He spun around and listened for it once more. 'Minotaur.' The beast could hardly believe what he was hearing. One of the doomed victims was calling for him. In an instant he considered that it must be a trap of some kind. Then he immediately dismissed the idea. What weapon forged could harm him? He did not fear any. He began to form the beginnings of an erection again. Soon he would have his way with the women and drain their life-essence from them. He felt powerful, invincible. With his arrogant self-confidence and newly renewed lust he treaded heavily towards the cavern at the centre of his shifting maze.

It took him only a few minutes to reach it. The network of interconnected caves was much wider than what was left by the Romans when they had abandoned it. He had ensured that it was more befitting as his residence and had carved many new tunnels. Eventually he had re-created an image of this first home, back in Greece, two thousand years ago. All of these stray thoughts filled his head as he entered the central cavern. There standing by his magical fire and miniature cauldron was the woman with red hair. There was something about the way that she was standing that unsettled him. She did not recoil when he entered the cavern. He looked about the room; the Sorceress was nowhere to be seen. But he could still feel her presence somewhere nearby.

"Where is the Sorceress?" demanded the Minotaur, his voice harsh. "Gone to fetch a friend that wishes to be reacquainted with ye," answered Gwenhwyvar. The exchange took the beast completely off-guard. "What foolishness is this?" he bellowed.

Lying flat on her back behind the altar and completely out of view, Morgan began the spell of beguilement, focussing within her mind a very specific image. There it was, she could see every detail now. All that remained was to wrap herself in the disguise.

The Minotaur was incensed at what he perceived was a stupid exchange of words. "What trickery is this?" he was even angrier now. "No trick Minotaur; see," Gwenhwyvar motioned with her arm. The Minotaur spun around. Standing behind him was the Lady of the Lake. "Matrona?" he actually took two steps backwards away from her, such was his shock at seeing the ancient faerie. She stood staring at him impassively. Her expression impossible to delineate, was she angry or not, he could not tell. This was the only being on earth that he needed to fear. She was ancient even by his standards. Mysterious and evasive, he had only had brief contact with her every now and again throughout his miserable lifetime. "What do ye want?" he probed, his voice now weak and unsure. The moments of absolute silence that filled the cavern that followed his question were unbearable to him. What could this powerful being possibly want with him? She was not prone to mercy or compassion when it came to her own kind. He was sure of that. Twice in his life he had sought her out and begged her to put to rights his abilities to transform into animals, but more importantly to take on his proper human form once more. She had refused him both times.

"What is mine," was the ominous reply. It took a second for him to realise what she was referring to. She pointed at his hand. He looked down; he was still carrying the 'magical' sword Excalibur. This formidable faerie had come to claim what rightly belonged to her. He knew better than to refuse such a potent creature. He bowed his head in a sign of respect and moved forward. Raising and outstretching his arm he offered it to Matrona. Without a further word she clasped both of her hands around the handle and drew it toward her. There was an expression on her face that could have been one of gratitude but it was impossible to tell with this mighty being. "Gwenhwyvar shall accompany me," said Matrona. Even though it was not in his best interests to argue, he did so. "No Matrona, leave the woman and Sorceress to me. Ye will not grant me the ability to transform back into a human. If I drain the essence of the Sorceress, I may yet reclaim that ability." In an instant the reason that the Minotaur had made the pact with Garlon became clear. The sword was to be bait for Merlin so that the old Sorcerer's powers could be ingested by this foul creature. Garlon would be rid of Merlin. Arthur would no longer have his sage and strategic commander. Excalibur would be the symbol to rally all of the Saxons in the land to annihilate his rightful rule.

Matrona's expression sullied, she practically frowned at the Minotaur. Exasperated with the unravelling of his plan, the beast snorted loudly and pounded the ground with his feet. She was not going to allow him to drain the Sorceress and the woman. He had lived for what felt like an eternity in this half-man half-beast form. When the opportunity of luring a powerful sorcerer into his labyrinth was offered to him he had dared to believe that it would be the solution to his transformational problem. Now the most powerful of all the faeries was going to deny him that prize.

He reluctantly stood aside to allow the Lady of the Lake to pass. She made to walk past him. He gave her a look of complete contempt and malevolence. And then something happened. Her face wrinkled like a piece of cloth in the wind. It was just the once and just for a fleeting moment. Leaning forward he looked more carefully at her features. It was then that he noticed it. There was fear in the eyes of the all-powerful Matrona, former Queen of the faeries and now immortal goddess. He couldn't believe what he was seeing. Why would so powerful and omnipotent being fear him? At first he thought that he must be mistaken. So he looked closer. She was about to walk past him when he subconsciously put up his hand to prevent her from doing so. She jerked her head to bring his face into alignment with his; albeit the size and inclination of a child looking up to it parent. There is was again, a look of fear.

The Minotaur looked her up and down, "What do I see in thine eyes Matrona? Is it fear?" For her part the Lady audibly drew in her breath. "Stand aside!" she commanded. It was then that the Minotaur noticed something else. Her voice was not as he remembered it.

There was something different about it. "Thine voice sounds different goddess." He practically spat the suspicion in her face. Raising his hand he pointed accusingly at her face. As he was forming his next sentence he saw that his finger had actually distorted the face of the Lady. It was though her features were some impossibly realistic tapestry and he was pushing his finger into it, depressing the image. "What trickery is this Matrona?" Once, twice more he prodded his finger in the air surrounding her face and it caused the same result. It was as if she was wearing a thick robe over her face that could not be seen. He could feel something though. It was malleable, but would bounce back into the shape of Matrona's face whenever he relented.

Using his filthy but long and sharp nails he clawed into the invisible cloth. Then in a single felled swoop he tore it away from the woman. Pieces of Matrona's face and neck shimmered and cracked. There in the places where Matrona's face had been were the tell-tale features of the Sorceress with long blonde hair. "Treachery!" he screamed. With both hands he grasped any more pieces of the imposed image and ripped them down and away from Matrona, revealing Morgan.

He was so enraged that he barely noticed that she was brandishing Excalibur. It was heavy in Morgan's hands she could barely lift it. But with both hands and the surge of fear that was flooding her entire body she swept it back over her right shoulder and brought it down in a beautiful arc; its blade heading in a blur of motion toward the beast's neck. The impact and resulting rebound from his magically reinforced hide was shattering. Morgan felt that her hands, wrists and lower part of her arms were going to fall away from her body. The pain was excruciating. Excalibur flew from her hands and disappeared from her view entirely.

The Minotaur grabbed Morgan with both arms and lifted her up so that she was level with his face. "First, I shall mate with ye perfidious woman. Then ye will feed me with thine powers." He carried her over to the altar and slammed her down on the hard stone surface. The blow knocked her senseless and the scream that was building in her lungs was beaten from her. He tore the garments from her body. She was naked and lying prone upon his stone bench,her genitals exposed for him to see. A surge of blood filled his penis and he became erect. Morgan felt her legs get brutally pushed apart. Partially recovered, she screamed as loudly as she could.

Gwenhwyvar had by this time run over to where Excalibur had fallen. She could not believe her eyes when the sword bounced off the body of the Minotaur. Now Morgan was going to be raped by this hideous creature and she had no idea what to do. If Excalibur's magic was useless against it then what hope was there? Unable to think of anything else to do she simply reacted. Leaning down she grasped the handle of the sword with one hand and lifted it up. It had almost no weight to it. Something happened in that instant. Gwenhwyvar felt that she was one with the sword. It was as if Excalibur was an extension of her arm. An image of the first time that Arthur had allowed her to hold the sword flashed into her mind.

Chapter 41: AD 488-Arthur and Gwenhwyvar's wedding night

Alone together for the first time since the announcement of their wedding, Arthur and Gwenhwyvar were in the most secluded part of King Rhydderch's castle in North Rheged. They were both only seventeen years of age. Still resplendent in their wedding attire, this was the moment that they could consummate their vows. There was so much emotion and expectation passing between them that it was difficult to think properly. Arthur removed his magical sword and placed it beside the wedding bed. Without even realising that she had done so, Gwenhwyvar held out her hand silently asking for the opportunity to hold the symbol of his power. Arthur, for his part did not hesitate. She was after all was his wife, the Queen of Northumbria and Wales. He held it so that she could take the handle from him. Magical; it looked so heavy but was unbelievably light. She instinctively knew exactly where the point of the sword was without the need to look. There was a power that came from being one with Excalibur. It made her feel strong, fearless, and invincible. No other words were spoken between them. There was an understanding that both knew the sovereignty of the weapon in a way that no other man or woman ever would.

Chapter 42: AD 494 - Earlier at Llyn Callyfyrth

The Lady of the lake addressed Gwenhwyvar. "Tis mine wish that Arthur remain in possession of Excalibur to compete his work. It will continue to serve the authority for which it was meant."

Chapter 43: AD 494: The Minotaur's Cavern in Gaul

Morgan's second scream of absolute desperation and fear snapped Gwenhwyvar from her momentary recollections. They had flashed before her eyes like the lightning in a summer storm. A feeling of power spread from Excalibur through her arm and into Gwenhwyvar's entire body. It was the same feeling that she had encountered on her wedding night with Arthur in North Rheged. Nobody else could understand or hope to know what the sword was capable of in the hands of Arthur the King or Gwenhwyvar the Queen. Looking over to the Minotaur, Gwenhwyvar could see the foul beast lean over and lick its slobbering tongue over Morgan's breasts. It left behind viscous animal saliva that oozed over her form.

Gwenhwyvar walked toward the creature. She did not feel anxious. She did not feel doubt. In a blur of time and motion she floated to a point where she stood directly behind the huge form of the Minotaur. His back was arched as he leant over his prize once more running his vile tongue over her naked torso. Judging the point of entry and exit precisely, Gwenhwyvar was cognoscente enough to ensure that Morgan would not suffer a single scratch from the blow that was to follow. And follow it did. Not a sharp warrior's stab, but a slow deliberate and carefully considered thrust from the entry point just below his left shoulder blade, through the muscle and sinew. She could feel the bones of his ribcage separate at the point of the sword as it passed through them, then into the side of the beating heart of the creature. It offered no resistance. Finally it slid through the front of the rib cage and more muscle before the point of Excalibur protruded out from beneath the Minotaur's left pectoral.

All this time the beast was screaming in shock, agony and terror. Gwenhwyvar had not even noticed it until now. For a brief moment she considered pushing on the handle of the sword, downwards. It was so tempting. The torture that the Minotaur would suffer with this move dangled before her like a forbidden fruit. Taking a deep breath, the Queen tried to quell the feeling of retribution that welled up within her. She was successful. There was no need to further torment this pathetic creature. She had afflicted a death blow to it, no more was required.

Morgan at first couldn't distinguish the sound of her screaming from that of the Minotaur. It took a few moments to realise that he had stopped ravaging her naked body. She could see that the beast was arching it's head backwards and crying out in excruciating pain. Then the reason became clear. The point of a sword burst through the chest of the creature. Blood poured out from the wound. It kept time in a rhythm, squirting at evenly speced intervals.

Gwenhwyvar pulled on the handle of Excalibur; it obeyed the simple instruction and withdrew from the body of the creature without a hint of resistance. Bringing it to a standing salute before her face, she followed the bloodied length of the sword with her eyes. Then looking back to their victim she watched and listened as the Minotaur choked off a final cry of torment. Its huge body fell over to its left side and thudded loudly on the soft ground of the cavern.

Morgan sat up and surveyed the scene. The Queen was standing impassively over the body of the fallen creature, holding Excalibur. Morgan was stunned. Gwenhwyvar had somehow succeeded where she had failed. In her hands the magical sword could not even make a mark on the hide of the Minotaur. Yet clearly, Gwenhwyvar had managed to run the beast through in a single blow. "Gwenhwyvar," began Morgan. "How….?" She trailed off feeling that she need not elaborate on the obvious question. Gwenhwyvar, ever the perfect woman and monarch, and now saviour, responded with her concerns. "Are ye injured?" She looked over Morgan's form hoping to find nothing that needed tending to. Morgan did a quick inspection of her body. "No injuries Gwenhwyvar." She wriggled her way off the slab of stone and manoeuvring herself over the body of the Minotaur, turned to gather her ruined clothes from the altar. Folding what was left of them around her as best she could, she couldn't help but ask her question again. "Gwenhwyvar, how did ye wield Excalibur in such a way as to kill the beast? I could barely lift its burdensome weight. The Minotaur's hide must be reinforced with magic. Not a single mark could I inflict upon it. Tell me please, how did ye manage to slay the creature?" Morgan realised as she spoke that her rambling and disjointed thoughts could hardly be considered cogent. But it delivered the meaning nevertheless.

Gwenhwyvar replied evenly. "It was something that the Lady of the Lake said when we asked her for help." Morgan did not understand and let it be known. Shaking her head she spread her hands in a gesture of inquiry for more information. Gwenhwyvar continued, "Excalibur was meant to go to Arthur to serve the authority that he represents. It's magic works for him. And I had gathered from Matrona's words that it was available to those that share in his authority." Morgan understood, she followed on with the trail of thought. "Excalibur's magic could be wielded therefore by both the King and Queen." Gwenhwyvar smiled "Exactly. I saw that ye could not scratch the beast's hide with Excalibur. But it looked heavy in thine hands. Yet when I lifted the sword, it was as though it were a part of me. In the same way that it is part of Arthur." The two women had in rescuing Excalibur from the clutches of the Minotaur and using it to slay the beast, uncovered another layer of the mysterious sword.

Gwenhwyvar's thoughts were of Arthur. She could hardly wait to tell him how she had used his sword to battle the fearsome creature. Morgan wanted desperately to impart this knowledge to Merlin. It was a fascinating revelation that must be added to his library of scrolls. Morgan looked down at the Minotaur. The silver shadow that she had seen fleetingly around a part of his head was there again. But this time it seemed to be oozing out of his head like molten silver. It beguiled her. She leant down and stretched out a finger to touch it. It was warm, seductive, and desirable. There welled up in Morgan a want to possess it. The feeling came upon her like a sudden fever. It filled her every thought. With both hands she began to pick at the surface of the silver liquid. Then just like a molten metal it solidified in her touch. She pulled at it. To her surprise and delight, more of it came from the head of the beast. Again she pulled and even more showed itself coming from somewhere deep within the creature's body. It was thin.

Unbelievably thin and delicate yet it felt stronger than any metal or stone that Morgan could compare it to. She gave it a wrench, once twice and the third time with all of her might. Pulling it from the creature it separated itself from the Minotaur's prone form. She held it high to view her prize more closely. It was completely reflective. It flashed with colours, blue, red and some that Morgan had never before seen. It was like a mirror but made from the finest of faerie silk. No finer still than that. Morgan had never before seen anything so completely enthralling. "Look at it Gwenhwyvar!" she practically screamed with excitement. "Hath ye ever seen the like of it before? It is so beautiful." Morgan spun the flimsy sheet around to see both sides of it. They were identical. It could not have been a more perfect sheet of.....exactly what, Morgan did not know.

Gwenhwyvar for her part was completely taken aback at Morgan's sudden outburst. She looked at Morgan holding up absolutely nothing. It was as though she were doing a pantomime of some description. The excitement in Morgan's voice was clear, but she was referring to something that simply was not there. "Morgan I can see nothing in ye hands." At first Morgan didn't hear the Queen; she was still too enraptured with her new found prize. Once more Gwenhwyvar repeated. "Morgan there is nothing in ye hands." Morgan spun around like she had been scalded. Her face twisted with disbelief; how could she not see this most amazing of materials in her hands. It was surely the most stunning piece of weaving that had ever come into being.

"Gwenhwyvar; it is a delight. A most striking....." words failed Morgan. She simply had no words to describe what she was seeing.

"Cloak." She finished the sentence as best as she was able. "Ye cannot see how magnificent it is?" Gwenhwyvar reiterated her inability to see that Morgan was indeed holding anything. There was a certain feeling that Morgan had when she used the word 'cloak' to describe the object. Yes, that was it, she thought. It should be worn as a cloak. Flinging it above her head she brought it down to rest upon her shoulders and back. It settled upon her form and wrapped itself around her. It felt soft and comforting but powerful and strong at the same time. She pulled it around her chest. This was exactly where the cloak was meant to be. Morgan looked down at the brilliant surface as it hugged her form, and then tightened. It found every curve of her torso and wrapped itself skilfully around her form. To Morgan this felt even better than when it first touched her body.

There was something else, another feeling, like it was integrating itself with her somehow. As she looked enraptured, the reflective surface began to absorb into the skin of her hands. Slowly but surely it was boring into every pore. And it felt good. Morgan let out a groan of pleasure. The reflective surface was disappearing into her clothes and forming on top of her skin beneath. Then bit by bit it became a part of Morgan and effectively disappeared from view. It was the most intense feeling of ecstasy that Morgan had ever experienced. It was as though this mysterious material was making love to her. Her nipples became hard. Her genitals were throbbing with pleasure. She drew in a long slow breath only to respire it as a rapturous orgasm shook her entire body. Morgan climaxed with such ferocity that her legs shook and buckled beneath her.

The next thing that she saw was Gwenhwyvar's concerned face hovering above her. "Morgan, what happened?" said the Queen clearly distressed at what she had seen. Morgan felt too good to answer; instead she sat up invigorated by the new-found energy that was pulsing through her body. She knew, she absolutely knew and understood exactly what had happened. The thin veil of silver silk that she had stripped from the Minotaur was a sizeable chunk of his magical power. She tried to put it into words. "I hath consumed magical prowess from the dead Minotaur" said Morgan. The statement dumbfounded Gwenhwyvar. "What?" she asked; "how is that possible?" But instead of answering, Morgan continued to explain what she understood to have happened; fighting to find the perfect words that would expound the remarkable situation. "I pulled the magic from the body of the beast and wrapped it around myself. It became a part of me. In that instant I knew what it was and how to use it." Morgan was elated. She sprang to her feet in a blur of motion so fast that it could not have been humanly possible. "I feel so powerful that nothing is beyond mine abilities." Morgan breathed in and out with a loud moan upon each breath. Suddenly turning to face Gwenhwyvar as though she had just noticed her standing there she spoke. "Gwenhwyvar, we hath succeeded beyond our wildest dreams. Excalibur is recovered and I know the way to return us to Briton faster than any water horse could imagine." The tone of Morgan's revelation was almost manic with happiness. It took Gwenhwyvar aback somewhat.

Trying her best to calm the Sorceress the Queen spoke in a low even tone. "Morgan, try to calmly tell me what ye mean. How can ye travel faster than a water horse?" Morgan was having none of it. She was invigorated beyond any level that she had previously encountered or imagined. This was more exciting than casting her first successful spell whilst in Merlin's chamber. The thought of Merlin changed her trail of thought. "Merlin" she said, "Merlin must be told of this amazing happening. We must explore the intricacies of this transfer of magical ability from the Minotaur to mine body." Closing her eyes she looked as though she were concentrating upon a distant sound, as if straining to hear it.

Opening her eyes she looked evenly at Gwenhwyvar. "Merlin is with Arthur, they are at North Rheged Castle. I can see them talking with King Rhydderch and Queen Ganieda." Although welcome news Gwenhwyvar almost refuted it, but thought the better of it; Morgan's abilities to see where Merlin was were known. She had no reason to doubt the Sorceress's abilities now. And she sounded so absolutely sure of what she was saying. "That is good news Morgan. Now ye said something about getting us to Briton quickly?" Morgan was calming slightly. She laughed a little, realising now that her behaviour must have seemed disconcerting to the Queen.

"I can use the new found power to help us travel a great distance in the blink of an eye. But first we have to stop and bid goodbye to our new friends." Morgan clutched her head with both her hands. Gwenhwyvar shook her head, what friends, she thought. Slowly caressing her cheeks, Morgan massaged her fingers over her face and looked up toward the entrance to the Minotaur's cavern. "It is done," she said simply. Gwenhwyvar turned to see where the Sorceress was looking. To her amazement the entrance to the cavern now led to the exterior of the Tavern in Avyze village instead of to a darkened chalk cave tunnel. Gwenhwyvar was stunned. She rubbed her eyes fearing that it was an illusion of some description. "Am I dreaming?" she asked Morgan. "No Gwenhwyvar. This is how the Minotaur has learnt to travel over the centuries. His powers far exceed those of an ordinary faerie. And now they are mine. This is but one side of the abilities that I have taken from the beast. It has many surfaces to explore." Morgan's tone got progressively darker as she spoke the words. Explaining the 'stolen' magic as an object with multiple surfaces was bewildering Gwenhwyvar. And Morgan's tenor was a cause of concern as well. However the proof of what she was saying lay before her. A few short steps away was the Tavern that they had left this very morning and taken half a day to travel to the chalk caves of the Minotaur.

Deciding that come what may, she would be able to face it; Gwenhwyvar gripped Excalibur more firmly and addressed the bewitched Sorceress. "Then let us waste no more time in this dreadful place Morgan." With all of her majesty, Gwenhwyvar strode forward, fearlessly leading the way. She walked up to and passed through the cavern entrance without so much as a brief hesitation. It took Morgan slightly unaware. Quickly she gathered herself and followed. They stood outside the tavern, but could then not help but look backwards at the way they had come. The image of the Minotaur's cavern floated behind then like the most realistic of tapestries. Then it began to fade. It was not dramatic, not like dispersing a beguilement spell. It was just suddenly no more.

There was nobody around, but many voices could be heard inside the tavern. "We should make our goodbye's brief" said Gwenhwyvar. "Can ye use the same magic to get us back to the knights in Wareham?" The Queen's question was responded to with vigour. "Aye mine Queen, ye can be certain of reaching our destination in just as quick a time."

Chapter 44: Avyze Village Tavern; Night

The door swung open and some of those closest to it looked up wondering who it was that was entering. To their dumfounded shock it was Gwen and Morgana. One of the men present actually screamed. This attracted the attention of everyone in the crowded inn. A shocked silence followed briefly before one of the men nearest to the door shouted, "Ye hath come to take revenge upon us for abandoning ye." This thought must have been prevalent in the tavern because a good number of those present murmured in trepidations agreement. Gwenhwyvar stepped forward still holding the sword, and must have looked the image of a woman seeking vengeance because it provoked a reaction from some who stepped back as she entered. "Calm good villagers. We hath returned triumphant!" announced Gwenhwyvar smiling broadly. Morgan carried on with the hail. "The beast hath been slain. It can no longer threaten the village of Avyze." Instead of a raucous cheer there was absolute silence. Not the effect that either of the women thought that their announcement of good cheer would bring. Garrone pushed his way through the crowd to address the two women. "Gwen, Morgana. We are sorry that we ran in fear and left ye to the mercy of that vile creature. Please forgive us." It was plain from the remorse upon his face and the look of guilt that he provoked in the villagers with his words, that he was sincere. That must have been the explanation for the anti-climactic response to the good news thought Morgan.

"Think no more of it Garrone" comforted Morgan, "In the end goodness prevailed. That is all that matters." Now there was a rowdy applaud from the villagers. It started off with all of the joyfulness and merriment that the women were expecting from the announcement. Then after the good spirits had almost subsided someone repeated that the 'beast was dead' which set off another round of loud praise and cheer.

"Come Morgan, Gwen; eat drink. Ye must be famished after such an ordeal." Garrone's words hit a note of accord with the women; both realising that they were indeed hungry and thirsty. Garrone organised a meal for the two heroines; ensuring that they had the very best that the village was able to offer of wine and mutton. Everybody wanted to talk to them and find out the details of the battle between the two women and the hideous Minotaur. Morgan shot a look to the Queen as if to bid her to take the lead. It was obvious that they did not want to reveal the exact details of how the beast came to be slain. Gwenhwyvar indulged them all with her story and the crowd sat and listed enraptured. She spoke of Morgan's abilities to enchant a sword to pierce the creature's flesh, and how bravely Morgan distracted the beast and allowed her to creep up behind it and run it through. The story must have been told over and over again many times. Each time though the villagers were just as smitten with the tale.

By the time that Gwenhwyvar finally put an end to it, insisting that they must re-commence their journey, it was midnight. Garrone insisted that they stay in the village for the night and that they could continue their journey in the morning. Morgan and Gwenhwyvar accepted the offer graciously. Just as they were to leave the tavern and be escorted to a hut that had been prepared for them a young boy burst in through the door. "The sky!" he shouted at everybody in the tavern. There was no follow-up explanation by the boy he simply looked dumbfounded and was very agitated. "What of it?" demanded Garrone. "tis red, the moon Garrone, it is red" said the boy.

This garnered a reaction from everybody. Some flung open the wooden shutters to better view the sky and others pushed past the nervous boy. Before any had ventured outside though there came a report from a few of the villagers that had positioned themselves to view the sky from the various windows in the tavern. "It is true!" shouted one villager. "Red as blood!" cried another. "It means that evil is upon us!" cried out one of the women.

Morgan realised that she would have to take command of the situation immediately before panic gripped the villagers. "No good people of Avyze," she said in a loud and authoritarian voice, "it means that evil hath been slain." Morgan indicated with a swish of her arm. "Come, let us all see the sign." She led the way outside with a string of people following her. Gwenhwyvar came up to stand beside Morgan. They looked up at Gaelach. She was in only one quarter crescent. But as the boy had said, the colour was not the usual soft white-yellow, but a deep blood red.

"See," said Morgan pointing dramatically at the moon, "a symbol that this very evening, evil hath died." The villagers were not going to disagree with Morgana's interpretation of this event. After all she was a powerful Sorceress that knew of such things. There was a general murmur of approval and acquiescence. It was as the Sorceress had said, evil has died and the moon has turned red to mark the occasion. There was nothing sinister to it at all.

Gwenhwyvar and Morgan could feel the tension dissipate. "Garrone. Ye were to escort us to a hut to rest for the night?" asked Morgan. "Aye, Morgana, Gwen; this way," he responded indicating the nearest hut to the tavern. With a last look at the wonder of the blood red moon, the women disappeared inside the hut. The plethora of villagers, now with nothing left to panic about, began to wander off to their own huts to prepare themselves for their first night free from the curse of the Minotaur.

Chapter 45: Avyze Village Tavern; Morning

Gwenhwyvar and Morgan were awake before first light and preparing themselves for the day ahead. Garrone had arranged for them to stay in one of the dwellings close to the tavern. He too must have been up prior to sunrise because he delivered a breakfast of bread, cheese and fruit to them. Morgan bid him to enter and eat with them. They sat at a small well-crafted wooden table together. "I shall see to it that ye receive two of our finest horses to aide ye journey." He announced proudly. Morgan and Gwenhwyvar were grateful but refused. "Why?" queried Garrone puzzled by the polite rejection of such a generous offer. "We shall journey on foot as is befitting a Sorceress and her apprentice," remarked Morgan, thinking that would be the end of it. But Garrone proved at this point to be a lot more astute than either of them had judged.

"Befitting for a Sorceress and her apprentice maybe," he said "But what of a Queen and a King's sister?" he let the accusation hang in the air like smoke on a rainy day. The two women were stunned. Gwenhwyvar began to repudiate the inference but he waved it away with a wry smile. "Please Gwen, or should I say Queen Gwenhwyvar; the legend of Arthur and his knights of the round table hath spread far and wide. And we know of Morgana, I mean Morgan, his sister from Gaul gone to Briton to be at his side. Simple tales told by simple folk around an evening meal." Morgan and Gwen were unsure what to do. The Queen spoke, "How long hath ye known?" her curiosity apparent. "Since I first saw ye with mine own two eyes. A red-haired woman clearly a native Briton and a blonde-haired

Sorceress that can speak Gaulish without an accent; it was easy to piece together." He was proud of his deductive reasoning. "Hath ye told anyone else in the village?" asked Morgan. He shook his head decisively. "No, no; there is no need for anybody else to know. Ye secret is safe with me. I shall not tell anyone after ye hath gone that it was Arthur's Queen and his Sister that saved us from the Minotaur. Although to this day, I am unsure why?" Morgan and Gwenhwyvar could hear the sincerity in his tone; they both believed him. "That is welcome news indeed," said a relieved Gwenhwyvar, not directly answering his question.

A quizzical look from Garrone to further enforce the query he had just posed proved too much for Morgan. "We had to undo some evil done by a brigand that was formerly in our employ Garrone. But it is done now and that what matters." He nodded and accepted the response even though it was far from resolving his original question. They finished their morning meal and Garrone said that he wanted to corral the villagers to give them a hearty goodbye. "No, Please Garrone, we wish to leave quietly," insisted Morgan. Although he protested at losing the chance for one final collective thank you from the villagers Garrone eventually acceded.

"Quickly then," bade Morgan, "Come outside and ye can witness on one more magical deed." Garrone was intrigued and dutifully followed them outside into the soft morning light. No doubt there were many of the villagers awake and already attending to their animals or crops but they were not to be seen. It was all but deserted. "Perfect," said Morgan. She hugged Garrone and wished him well. Gwenhwyvar too did the same. Morgan was practically bristling with excitement at the thought of once more using her newly acquired magical power. She chose their destination with care, Cawshall's hut outside of Wareham. The three brother Knights would be awaiting the return of the Queen and Sorceress. Gwenhwyvar and Garrone were looking expectantly at Morgan as she concentrated. It seemed to take longer this time for something to happen. Morgan's face twisted in what could almost be described as pain, or confusion. "What is it Morgan?" queried Gwenhwyvar. Morgan shook her head and waved the question away with her hand. "I shall explain later," she said.

Her face became set in a fiercely determined pose. Then Garrone noticed that the air ahead of them was shimmering; like there was an impossibly thin tapestry hanging before them. An image formed. It was of a hut somewhere near the sea. The three of them could smell the sea air. The hut had a light burning in the window. Clearly somebody was home. Garrone had never seen the like before. "Ahhhhaaaaa," was all that he could manage as words failed him. He thought that he should be saying something more expressive but could not think for the like of him what that should be. The image solidified. It was as clear as the vista that was behind the image or to the side. The only delineation was that the edge of the image shimmered ever so slightly. It formed a perfect square, tall enough for a man mounted on horseback to ride through without ducking his head.

With a final farewell to an astounded Garrone Gwenhwyvar walked boldly up to and then into the image. She became part of the scene that was suspended before him. Morgan too bade Garrone a final goodbye and followed Gwenhwyvar into the image. When they were safely inside the scene they turned back to look at him; both raising a hand to wave. Garrone instinctively did so as well. As he did, the scene faded away. In a matter of moments it was no more. He was left alone waving at nothing in particular. Contemplating the occurrence for a moment, he summarised it in a single phrase. "A powerful Sorceress indeed."

Chapter 46: Cawshall's Hut, Outside Wareham, Briton; Morning

Gwenhwyvar and Morgan were walking toward the entrance to Cawshall's hut. Gwenhwyvar was excited to once more see the Knight's that she had instructed to return here from Insula Vectis to await their return. She noticed after a while that Morgan was no longer following closely behind. Turning she saw that Morgan had stopped to catch her breath as though she had just been exerting herself. "Morgan?" she queried. Morgan looked up clutching her chest. She looked pale and drawn. "What is it; what is wrong?" she asked, concern overtaking her. "It hath taken a moment to catch up with me. But the effort of casting that spell was greater than I thought. I shall regain mine strength in a short time, I am sure." Morgan finished off her explanation with a faint smile to help reassure the Queen of her assessment. For her part, Gwenhwyvar was far from convinced, Morgan looked positively ill.

The women's conversation had alerted the inhabitants of the hut. The door swung open and a big burley man came out to see what was happening. It was Sir Galahallt. "Gwenhwyvar!" he shouted in surprise. Correcting himself immediately he said "I mean Queen Gwenhwyvar, and Lady Morgan." The revelation brought Cawshall, Guaen and Garethe scurrying out into the morning light as well.

Gwenhwyvar held up Excalibur for them all to see. "Success," she said. They ran toward her and had to stop themselves from embracing both of the women. "As I live and breathe, mine Queen, I should never hath doubted ye for a single moment," confessed

Galahallt. His face alight with glee and awe at the triumphantly returning monarch. Guaen was the next to add his delight at seeing the two women. "Tell us all everything that happened since we last saw ye. This is a joyous day. A joyous day mine Queen." He looked to Morgan who had managed to recover her composure in the meantime. Garethe did his best to add to the brother's tidings. "What dangers did ye face mine Queen, Lady Morgan? How did ye overcome them and reclaim Excalibur victoriously?"

Cawshall too was astounded to see the women. "When the knights returned to mine hut and said that ye had gone on without them I feared the worst…." But Gwenhwyvar calmed them. "We are safe and we hath returned with Excalibur. Dispatching a Minotaur and saving a Gaulish village from its evil in the process." Gwenhwyvar was not above a little boasting. She had after all achieved an amazing result in the time that they had separated from their Knightly guards. Unfortunately her reference to an ancient Greek myth was lost on all of the men present. "Mina-tor?" said Guaen unsure of what the word meant and even if he was repeating it correctly. Gwenhwyvar almost rolled her eyes. She had achieved a feat that no other woman alive had come close to paralleling, and the very men she thought to impress were clueless as to the magnitude of her accomplishment.

"Come inside, I shall tell ye everything of our adventures," said Gwenhwyvar after a monumental sigh. The men were so eager to hear all of the details of the quest they practically fell over each other to lead the way and open the door to the hut for the women. Gwenhwyvar gave a quick look to Morgan to reassure herself that the Sorceress was looking better than she had only a short time before. She did.

Cawshall played the perfect host, preparing them a meal in spite of their objections that they had already eaten. Aided by Morgan, Gwenhwyvar repeated their tale from the point of riding on the back of Alus across the water to Gaul. No detail was left out. The point of the story where the women were hiding in the secret room in Avyze village and the Roman soldier entered was mesmerising for the men. Morgan's keen eyes saw the hairs on the men's arms stand up at various points of the story, and that one in particular. Even as she retold their story to the men, Gwenhwyvar was aware of the effect that it was having on the men. This, she knew, would help solidify her position as Queen and ruler at Arthur's side. Not that there was ever any doubt, but up until this point she had not been seen as a warrior queen like those of the tribes of old Briton, prior to the Roman invasion. However, now was the time and opportunity to solidify her position in the hearts and minds of the Knights as a Queen that was fit for more than just a simple courtly life.

The retelling of their exploits took a lot longer than either of the women had anticipated. The length of time was aided by the fact that the climax of the story where the hideous beast met its death at the hands of Excalibur, expertly wielded by the Queen, had to be told from beginning to end at least three times. Eventually though the men were satisfied that they had extracted every facet of the escapade from the Queen and Sorceress. This, thought the men, was a story that they could hardly wait to tell the other Knights. Gwenhwyvar was very aware of what they were thinking and cautioned them to first seek Arthur's approval before repeating any of it. She felt that Arthur would forgo the secrecy surrounding the stealing of Excalibur once it was safely returned to his hands, but she was not absolutely certain. It was something that she could deal with when they were safely ensconced at Caerleon castle.

It was close to noon before Gwenhwyvar finally gave the order that the horses be prepared for the return journey. Before leaving to do so with his brothers, Sir Guaen posed the question to Morgan, "Shall we travel using this new magic that ye hath acquired mine Lady?" Morgan was non-committal with her response; shrugging off the question with "We shall see." When they had left the hut and Cawshall too, Gwenhwyvar probed Morgan for more information. "Morgan, ye looked pale and drawn after we had arrived back in Briton; after ye had used the new magic for the second time." It was an open-ended question designed to draw information out of the Sorceress.

Morgan responded, "This magic that I hath taken from the Minotaur is like holding two handfuls of sand; it falls away from ye grasp no matter how tightly 'tis held." I did not notice it the first time that I used the power. But the second time, I knew that it was diminished. The effort that it took to reinvigorate the spell the second time was substantial. I am unsure if I could do it once more, and over such a similarly great distance." Morgan looked to Gwenhwyvar for direction, or maybe permission to not try to use the spell again. Gwenhwyvar could see that Morgan was fretful about the thought of casting the spell for a third time. She comforted her sister-in-law. "Do not trouble thineself Morgan. Ye said that Arthur and Merlin are with King Rhydderch and Queen Ganieda? It will be the better part of a week before they return to Caerleon. We can make it back to Wales in two days, or maybe two and a half. We shall ride." The reprieve was welcome to Morgan. "Mine thanks Gwenhwyvar."

"Let us help the men prepare the mounts. We should leave and get in a good half-days ride," instructed Gwenhwyvar. They gathered up their belongings and went to do so.

***

It did not take long with the expert help of Cawshall to get everything ready for their journey. Even though he assured the Queen that his services not be paid for, Gwenhwyvar insisted that he take recompense for aiding them. He was paid with a combination of roman currency, still valued in these parts and some coins prepared by the Caerleon ironmonger. He could easily use them in Wareham, citing that passing traders had paid for his services with them. Nobody would be suspicious; Caerleon coins had found their way throughout Briton since Arthur introduced them after his ordination as King.

Cawshall gave a reverential farewell to the Queen and Sorceress. A more boisterous farewell between the knights and he followed. It was good for all of them to know that they had supporters in the land this far south and into the Saxon held areas of Briton. They ambled up the pathway to the main road turning occasionally to wave to Cawshall until they could no longer see him through the trees and scrub. Once more disguised in their grey riding clothes they made their way back on what now seemed a familiar track. They would need to follow it for some time before finally turning northward and traversing the Saxon held land of Wessex, and then over the border through the lands of the South Angles. Only then would they reach the safety of Wales.

Chapter 47: The Minotaur's Labyrinth; Early Afternoon

Garlon was nervous. He had called and called for the Minotaur from the entrance of the Labyrinth, hoping to get some sign that it was safe to enter. There was no response. If all had gone to plan, the beast would have had its fill of Merlin and, having made good on his bargain, he could collect Excalibur. Now he was moving forward warily with a flaming torch in hand. It was barely lighting the way ahead. He could not remember the way that he had taken to find the beast's chamber, but he was certain that it had not taken this long last time. Turn after turn he could feel the uneasiness welling up within him. He was unsure if he would be able to find his way back to the entrance.

After a while he saw a familiar glow from ahead of him. He remembered the spectacle of the glow-worms lighting up the Minotaur's chamber. This was it for sure. He walked in through the arched entrance. There was no fire lighting the pot on the tripod over to the right. He ran his eyes from the pot up to the ceiling to once more look upon the uncountable number of lights that the glow-worms afforded the room. Then as his vision descended to the beast's altar and below he saw the prone form of the Minotaur. Garlon could hardly believe his eyes. Had Merlin slain the beast and recovered Excalibur. He felt sick. He had arranged with the Saxon leaders to meet them in under two weeks' time. He had assured them that he would bring proof of the death of Arthur's Sorcerer, Merlin and present to them Arthur's sword. It would be a fitting symbol to show how weak the young king really was, and ripe for conquest.

Everything that he had planned and hoped for was lying in ruins before him. "No," he said feebly to nobody. He walked forward to inspect the body of the creature more closely. There was some vague hope that somehow this was some other beast and not the one with which he had struck his bargain. Even as he walked forward he knew it was a foolish hope. As he approached he could see the head of the Minotaur lying face down. There was a wound in his back. Dried blood had congealed in it. He could smell it. Kneeling down he rested his flaming torch upon the stone altar.

Faster than he could register the beast's hand flicked out and grabbed him around his throat. With every last vestige of energy that the Minotaur had he drained Garlon of his life-force. Garlon knew only in that instant that he had made a fatal mistake. It took less than three seconds of absolute terror for his life to come to an agonising end. The very energy that held his form together was sucked out of him by the mortally wounded beast. What was left began to liquefy and oozed from the grip of the Minotaur and congealed in a pile near to his head. The beast was still once more. It was not enough to reverse the damage that the sword had done. His heart was still broken. The strength that he drew from the life of Garlon was insufficient to heal him completely. He would just be able to subsist and hope that a villager happened into his lair. Maybe another life-force would help him recover? Surely it would. He needed to comfort himself that his long life was not going to end here.

There was something else. Now that he had half-mended his ruptured faerie heart, he was able to concentrate on other aspects of his being. Something was missing. He pondered upon it as he lay motionless upon the cold ground. It dawned upon him like a sunrise. Magic; he had lost a considerable portion of his magical powers. Its absence, now that he had realised it, gaped more openly than his injured heart. How could this possibly be? Never in his life had he heard of a faerie losing any magical ability. His fevered mind searched for an explanation. The only conclusion that he could reach was that the Sorceress must have had something to do with it. He became angry. If he ever recovered he would hunt-down that Sorceress and strangle her with his bare hands, forcing her to return what was his before he ended her worthless life. The beast's angry musings took more energy than he had to spare. He succumbed to his injuries and slipped into a state of deep hibernation.

Chapter 48: Caerleon Castle. Three Days Later

The trip back to Caerleon was not without its small dramas. More than once the party had to scurry away from the prying eyes of Saxon warlords' forces patrolling their land-holdings. But each time they had managed to either outwit or outmanoeuvre the dangers. Now safely back at Caerleon castle, Gwenhwyvar was feeling a little morose at returning to the routine of court-life. She kept replaying the moment that she slew the Minotaur in her head. Sometimes she wondered what would have happened if the beast did not die immediately. In that case, she would have bravely withdrew the sword and then with a single swoop sever the head of the hideous creature. A tapestry needle prick to her finger brought Gwenhwyvar back to the present. She exclaimed a small "Ouch!" which attracted the attention of Florie, Elamite and Lyonors. They all looked over at the Queen to see what had caused the minor outburst. Amhar who had been playing at the edge of the tapestry too looked up to see what had hurt his mother.

Seeing the various sets of eyes inquiring as to the problem she smiled it away. "Not concentrating enough on the task at hand," she explained to the women. Then she reassured her son, "I am not injured little one." Also since her return she had kept Amhar close by, day and night; seeing him again was a gift that she had secretly treasured more than recovering Arthur's sword. He seemed satisfied that his mother was indeed unharmed and went back to playing with the dowels of thread that were so occupying his attention.

At that moment Morgan entered the Queen's antechamber with Mordrede in tow. Once again work on the tapestry came to an immediate halt. Just like Gwenhwyvar, since being reunited with her son, the Sorceress was spending every moment with him. "Mine Queen," began Morgan in her formal courtly tone. "I hath had a vision of Arthur and Merlin's return to Caerleon." This caused excitement in the room. Servants and maids standing nearby were suddenly very attentive. "Do tell us Morgan; when is it to be?" asked Gwenhwyvar. "Tomorrow; before noon," came her reply. This elicited a mumbling of approval at the thought of the King returning to his castle.

"Excellent!" said Gwenhwyvar, we shall be ready to receive the King. Looking over to her head maid all she had to do was nod and the woman swept out of the room, no doubt to spread the word, but also to alert all of the staff to prepare. Morgan looked down at the intricate pattern being stitched into parts of the tapestry. "An exciting scene," she said knowingly. "It must be rousing to perform such work." Morgan gave a wry smile. Gwenhwyvar knew that she was being teased by her sister-in-law. Everybody had been curious as to where the Queen and Sorceress had gone with Guaen, Garethe and Galahallt. But she had ordered none of them to talk about their adventures. She wanted to relay everything to Arthur and Merlin first. The comparison of weaving a tapestry to their recent adventures was as marked as the difference between the sun and moon. But still, beneath an oath to remain silent, Morgan was at least free to hint at their recent sensational journey. "Aye Morgan, very exciting indeed," responded the Queen in a droll tone.

Chapter 49: Caerleon Castle; The Next Day

It was mid-morning before the lookout signalled the sighting of Arthur and his party. The excitement had been building since the early morning meal. As anticipated, word of Morgan's vision had spread throughout the castle and to Caerleon village as well. Upon the confirmation that it was definitely the return of the King, knights and soldiers hurried in various directions in last minute preparation to receive their lord. From the vantage point of the battlements of Caerleon, Arthur and Merlin could be seen riding side by side at the front of the knights and the foot soldiers obediently marching behind.

One would have thought that it would have taken longer for the arriving band to traverse the final leg home. But there seemed to be so much yet to be done to ensure that all was ready for the King that hardly anybody noticed.

When in good time Arthur and Merlin rode through the main Gate, all of the castle’s inhabitants had assembled. Arthur was clearly very happy to be home and it showed clearly on his face. Merlin too was a picture of relief and contentment at having returned safely from their mission to North Rheged. Arthur raised his hand in greeting to everyone present. "We return to Caerleon having secured a new land for the Kingdom. Galloway now counts itself united with us." The surprise announcement from the king drew a rapturous hurrah from the gathered crowd. As he was dismounting, Gwenhwyvar came forward to greet her husband. "I give thanks that ye hath returned to Caerleon safely," she said for all to hear. They embraced and Gwenhwyvar whispered in his ear, "We hath recovered Excalibur." Arthur had to keep himself from reacting, although those closest to him would have seen some signs on his face. Amhar's maid presented the young prince to his father. Arthur warmly picked up the toddler and in a very fatherly gesture pretended to throw the little one into the air and brought him back down for a big hug. Amhar was very amused and laughed loudly. "How is mine little boy?" he asked. Amhar was quick to respond about how he had been playing all morning and so much other information that his father could only smile.

The welcome continued for quite some time before Gwenhwyvar announced that a midday feast had been prepared. "How..." Arthur started to ask how their arrival was so well known about and prepared for, when he was given a look by his wife. "Morgan." He stated, answering his own question. He looked around for his sister and found her with Mordrede. He made a point of warmly greeting them both. The party was moving in through the main doors in dribs and drabs, the crowd began to thin out. Arthur seized upon the opportunity to quiz Gwenhwyvar more about the recovery of Excalibur. "How did ye come by it; was it a vision of Morgan's"? He looked about him to ensure that nobody else was in hearing distance. "It was recovered in Gaul," the approaching proximity of Sir Lyonell prevented the Queen from elaborating upon the statement. For Arthur this only raised more questions than it answered.

"Mine King," said Sir Lyonell as he passed by the both of them on his way inside. And that is how the conversation continued between Arthur and Gwenhwyvar. They stole every moment that they could. Gwenhwyvar using each precious point in time to give just a little more of the story, from the time that they rode to Cellewig and then onwards to the seek guidance from the Lady of the Lake through to their travels in Sussex, to Insula Vectis and onwards to Gaul. During the feast, more of the story came to light. Arthur found that he was creating opportunities for he and Gwenhwyvar to be alone, often sending those sitting closest to them on petty errands for anything that he could think of. Ensure that the mare is properly watered after the journey. Go to the kitchen and see if they have any more of the previous course left. Arthur's behaviour was unusual to say the least. There were plenty of servants that could have done his bidding. But in each case he made the recipient feel as though he were entrusting this particular task directly to them.

By the time Gwenhwyvar had reached the part about the Minotaur, Arthur had run out of excuses to send those situated closest to them away. He was clearly agitated and struggled to contain himself. He was completely absorbed in Gwenhwyvar's tale. Also intrusive were people's questions about his journey to North Rheged, which now, by comparison to his wife's travels, seemed inconsequential. The battle at sea drew most of the comments and questions from the feasters. Eventually Arthur waved away all questions about it and stated that the Knights could tell the story better than he.

At one point, well into the meal, Gwenhwyvar looked over to Morgan, she was listening intently to everything that Merlin was telling her. It must have been about the journey north to Pen Rhionydd. Gwenhwyvar knew that Morgan would not tell Merlin about the journey to recover Excalibur until she was given leave to do so. It must have been very frustrating for her. However, Gwenhwyvar also knew that Morgan was a patient woman. The meal would end in good time. And eventually it did.

Arthur rose to give the final blessing for the bounty of their land and the success of their journey. He finished off his short speech with an unexpected epilogue. "Now Merlin and Morgan please accompany Gwenhwyvar and me to mine study so that we may discuss the tactical implications of bringing Galloway into our fold," he said. There was a murmur of feint surprise from the crowd. When were Morgan and Gwenhwyvar ever included in Merlin and Arthur's strategy sessions? It was really quite unprecedented; there would be talk of it throughout the castle.

Pretending to not notice the minor ruckus that he had caused with his announcement, he offered his hand to his wife who dutifully took it. They gracefully left the banquet table and exited the hall. Merlin, a little perplexed at the sudden need to once more strategise with the King, did the same for Morgan. They followed the King and Queen from the room.

On the way to the King's study, Merlin sought to quiz Morgan on the need for this session. "Surely the King and Queen would hath better use for this time than a military planning session?" he looked curiously at Morgan hoping to get some hint as to whether or not she knew something about the meeting. "The King hath had the Queen's ear for the entire banquet Merlin. Gwenhwyvar hath been relaying a story that no-doubt he wished to impart to ye." Morgan's answer was mysterious to say the least. "Story?" he further enquired. "Patience

Merlin, all in good time" she responded. A little irritated at the lack of forthcoming information he contented himself that the King's library was not that far away and all would soon be revealed. He gave Morgan a peeved look hoping that it would result in further clarification from his former pupil. It did not. He sighed, making her smile.

"Does this story have something to do with the recovery of Excalibur?" asked the cunning old man. Morgan almost stopped in her tracks, but managed to shoot Merlin a forced vexed look and inquired, "Excalibur hath been recovered?" she said as innocently as she could manage. The obvious ploy of pretending not to know what he was talking about resulted in him giving one final snort of displeasure.

Chapter 50: The King's Library; Afternoon

Merlin was obviously confused and becoming more and more irate at the secrecy that surrounded this sudden need for a military planning session that included the Queen and Morgan. Before anything was said however, Morgan recited the faerie expulsion spell. It was done without prompting from anyone. At its conclusion, there was no obvious faerie suddenly appearing and making a hasty exit. They knew that they were not being spied upon. All eyes turned to Merlin. The other three were looking at him almost waiting for him to make the first verbal move. He did not disappoint and went straight to the heart of the matter. "How was Excalibur recovered? I can sense in both the Queen and mine over-confident former pupil that it hath indeed been rescued from the thieves hands. So what is the story behind this wonderful happening?" Arthur, Gwenhwyvar and Morgan knew that there was no fooling Merlin. Signalling that his wife should begin the proceedings, Gwenhwyvar dutifully began the story at the point where Arthur and his party left Caerleon for North Rheged. Morgan intervened with every second sentence, just as though it had been some well-rehearsed pantomime. And so the complete story unfolded before the ever-growing incredulousness of the men. At the point where Gwenhwyvar suggested to Morgan that they seek guidance from the Lady of the Lake, Merlin visibly stiffened. Unsure if it was disapproval at the very idea or just plain shock that they would do such a thing, neither of the women knew. But they did not stop their re-telling of the events to find out.

Not a detail was left out about the journey to Cellewig and trying their best to not let on to the three brothers about the real intention of their mission to West Wales. The meeting with Nimue and how events in the faerie kingdom had unfolded after the battle of Anderidae was another point where Merlin was visibly tense. Any mention of the faeries however drew a similar response since Arthur's defeat at the hands of Aelle those few short years ago. Both Merlin and Arthur were leaning forward as Gwenhwyvar related the scene of them arriving at the shore of Llyn Callyfyrth and Gwenhwyvar calling for the Lady of the Lake. Merlin could not help himself any longer; he interjected. "Did she appear?" he said, the desperate need for an answer clear in his tone. "Aye," responded the Queen. Merlin drew in his breath in awe.

Both Morgan and Gwenhwyvar carefully spoke about everything that they had discussed with the ancient mysterious being. The most pertinent part after they had found out the whereabouts of the sword was the question about the faerie involvement in Arthur's defeat. When the women revealed that it was a plot between Hellekin and Aelle and only a few choice faeries both Arthur and Merlin erupted in flood of follow-up questions. Morgan and Gwenhwyvar had to deflect all of them though. "The Lady simply disappeared. Our audience was at an end," explained Morgan. The disappointment on both Arthur and Merlin's faces was understandable. Gwenhwyvar offered a quantum of solace; "We too would like to hath know much more about the situation, but it was just not to be. I am sorry Arthur." Gwenhwyvar touched Arthur's cheek with her hand. He raised his to clasp her hand and asked her to continue with the story.

Merlin however was lost in wonderment. "The Lady is Matrona, the faerie Queen from an eon ago. 'tis hard to fathom." Realising that he was interrupting the flow of the retelling of events he apologised and begged for the women to continue their recount.

The journey through Saxon-filled Wessex and Sussex to Cahshall's hut and then onwards by boat to the island of Vectis once more had Arthur and Merlin entranced. The meeting with Alus and the bargain of safe passage across the water to Gaul was handled as modestly as possible by Morgan. Both women could see that Merlin was itching to find out more about the water horse, but it would have interrupted the flow of the story and he was too enraptured with the magnificence of the women's bravery and shrewdness to do so. The acceptance of the villagers of Avyze and hiding from the Roman soldiers brought Merlin into the story. "Morgan, ye say that ye saw me die in a dream?" "Aye Merlin, I was not sure if it was a vision of what was to happen or what had happened already; but I felt that ye were still alive somewhere and had no other course of action to take other than concluding that I was helpless in Gaul to offer ye assistance."

Merlin walked forward and took hold of both of Morgan's hands. "Morgan, ye did give me assistance. When I saw ye in mine dream, I thought that it was a signal that ye hath found Excalibur. But the clarity of the dream and thine presence in it gave me the clue that it was a foretelling of the near future; and it meant that I was free to plan for the Gael raider. I convinced Arthur to take all of the knights and as many soldiers with us across the sea to Mann. We battled with them just as happened in ye dream." He leaned forward with a sly smile, "But we were victorious. This time it was Morgan and Gwenhwyvar's turn to breathe a sigh of relief. "Continue," asked the old Sorcerer.

Gwenhwyvar was careful to squeeze Arthur's hand during the retelling of her killing the Roman that could have brought his compatriots into the hiding place in the grain store. Arthur was proud of his wife, but could not help the feeling of dread as he imagined how that scene could have gone horribly wrong. The mood was lifted however when they spoke of how they gathered the able-bodied villagers to mount an attack on the Minotaur's lair. "Good work Gwenhwyvar," praised Arthur "gathering a battle force to slay this foul beast. And ye were successful?" he finished assuming that somehow the villagers together with Morgan and Gwenhwyvar had then killed the Minotaur. "No," replied the Queen. "When we finally encountered the beast in his labyrinth his body could not be pierced with swords or pitch-forks or scythes.

Morgan chipped-in about how the young villager was ambushed by the beast and drained of his life-force. This almost provoked Merlin to seek more information but yet again he contained himself for the sake of not interrupting the story. The flight of the villagers and then of the women through the labyrinth and Morgan's unsuccessful attempt to use magic to tunnel their way to the surface almost had Arthur and Merlin falling forward they were leaning toward the women and concentrating so fiercely on what was being said. When Morgan revealed her plan to use the beguilement spell to imitate the chalk-cave walls Merlin could finally not help himself any longer. He clapped his hands gleefully together at the very thought of the spell being used in such a way. "Brilliant Morgan!" he praised clearly delighted with her ingenuity. "And the beast could not see ye?" he asked seeking confirmation that it had indeed worked as she had surmised that it could.

Morgan continued, "It was then that I had the idea of confronting the beast disguised as Matrona. Surely even he would tremble at the thought of defying a former faerie Queen and an immortal one at that." Morgan and Gwenhwyvar then split the retelling of the climax of the confrontation with the Minotaur. Morgan telling the events leading up to and including her clever disguise being stripped away by the beast; followed by Gwenhwyvar taking up the scene from there. She explained how her former experience with Excalibur, and Matrona's reference to it being in service to the authority that she wishes to govern a united land, were combined into realisation that she could wield the sword as effectively as if Arthur was holding it.

Gwenhwyvar seemed far away, the three of them could see it in her eyes. She physically re-enacted her moment of triumph, driving the sword through the beast's back and through his heart. "The Minotaur fell to the ground; dead," said Gwenhwyvar completing the tale of their recent adventure. The silence and obvious awe from Merlin and Arthur was more resonant than the loudest applause. Gwenhwyvar could feel the love and admiration emanating from Arthur directed at his sister and at herself. She could actually feel it touching her body as if it were a tangible thing that was created and handed to her like the finest of all gowns or the most precious of all jewellery.

Arthur moved forward and embraced his wife at length. Merlin too could not help but hold Morgan in his arms again, as though they had never separated. Merlin was the first to break the mood though. He was proud of Morgan but did not want to reignite the flame of their love. He had more important matters to attend to; staying at Arthur's side until the country was one, united beneath King Arthur Pendragon. He pulled away and began what could easily have been a flood of questions and statements. "There is so much information to consider here that it is difficult to know where to begin." He paused only for a brief moment, clearly centering on exactly what he thought was the most important aspect of the information gathered from the women. "Firstly; we now know that the entire faerie people are not conspiring against us. This evil King Hellekin will need to be dealt with. And any king that hath deceived his people is in a precarious position, when his deception is discovered." He stopped and changed the subject, a result of so many thoughts colliding and crossing over in his mind. "Where then is Excalibur?" he asked.

"In our chamber since our return; standing guard outside the royal chamber day and night are Guaen, Galahallt and Garethe in turn. They refuse to hand over the duty to a soldier," explained the Queen. Merlin nodded in understanding, he had wondered where Guaen was during the banquet; it must have been his turn to stand guard, he surmised. Merlin's thoughts now encompassed the recent journey to Galloway and the discovery he made there. "We no longer need to consider the deployment of Christians in Northumbria or Wales, Arthur. It is a small battle with Hellekin and his conspirers that we should plan for." This explanation made absolutely no sense at all to either Morgan or Gwenhwyvar. Morgan interceded, "Christians Merlin; the Roman religion from Antioch?" her perplexed tone apparent. Merlin realised that he had not briefed her about his discovery and planned use for the magical cancelling abilities of these mysterious religious people. "Morgan, we must talk at length regarding the Roman religion from Antioch. There are aspects to it that defy explanation. Magical people that cannot perform magic, in fact they seem blissfully unaware of its presence and prevent it from occurring without knowing that they do." He completed his abridged explanation leaving Morgan none the wiser. "As ye say Merlin, we shall need to speak at length," she said, not wanting to deflect the subject of conversation. Hellekin's conspiring with Aelle to defeat Arthur in battle was quite a lot to think about already..

Merlin was pacing up and down while his mind raced through possibilities. "Hellekin made an alliance with Aelle for the battle at Anderidae. If he hath done so once, then he may do so again. We do not yet know his reasons for forging this alliance with the Saxon? Will there be more secret alliances with Aelle or other Saxons? The four of them engaged in a game of strategy each offering circumstances and possible explanations for the faerie King's actions.

Merlin brought the proceedings to order. "Tell me once more what Nimue said when ye encountered her in the forest?" he asked to either Gwenhwyvar or Morgan. It was Gwenhwyvar that responded. "Twas a band of renegade faeries that assisted Hellekin in the defeat of Arthur. We hath offered an ultimatum that if he turns over the renegades to us, then we may consider allowing ye to help them with their fertility problem." The Queen finished the summary and took position on a stool next to Merlin. The conniving old Sorcerer pondered the information for a few moments, doing his usual pose of stroking his neatly beard. He seemed to reach a conclusion and he imparted it to the trio. "Nimue will hath delivered the ultimatum to Hellekin by now. He hath no way of delivering the renegades to us because they simply do not exist. How will he meet the obligation that ye hath put forward Gwenhwyvar?" It was a rhetorical question; none of them expected that they would know the devious answer.

Merlin continued to outline his scheme. "He will not." It was somewhat of an anti-climax for the audience. There was just about to be an objection from all three when he added "We give Nimue the proof that she needs to undermine Hellekin's rule. She and the faerie authority whomever they are, can take care of this insolent faerie on our behalf. We need only plant the seed and wait for events to unfold." He completed his plan with such a confident tone and smile that it was difficult to find fault with it. Arthur, Gwenhwyvar and Morgan all exchanged looks. It was as though they were challenging each other to come up with some reason why this course of action would not succeed. There was silence.

Merlin knew that he had devised a certain plot to unravel the rule of the current faerie King. This as he had said at the beginning of their discussions, was the first order of business. Remove the most apparent threat. This would see to that. There was a further moment of contemplation between the four of them. If this indeed would remove the threat that King Hellekin had proved himself to be, what was next? Merlin interjected with what was next on his list of things to take care of. "There shall be no help for the faerie population from mine magic; nor yours Morgan," he all but commanded, adding, "If the Lady of the Lake sees no value in the continuance of the faerie people, then neither do I."

There was a collective sigh. The events of the afternoon had been exhausting. It was lucky that they had all feasted beforehand, otherwise it would have been time to eat once more. All four of them felt drained somehow. There still seemed so much to consider from the events that had unfolded since the theft of Excalibur. Now that his one component had a plan of action, the rest of the events would have to be reckoned with. What of Galloway, a Christian outpost; should it be left to follow its strange Roman religion? Now that the Lady of the Lake has been secured as a source of information, what more could they hope to obtain from her? Sirs Galahallt, Guaen and Garethe were in receipt of confidential information, should they be allowed to disseminate it to the knights, and then onwards to the soldiers, staff and greater Caerleon village? Once King Hellekin is dealt with, shall Aelle be challenged for his hold upon Anderidae? Without a faerie King ally, what hope would he have if the battle was fought once more?

Morgan held on to her own questions that were not shared by the group. Would Gwenhwyvar make it known that magical powers were stolen from the Minotaur and used successfully to travel hundreds of miles in a matter of moments? What would Merlin make of the theft of another magical being's power? Had this kind of thing ever been recorded in his vast library of scrolls? Had he ever head of such an occurrence before? What would he think of her new ability to steal magical prowess?

The pondering could have gone on for much longer, but Merlin brought everybody's thoughts back into the room. "Let us dispense with the evil King Hellekin immediately." There was a shocked response from all three. A triumvirate of "How?" erupted from them. Merlin was sanguine with his response. He produced a small stone from within his robes and offered it to Morgan. Arthur and Gwenhwyvar were none the wiser. "What is it," asked Arthur. "A memory stone," replied Morgan. She looked to Merlin for more specific guidance on exactly how he wanted it to be used. He said, "Recall your conversation with Matrona, only the part where she reveals Hellekin's deception; no more." He saw Morgan placing the stone to her forehead. He looked at the King and Queen and told them what was happening. "Morgan will place the memory in the stone. It is a magical device that cannot be corrupted or fooled. The very words of Matrona and yourself," he motioned to Gwenhwyvar; "and Morgan's thoughts at the time will be transcribed into the stone. We shall give it to Nimue as proof of Hellekin's treachery. She will be able to read it, and more importantly share it with all of her kind. Hellekin will hath no recourse, his trickery will be revealed to his people." Merlin's expression showed his satisfaction at causing the dishonest leader the absolute level of mayhem that would follow such a revelation.

He stood up from his stool and walked over to the window. It was sunset. He realised that they had spent the entire afternoon talking. Summoning his vocal strength he called out Nimue's name in a pitch and volume that only a bird, or fox, or faerie could possibly hear. Arthur and Gwenhwyvar perceived the call without actually being able to hear it.

"How will ye handle this transfer of knowledge?" inquired Arthur. "With great care" replied the old man, clearly not willing to clarify his intentions any further. Arthur rolled his eyes. There was a moment of silence and then Merlin questioned Morgan. "Ye said that Nimue took the form of a stag to kill Aelle's spies whilst ye were travelling to Cellewig?" Morgan indicated that was indeed what had happened. "Curious," he said. "Faeries cannot change gender; at least not that I know of." He trailed off pondering the conundrum. Morgan took up the point with her former teacher. "Aye Merlin; surely that is described in thine scrolls. Do ye think that Nimue hath exceptional powers compared to her faerie brethren? Or do ye think that it is something else?" Morgan's question looked in danger of being unanswered, but eventually Merlin came back from his meditative state. "I think that Nimue hath unique abilities even amongst her own kind." That appeared to be the end of the topic. Neither Morgan nor Merlin said another word about it.

The time passed slowly. Without realising it all four of them were now looking out the window at the setting sun. It was precisely why Arthur had his library built on this side of the Castle. He had often watched the sun go down from his favourite place in the room. The window was high-up as the castle wall and the hill dropped off quite dramatically from this point. It would have taken a ladder to reach it, if the Castle were ever under attack. Nevertheless, the shutter was much thicker than normal, as it was still classified as a low-lying window by military tactical standards.

Whatever thoughts were going through the minds of the four, they were interrupted by a white dove fluttering noisily to the window ledge. It must have been Nimue. The dove regarded the inhabitants of the room for a moment before flapping into the room and transforming into human form. Nimue took a single step forward and bowed gracefully before Arthur and then Gwenhwyvar. She accompanied the show of courtly custom with a gently spoken "King Arthur" and "Queen Gwenhwyvar." It was clear that Nimue was being particularly courteous and genial. Arthur did not acknowledge the faerie; instead he turned to Merlin as if motioning for him to take over the situation.

"Nimue," began Merlin as he walked forward to position himself between her and the Royal couple. "The Queen and Morgan hath told me of ye plight and the deal that ye wishes to strike with King Arthur." This provoked from Nimue an expression of expectant hope, her eyes widened as if she were about to hear exactly the news that she so desperately wanted to. "Information is power Nimue. And I wish to give ye the power to help the faerie people. Help them move beyond the tyrannical leadership of Hellekin, the liar." Merlin let his final sentence hang before the shocked faerie. She looked as though she were about to shake her head from her shoulders. "What say ye Merlin? Power to….Hellekin a liar?" she was totally confused.

"Who is the one faerie above all others that ye would trust Nimue?" asked Merlin. This further muddied the conversational waters for the mystified faerie. "Trust?" she said. Then appearing to clutch at thoughts that were unable to be commandeered, she threw her hands up in the air. "Merlin ye are speaking in riddles. I trust mine own judgement and I trust that King Hellekin hath the best interests of his people at heart." Her tone had an inflection of irritation. This was not working out as she had anticipated when she heard Merlin's call.

"Matrona surely," stated Merlin as if it were an undeniable fact. The very mention of the now mythical former Queen of the faerie people who had supposedly attained immortality and then completely disappeared from the faerie populous brought Nimue to a frozen halt. "What do ye know Merlin? What do ye know of Matrona? Tell me!" her words were both demanding and pleading simultaneously.

"Matrona knows what is in the hearts of faeries Nimue; Hellekin's especially." The thought was beyond tempting. To consult with Matrona herself about their problem; she would know the location of the lost spell of fertility. Surely she would help them. Merlin must have found a way to contact the immortal former Queen. "Merlin!" she shouted, all of her previous graciousness now abandoned. "What do ye know of Matrona?" Nimue was edging towards rage at having such a thought dangled before her. Merlin extended his left hand to Morgan. She responded by moving forward and giving Nimue a contemptuous glare, she placed a small white stone into the palm of his hand.

Merlin then brought it up to his face as if to study it for a brief moment before extending his hand forward to Nimue, offering the stone to her. Perplexed she gingerly reached for it. Her movements suggested that she was expecting it to disappear before she could touch it. But nothing happened. She held it before her eyes. She could feel that there were thoughts held within the stone. Looking at Merlin she sought confirmation of her assessment, "A memory stone?" she asked. Merlin nodded, "A memory stone. Read it Nimue as if it were the most valuable scroll known to the faerie people. For it contains words from Matrona herself."

Nimue needed no further encouragement. She quickly placed the stone to her forehead and allowed the coherent stream of thoughts to enter her mind. It was true. Matrona! It was unbelievable. Nimue could see her as though she were in Morgan's place during the actual conversation with the immortal being. She could see Matrona clearly standing on the water of a lake somewhere she did not recognise. "King Hellekin in collusion with King Aelle, engineered the defeat of Arthur at Anderidae, using his own personal guards to substitute Arthur's horses on the night before battle. The ruler hath convinced his people that it was the interference of outsiders. But there are many now that question his veracity." Morgan's thoughts at that very moment in time could also be heard. "The faeries hath been betrayed by their own king." The memory was concluded, there was nothing more stored within the stone.

That seemed to be the conclusion of the stream of thought, but then something else crystallised in Nimue's mind's eye. Matrona was speaking once more. "Indeed her unborn child was aborted by Hellekin in fear of what the future held for the baby. He had a vision that the girl would grow into a powerful sorceress that recovered the spell of fertility and sacrificed his body to ensure its success. It was a display of degenerated selfishness that strengthens my resolve to no longer give assistance to the faeries."

Nimue's eyes snapped open. She brought the stone down from her forehead and clutched it with such ferocity it was in danger of breaking her skin. There was silence in the room. Nobody dared to speak. Nimue was shaking with anger; it oozed from every pore of her flawless skin. Her child murdered by Hellekin, the king that she had put her trust in to help all of the faerie people. Without a word Nimue turned and strode toward the window, stopping only to conceal the stone within her faerie silk robes. Merlin interrupted her exit. "What will ye do Nimue?" There was a long pause. For a while it seemed that Nimue was too upset to speak or formulate a coherent response to Merlin's question. But then she responded without turning around. "Present Matrona's words to mine people." With that, she transformed into an owl and flapped into the twilight.

"What now?" queried Arthur. "How shall we see what effect the news has on the faerie people?" It was the question that they were all thinking. Gwenhwyvar offered a solution. "Morgan, use the magic that ye took from the Minotaur to follow Nimue. Let us know what happens." Morgan dreaded the effect that the words would have even as they were spoken by the Queen. Merlin spun around to face Morgan. "Magic taken from the Minotaur?" he said in a baffled tone. Morgan was hoping to avoid telling Merlin about her new-found ability until a future time. Now it seemed that an explanation was required. Merlin continued, "There was no mention of taking magic from the Minotaur in the recounting of ye adventures." He was now addressing both Morgan and Gwenhwyvar.

The Queen nodded and apologised. "Mine apologies Merlin; I hath completely forgotten until this moment. Morgan can explain what happened and what wondrous things she can now do." Arthur, Merlin and Gwenhwyvar waited expectantly for Morgan to describe the events in question. In order to prevent a lengthy story she summarised it as best as she could. "I found that I could remove magic from the dead beast and wrap mine body in it like it was a fine cloth. I can feel that a portion of the creature's magical prowess is now mine to command. But each time I use it, the magic diminishes." Merlin was astounded, even more than he was that the women sought out the Lady of the Lake for assistance in recovering Excalibur.

"Never hath I head of such an occurrence in all of mine studies throughout all of mine life," concluded the old Sorcerer. "What is it that ye can do with this magic?" he asked. "Travel great distances in the blink of an eye; but it takes a great effort. Her caveat fell upon deaf ears. Arthur looked to Merlin for guidance in this situation. The delay in potentially once more experiencing the thrill of travelling so far in such a short time was too much for Gwenhwyvar. "Come Morgan, take us to the faerie forest. We could arrive before Nimue," she suggested.

Strangely it was Merlin that put an end to the idea. "No mine Queen. We do not need to see what Nimue does with this information. We shall let it find its own course, and in time discover what recourse the faerie people hath with their treacherous king." He turned to address Morgan. "We should talk about this at length. And there is much that I wish to tell ye about mine experiences at Pen

Rhionydd. Come to mine chambers tomorrow at noon and we shall document them together." Merlin's words seemed to put an end to any further discussion on the subject. Morgan was relieved. She wanted nothing more than to see Mordrede put to bed this evening, and tell him a bed-time story. Travelling to the faerie forest in the hope of spying on Nimue in the growing darkness was very unappealing to her.

Hoping that her motherly instincts would deflect any further want of a magical display from the Queen, Morgan added voice to her thoughts. "I should be leaving to see to Mordrede. It is time for him to go to sleep." She bowed to the King and Queen. Morgan's ploy was effective. Gwenhwyvar's thoughts now instantaneously turned to Amhar. "Aye Morgan, and we should see Amhar safely to sleep as well. The four of them left the King's library together to see to their immediate business.

Chapter 51: One Month Later; Early Afternoon

King Hellekin's birthday celebration was becoming a yearly event. This was unusual in the faerie kingdom as faeries life-spans were so long that they only celebrated significant birthdays. But Hellekin had made a proclamation that given the dark times that the faeries were facing celebrations should abound to keep their minds from dwelling upon their plight too much. Nimue had insisted on organising the entire gathering for Hellekin and had forbidden him from seeing her final preparations. She made him promise to leave the King's hollow at first light and not return until the celebration was in full-swing in the early afternoon, so that he could make a grand entrance.

Hellekin had noticed Nimue's absence on an almost daily basis in the month leading up to his birthday. He had questioned her on her whereabouts many times, but she had laughed it off saying that it had something to do with the preparations for the banquet. He had dutifully spent the day with some of his closest advisors running in the eastern most part of the forest as horses. The freedom that he felt striding along was exhilarating. Nevertheless his thoughts kept turning back upon his own selfishness to be pleased. Whatever Nimue had planned it was sure to be quite a sight. If he had not been so completely self-absorbed he may have noticed the look of pure contempt that Nimue occasionally shot at Hellekin over the past month. It was coming on to the time when he was due to make his grand entrance to his birthday party.

Transforming himself into his full-sized human form he waited for his advisors to catch up with him and they too took on their human forms. "Let us return to mine hollow for the celebrations" he said. The advisor closest to him did not fail to take the opportunity to ingratiate himself to the King. "An excellent decision sire; Nimue will hath surely prepared the most splendid of gatherings in thine honour." With that, they transformed into sparrows and flew toward the faerie forest.

***

Even as he approached he knew that there was a sizeable gathering in the hollow. He could feel the faerie presence from far away. It pleased him to be the cause for so much gaiety. Landing on the lip of the hole that was the entrance he gently thrust himself downwards whilst simultaneously taking on his miniature faerie form. The celebration was indeed in full swing, faeries filled the hollow, more than he had ever seen come to the hollow before. The cacophony of their talking was so loud that he could hardly believe it. There was almost no place for him to land, but he found a space and dramatically dropped to the floor raising his arms as if to embrace the closest of his subjects. "I hath arrived mine good subjects" he gleefully announced in the loudest voice that he could muster, hoping that it would be heard above the din.

There was a collective gasp from what sounded like everyone in the room. Then dead silence. The faeries nearest to him backed away from him as though he was diseased. Hellekin was dumbfounded. This was not the reaction that he had expected. Surely they were expecting him at his own birthday celebrations? He looked around at the faces of those surrounding him. They were positively hostile. Their expressions ones of disgust, revile, and pure hatred. Hellekin was now irate at such an inhospitable welcome from his lowly subjects. "What is the meaning of this?" he demanded. Nobody answered. This aggravated him all the more. "Somebody answer me I command it!" he shouted.

"Ye are no longer in a position to give demands Hellekin," it was Nimue's voice. But he could not immediately see where it came from. As if by some hidden signal, faeries now parted so that Hellekin had a direct line of sight to Nimue. She was seated on his throne wearing the faerie crown. Hellekin was shocked. He took a few moments to overcome the absolute bewilderment that he felt at seeing his concubine seated on *his* throne. Then he became angry once more. He pointed an accusing finger at her "How dare ye sit upon mine throne Nimue!" The confrontational gesture was insulting beyond words. "Get up and give me mine crown immediately or I shall hath ye punished."

Unwilling to wait for a response because he was so enraged, he then called for his men. "Guards!" he shouted. In an instant the royal guards that were hanging as moths above the gathering fluttered downwards and took on their faerie forms. He clenched his fist and ordered them, "Drag Nimue off mine throne and give me mine crown!" he was absolutely livid. The guards made no effort to obey him. "What are you waiting for?" he said looking at the nearest one. He did not recognise the guard though. Looking from one to the other, he realised that all of these guards were new. He had not seen any of them before. "Where are mine guards?" he demanded.

"They hath been replaced Hellekin, just as ye hath been." Nimue had a look of contempt on her face that was more than Hellekin's ego could bear. He made to stride toward her and forcibly eject her from the throne himself. Two of the guards closest to him grabbed him by his arms preventing him from approaching Nimue. He struggled with them and shouted louder, "I am thine king release me or I shall hath ye flogged!"

Nimue stood up from the throne. She took steps slowly toward him as she spoke. "I hath been declared Queen in thine absence Hellekin." Hellekin was further enraged at the very prospect of his being replaced. "What nonsense is this? Queen Nimue? I am the King of the faerie people by right of magical competition. Do ye challenge me? I shall defeat any challenger to mine rule" he struggled more with his captors who held him securely.

"It was ye who made me Queen, Hellekin," replied Nimue rather mysteriously "By taking away mine future, Ellergia, I hath nothing to live for except to see the faerie people able to once more procreate." She had now closed the distance between them. She took his face in one hand and continued "I shall give mine life to ensure the continuance of the faerie people." Her grip tightened. Hellekin froze. The very mention of Ellergia drew the blood from his face. "I can see it in thine eyes even as I say her name, the guilt of murdering an unborn child." Nimue pushed his face to one side in disgust unable to look upon it any more. She turned and made her way back to her throne.

Hellekin knew that he had to think quickly. "What proof do ye hath of such a cruel accusation?" he would have continued but

Nimue spun around and threw down a small stone to the floor. It rolled toward Hellekin. He looked at it with some trepidation. Nimue had stretched out her hand and was reciting a spell. He recognised it; it was a spell that only he should have known. One that was included in the faerie magical spell archives. Nimue must have already availed herself of the wealth of knowledge that it offered.

The stone began to glow brightly. Then a scene filled the hollow. It was a lake somewhere. There were two women; one standing at the shore and the other standing on the water. He recognised one as Queen Gwenhwyvar, the other he did not. She was speaking,"King Hellekin in collusion with King Aelle, engineered the defeat of Arthur at Anderidae, using his own personal guards to substitute Arthur's horses on the night before battle. The ruler hath convinced his people that it was the interference of outsiders. But there are many now that question his veracity." Hellekin looked around him uneasily. "Her unborn child was aborted by Hellekin in fear of what the future held for the baby. He had a vision that the girl would grow into a powerful sorceress that recovered the spell of fertility and sacrificed his body to ensure its success. It was a display of degenerated selfishness that strengthens my resolve to no longer give assistance to the faeries."

Hellekin was appalled. His secrets had been laid bare before his subjects. He grasped at whatever small hope he could think of. "Lies!" he screamed "Who is this woman that accuses me of such treachery. I shall hath her executed for such a heinous crime" Nimue was unimpressed. "Matrona" replied Nimue, causing Hellekin to choke on his words of threat. He looked this way and that hoping for something from the onlookers to aide him. Finding nothing he continued with his argument to place doubt in the accusation "How could that possibly be Matrona, she is a legend nothing more."

"I discovered the whereabouts of the lake in this memory; it was recognised by one of the oldest of our kind. So I journeyed there to seek out Matrona for help." Hellekin could see that he had achieved nothing. He had not managed to cast the slightest doubt on the vision. Nimue drew out another memory stone and flicked it on to the floor, it landed expertly beside the first. Once more reciting the secret spell, the contents were made visible to everyone in the hollow.

Chapter 52: Llyn Callyfyrth One Week Earlier - Noon

Nimue stood at the shore of the lake and beheld its striking beauty. She called "Matrona; Matrona please grant me an audience." There was silence. Nimue's thoughts could be heard "If Matrona will not speak with me I shall not hath the evidence that I need to depose the King." Once more and with desperation in her voice she called "Matrona, I seek the truth of our existence, I beg ye please hear mine plea."

The water before Nimue formed itself into the shape of a woman. Features appeared and became defined. She was more beautiful in reality than she had appeared in the vision contained within the memory stone. There was a moment of exaltation that Nimue felt that was recorded in the stone and felt by the faeries now witnessing its recital. "Queen Matrona," began Nimue, "I hath seen the record of thine meeting with Queen Gwenhwyvar and Morgan Le Fay the Sorceress. Now I hath come to beg for the spell of fertility for the faerie people. Please do not turn away from us in our hour of need."

Matrona responded, "No help will the faerie people derive from me Nimue. King Hellekin is the embodiment of all that is wrong with the faerie nation. Do not come here again, and spread the word throughout the faerie people to leave me in peace."

Nimue was ready for this contingency and skilfully countered. "I shall depose King Hellekin with the help of the senior advisors and then willingly give mine life to ensure the success of the fertility spell once more." Nimue's act of selflessness surprised Matrona. She regarded Nimue more closely. "If only more faeries were like ye Nimue, then perhaps our race would not be doomed to extinction." This was not the response that Nimue had anticipated. She had no more strategy to display; this was a one-shot battle that had not resulted in the victory that she had predicted.

"Go Nimue, leave this place and do not return," said Matrona. Nimue pleaded just once more. "Is there no hope of us recovering the spell?" Paradoxically Matrona offered Nimue a glimmer of hope. "There is always hope Nimue" she said. Her features dissolved into the clear water of the lake and her form returned from whence it came. Nimue was alone.

Epilogue: The Queen's Hollow

Hellekin knew that he was defeated, absolutely, and without any hope of redemption. He was embarrassed, humiliated, his indiscretions and deceitfulness laid bare for all to see. He could barely lift his head to address Nimue. "What of me?" he enquired. His voice was barely audible. She did not answer him directly but spoke the answer to her subjects as the first of her royal commands. "Let Hellekin former king of the faerie people be banished from the faerie nation. No faerie in this country is to fraternise with him or help him in any way. Should he be seen by another faerie, he should be moved on from that area to wander the land alone, rejected by all."

At first Hellekin could not believe how easily he was being punished. Nimue had the right to see him executed for his crimes. Aborting an unborn faerie, even a half-human faerie hybrid was punishable by death. His crimes were many; misuse of a privileged faerie spell, the abortion spell; not to mention involving faeries in a human battle. These were the most deplorable of things that any faerie could do. This explained the reception that had greeted him when he arrived. But to simply be banished, the punishment did not seem to fit the magnitude of his crimes.

He looked at Nimue, vexed by her compassion. But slowly he began to realise that she had thought through his punishment very carefully. He was accustomed to a life of privilege. He had never had to forage for food. Never felt the cold of winter, he was always wrapped in exquisite faerie silken gowns. He was born into a powerful family and was raised as an only son tends to be raised; believing that he was the centre of the world. When he had attained the position of absolute monarch of the faerie nation his aged parents were very proud. They were no longer alive to help him now. He had nowhere to go. No friends to fall back upon. The entire faerie people that he had contemptuously treated as his inferior subjects for his entire reign were all that he had in this world. Without them he had no way to fend for himself. He would no longer be able to satisfy his carnal lust. He would have to steal food from grain stores and village markets perhaps as a bird or a small creature that would not be noticed.

Nimue was very aware of what Hellekin must have been thinking. She allowed him to dwell upon the proposition of becoming a complete outcast from a people that he once ruled.

"Go now Hellekin, lest my compassion runs dry and I order ye execution instead." Nimue's words interrupted Hellekin's introspection. Hellekin walked toward the exit. Faeries moved aside not wanting to touch him. He was beginning to become angry again. This was more humiliating than he could have possibly imagined in his worst dreams. One of the faeries closest to him actually spat on the disgraced former ruler. Hellekin's eyes flashed with anger. He took flight and in the form of a sparrow fluttered out of the hollow.

***

Flying as fast as he could he made a vow to himself to take revenge upon Nimue for making him suffer like this. If it was the last thing he ever did in his life, he would see that Nimue paid dearly for her insolence. And however, Queen Gwenhwyvar and Sorceress Morgan Le Fay were involved, they too would be dealt with. He would see them humbled before him. They'd plead and beg for mercy; mercies which he had no intention of granting. It was only a matter of time.

The End

Connect with Aenghus Chisholme

Visit my website on www.aenghuschisholme.com

Works by Aenghus Chisholme

Merlin the Sorcerer AD491

King Arthur is facing a war with the murderous Saxon Lord Aelle over the artisan land of Anderidae. Unknown to him magical forces have conspired with Aelle to ensure Arthur's defeat.

Guinevere the Queen AD494

Queen Gwenhwyvar and Sorceress Morgan Le Fay pursue the stolen Excalibur to a magical labyrinth where it is guarded by powerful Minotaur.

Gawain and the Green Knight AD499

An animated corpse has Sir Guaen in its sights. How can you kill something that is already dead?

Arthur the King AD517

Caught in an untenable situation King Arthur is manoeuvred into a battle he cannot possibly win.

Murder on the Mary Celeste

One by one, the passengers and crew aboard the merchant ship Mary Celeste are being picked-off by an unseen assassin.

Jack the Ripper: The murder of Madam Athalia

A clever young detective thinks that he can outwit the most cunning killer in the history of London.

The Best Things in Life Begin with the Letter B

Consumerism can lead to happiness, providing you know exactly what it is that will make you happy. Enjoy a tour of the material and immaterial world of the exclusive and the everyday.

Commissioned works

I am available to write something for you; fiction or non-fiction. Contact me through my website and tell me what you have in mind.

www.ingramcontent.com/pod-product-compliance
Lightning Source LLC
LaVergne TN
LVHW041114080826
845145LV00007B/1814

* 9 7 8 0 6 4 8 0 7 8 9 1 3 *